A LONG
TIME
COMING

OTHER TITLES BY AARON ELKINS

Gideon Oliver Mysteries

Chris Norgren Mysteries

Thrillers

Loot

Turncoat

The Worst Thing

Lee Ofsted Mysteries (with Charlotte Elkins)

A Wicked Slice

Rotten Lies

Nasty Breaks

Where Have All the Birdies Gone?

On the Fringe

Alix London Mysteries (with Charlotte Elkins)

A Dangerous Talent

A Cruise to Die For

The Art Whisperer

The Trouble with Mirrors

A LONG TIME COMING

AARON ELKINS

THOMAS & MERCER

Published by Thomas & Mercer, Seattle

www.apub.com

Amazon, the Amazon logo, and Thomas & Mercer are trademarks of Amazon.com, Inc., or its affiliates.

ISBN-13: 9781503902381
ISBN-10: 1503902382

Cover design by David Drummond

Printed in the United States of America

For me a picture has to be something pleasant, delightful, and pretty—yes, pretty. There are enough unpleasant things in the world without us producing even more.

—Pierre-Auguste Renoir, 1841–1919

Prologue

The most intriguing art heist I ever heard of happened at the Louvre Museum in Paris, early on the morning of August 21, 1911.

When the cleaning crew arrived at the celebrated gallery known as the Salon Carré, they were met with a blood-chilling sight: between Correggio's Marriage of Saint Catherine *and Titian's* Allegory of Alfonso d'Avalos *was a blank space five feet wide. In that space, for as long as anyone could remember, had been the most famous painting in the world, then as now: Leonardo da Vinci's* Mona Lisa, La Gioconda.

Gone.

Its widely reported disappearance was an international sensation and, in Paris, a source of consternation and woe. The museum's director was booted out the door before the week was out, to be followed in short order by its head of security. And in the subsequent investigations, the police, for all their frantic work, did not come up with a single clue that led anywhere. The Paris chief of police was soon sacked as well.

Two years passed with no progress, and then, in November 1913, a Florence art dealer named Alfredo Geri was contacted by one Vincenzo Peruggia, who had been a carpenter at the Louvre at the time of the theft. Peruggia now had the Mona Lisa, *he claimed, and offered to sell it to the Republic of Italy for 500,000 lire. Geri informed the police, who promptly arrested Peruggia.*

A confession was not long in coming—I took it off the wall, tucked it under my smock, and just walked out with it, he says (the painting weighs only a few pounds)—and led the police to where it was hidden: a trunk in his rented room. He'd taken it out of patriotism for his native land, he declared. The great Leonardo was Italian through and through, and it was in Italy that his greatest work belonged, not in some museum in France.

Peruggia was brought before a judge, declared mentally unstable, and given a few months in jail. To great fanfare, the painting, fully authenticated, was given a star-spangled tour of Italy and then returned to France, where, in a solemn ceremony, it was rehung in the Louvre.

The Mona Lisa *was back where it belonged, everybody was off the hook, and happiness and contentment reigned.*

For a while. But it didn't take long for some provocative new questions to percolate up into the national consciousness. Why had Peruggia taken more than two years to come forward? And if his motive was patriotic, why did he take only that one picture? There were other celebrated Italian painters represented in the same room: in addition to the Correggio and the Titian, there were two more Titians and a Raphael. Weren't they too part of Italy's artistic patrimony? Some of them were no larger than the Mona Lisa's *21 by 30 inches. How much harder would it have been to pluck another one or two of them off the walls and "just walk out" with them?*

The questions were logical enough, but with no logical answers forthcoming, outlandish rumors and cockeyed theories naturally sprang up. The most credible of them coalesced around a shadowy nobleman known as the Marqués de Valfierno, and on a central idea, one that maybe wasn't so cockeyed.

That the theft itself wasn't the point.

Chapter 1

My name is Val Caruso and I'm a curator at the Metropolitan Museum of Art. I have been having one hell of a day, and I don't mean in a good way.

First, my divorce decree became final after seven years of marriage, four of them wonderful, one not so wonderful, one hellish, and one separated and thus bearable. These were followed by three months of vicious, soul-sucking lawyering. With Sue herself being a lawyer—a divorce lawyer, if you can believe it; how's that for karma?—I was outfoxed, outplayed, and methodically hammered at every turn. In a way, of course, getting over with it was a relief, but it doesn't exactly leave me feeling as if I have much of a handle on my life.

And this, bear in mind, was my second divorce, which has to mean either that I'm a slow learner or that I make a lousy husband.

Yes, I know: or both.

Second, my expected promotion from associate curator to full curator fell through as of this morning, when the endower's will that provided for the position was contested by a slavering army of relatives near and distant. This struck a blow not only to my anticipated lifestyle changes (the salary difference is $40,000), but equally important, to my ego. Look, I love my work. I mean, a curator of nineteenth-century

European painting at the Met, for God's sake? What could be better? I live my days among the most beautiful works of art on earth. And if I get tired of Monet and Van Gogh and Ingres and Turner (which I can't imagine), I can wander around the whole rest of this fantastic treasure palace on my own, anytime I want, even after it closes. Talk about perks.

But I've been an associate curator for going on six years now and, well, I'm beginning to feel kind of stuck. Associate curators don't really have ultimate responsibility for much of anything. Aside from lesser tasks—participating in exhibitions, preparing literature, doing library research, and so on—we are under the thumbs of our seniors, and although in my case it's a kindly thumb, boy, am I ready for some ultimate responsibility of my own.

And third, today I turned forty, not inherently a bad thing, I suppose, but here I am, embarking on the fifth decade of my life; beyond the halfway point in the journey according to the actuaries. And career-wise, relationshipwise, and every other -wise, where am I, exactly? Running in place would be putting a charitable spin on it.

To "celebrate" the birthday, a few of my fellow-toilers at the Met treated me to after-work drinks at Bemelmans Bar in the Carlyle Hotel, a few blocks from the museum. Bemelmans, with its lighthearted murals, is the sort of place that encourages whimsy, and so there was lots of laughter, bonhomie, and, what with my being the eldest of the bunch, a good many friendly jokes and jibes about getting old and what great fun it was. These provoked much hilarity from my colleagues.

By the time I left to slouch the few blocks to my fourth-floor condo on East Seventy-Eighth Street (borrowed from a compassionate, wealthy friend while he was in Europe for a few months; Sue got the house in Queens), I felt as ancient and fusty as one of those Middle Kingdom mummies back at the Met.

Half an hour later, I was looking down on this pleasantly leafy block from Gerry's fourth-floor dining room, sitting at his splendid, marble-topped, eighteenth-century Empire dining table. (Or so Gerry thought; in actuality it was a fake, but I didn't have the heart to tell him. Besides, it was a good fake.) I was doing what any mature, reasonably intelligent adult who'd had a day like this would do to bring things into perspective: drinking some more Scotch. And musing about Gauguin.

There's an enigmatic, oddly static Gauguin painting in Boston's Museum of Fine Arts. Painted in his Tahiti years, it's called *Where Do We Come From? What Are We? Where Are We Going?* And those are the questions, particularly the last two, that I found myself asking. I had been clobbered today, or so it seemed to me, by an unholy trifecta—the disastrous ending of a marriage, a promotion gone awry, and my official entry into middle age—that had left me purposeless and depressed. Was I in the wrong occupation? Was it time to call myself a failure and move on? (To what?) Had I lost my confidence, my trust in myself? Had I ever really had it?

I don't know that I'd ever been big on verve or self-esteem, but however much I'd had, I didn't have it now. During the rocky latter years of our relationship, Sue had more than once told me I needed to see a psychotherapist. Was she right?

Highball glass in front of me, opened bottle at the ready beside it, I was sipping away, munching clam dip and crackers, and engaging in these and equally maudlin thoughts, feeling sorrier for myself with every Triscuit-load of clam dip. When the landline in the kitchen rang, I didn't trouble myself to get up. Probably for Gerry anyway. And even if it was for me, well, given the way things had gone so far today, what were the odds of this being anything good?

"Val, you come pick up the phone; I'm waiting." A two-second pause. "Or if you're really not there, which I don't believe for a minute, you call me the first chance you get, you hear me? Have I got a job for you!"

She wasn't five words into it before I was on my feet and making for the phone with a half-smile—closest thing to a whole one that had been on my face all day. Esther Lindauer, five foot two and built like a fireplug, was a blunt, bossy, irrepressibly upbeat woman I'd known for a long time. Somewhere in her mid-sixties, she was in her second decade as the director of IRSA, the Institute for the Recovery of Stolen Art. This was a formidable organization mostly focused on helping its clients in the retrieval of art looted, confiscated, "purchased" under duress, or otherwise forcibly taken from them during the Second World War. But that had been more than seventy years ago now, and the passage of time has done what the passage of time always does when it comes to old grievances; nowadays, IRSA lost more often than it won, but Esther was burnout-proof. Every new case filled her with the same righteous fervor and contagious optimism that the last one had.

And a little contagious optimism was just the ticket at this point. "Okay, Esther," I said into the phone, "you win, I'm here. What can I do for you?"

"Val! Hah, didn't I tell you you were there?" Having grown up in Lower Manhattan, she often fell back on an offbeat sort of Italian-Jewish-New-Yorkese speech pattern that added to her charm—for me, anyway, but then I'm a Brooklyn boy myself.

"You did, indeed," I said. "What's up?"

"What's up is I've got a—"

"—job for me that I'm going to love."

"That's right, you will! Believe me, I'm telling you—"

"—it's right up my alley."

"That's *exactly* right! This one was—"

"—made for me."

She sighed, paused. "Valentino, do you have any idea what an annoying habit that is that you have?"

"Really? You don't suppose it could be because you always say the same thing?"

"Don't be ridiculous." *Ree-dickaluss* is the way she said it, and the way she invariably said it, and she said it a lot. Talk about an annoying habit. But for some reason it didn't get on my nerves. Well, hardly.

"Listen," she went on, "I understand you're going to Milan."

"Yes, I'll be there for a week, maybe a little more."

The Pinacoteca di Brera, Milan's world-class art museum, was putting together *Treasures of the Brera: Five Centuries of Italian Masterworks*, a major exhibition that would be coming to five cities in the United States, starting with a splashy debut at the Met. When a touring exhibit from another country comes to the U.S., it's customary for the first museum on the itinerary to take the responsibility for coordinating logistics with all the others and with the originating institution. So with us kicking it off, Roger van Polden, the Met's director, had designated me as the American liaison to the Brera. A traveling show like that takes a lot of preparation and coordination—a whole lot of things can go wrong, and usually do—so I'd been given the time to meet with the Brera's senior-level planning committee to get things in order.

It was one of those high-level "ultimate" responsibilities I mentioned earlier, but it didn't signify; it had been entrusted to me only because our curator of European paintings had been unavailable. Besides, when it came down to it, it was just another administrative/logistical chore. What I needed was a *mission*—a purpose, something *important*, something I deeply cared about . . . and this wasn't it.

But it was a golden opportunity, so I was told, to show myself worthy of the newly bequeathed curator's position that would be coming to me shortly.

Except, of course, that it didn't.

"So then," Esther said, "how much trouble would it be to take an hour, okay, maybe two, out of your busy schedule—"

"It *is* a busy schedule," I said, "and I object to your tone."

"—to help an ailing, deserving, wonderful old man nearing the end of his life, to retrieve beloved possessions that were brutally ripped from his family in his youth? Would that be too much trouble?"

"No, it would not be too much trouble," I said, as we both knew I would. "Okay, let's hear it." I took the phone back to the dining table, and poured myself another tipple of J&B. "What's the story?"

"One more thing first. You know the way I am, Val—full disclosure. IRSA's been carrying this case for two years now and . . ."

"And?" I repeated when she didn't continue.

"What, you don't want to finish this sentence for me too?"

I complied. "'And we've used up our allocation for it and then some, so I'm afraid I can't offer you any kind of consulting fee for your help.' That about it?"

"That's it. Is it a problem?"

"Has it ever been a problem?" Four or five times a year, Esther would call on me for help of one kind or another—everything from mediating a meeting between antagonists to expert-witnessing in court on Impressionist and Post-Impressionist art, my specialties. It was always in a good cause, and as long as it didn't interfere with my job I was glad to do it; I had yet to charge them anything.

"Val, you truly are one of the good guys."

"Thank you."

"Despite what they say about you."

"Sigh."

"All right. Good. Thank *you*. So. You know about the Bezzecca case, am I right? The Renoirs?"

"Sure. Well, the general outlines anyway."

As I understood it, a Mr. Solomon Bezzecca of New York was trying to recover two paintings by Pierre-Auguste Renoir that had been looted by the Nazis from his great-grandfather's home in Milan during the war. Like so much other Nazi-looted art, they had then dropped out of sight for decades. Then, just two years ago, Bezzecca's niece—grand-niece, I think it was—came across a *New York Times* Sunday magazine piece about them, and about Ulisse Agnello, the Milanese art supplier who now owned them, having picked them up at a giant flea market in Hungary at €90 for the pair.

Why the bargain? Because nobody knew they were Renoirs. They had both been overpainted with mediocre (at best) seascapes. Agnello had bought them for their carved, gilded frames. At the time—2013, I believe it was—he was heard to exult about what a good deal he'd gotten.

He had no idea.

It wasn't until two years later, when he'd finally gotten around to removing the frames for use in his business, that he'd spotted indications that there were older paintings underneath the seascapes. After a little judicious scraping at one of them, his practiced eye—he had at one time been an art appraiser—told him that what lay underneath was something special and strongly suggested that they might actually be early Renoirs.

This business of covering valuable old paintings with not-so-valuable ones isn't all that uncommon, by the way, and has been around for a long time, the idea being to get around national and international laws prohibiting their export or levying heavy taxes on them when it comes to importing them.

Anyway, when Agnello got a glimpse of the paintings underneath, he very naturally dropped the scraper in a hurry. Then he submitted the canvases to Florence's prestigious *Laboratorio di Tecniche Nucleari per l'Ambiente e i Beni Culturali*, where analysts subjected them to accelerated ion-beaming, UV infrared reflectoscopy, scanning electron microscopy, energy-dispersive spectrometry, and a half-dozen equally arcane technologies from the forensic arsenal. Their conclusion: *"Our exhaustive evaluation of the methods, materials, and techniques of these paintings indicates that they are in no way whatever inconsistent with those of Pierre-Auguste Renoir."*

I'm guessing that seems a little weaselly to you. After all, why not say that the methods, etc., are *consistent* with those of Renoir, instead of going about it backward like that? For that matter, why not put their money where their mouth is and simply say that these two paintings are *by* Renoir?

Well, don't be too hard on them. What they said is really about the best you can hope for from art forensics. It's not like criminal forensics, where they can say that this hair, this tooth, this fingerprint definitely came from this one person and no other. When it comes to art, the scientists can only tell you what a painting *isn't*, not what it *is*. That is, they can say with absolute certainty that a picture is *not* by a particular artist. If, say, they'd found that the pigments used in these had included titanium white, they could say with utter certainty that whoever painted them, it most assuredly was *not* Pierre-Auguste Renoir, since titanium white wasn't developed until 1930, when he'd been dead for more than ten years.

But how can they say with equal certainty that a painting *is* by Renoir . . . and not by one of his many talented contemporaries, who would have used the same methods, materials, and techniques that he used, and might very well in fact have been trying to emulate him?

Well, they can't.

Art scholars to the rescue. That is, experts who might not know anything about spectroscopy or the physical or chemical makeup of pigments, but who know everything there is to know about the styles, approaches, quirks, and artistic aims and evolution of whichever artists they are expert in. And so in they came, the Renoir experts of Paris's Musée d'Orsay, the world's preeminent museum of Impressionist art. And they agreed: the pictures were surely the work of the young Renoir, painted somewhere between 1863 and 1867.

A side note: The fact that art scholars can be "sure" is no guarantee that they're right. They've been wrong plenty of times. (Google "Vermeer" and "Van Meegeren" for a particularly egregious example.) But mostly they're right, and when they agree unanimously and are backed up by the scientific findings, then that's the end of it. And that was the way it was here.

One of the paintings was a sketch, really, a cavalierly dashed-off testament to the artist's virtuosity, of a café scene—a café *sans pretensions*, as the French say—with a young man smoking a pipe and reading a newspaper in the foreground, and in the background two other tables, one with two men playing cards, the other with a lone woman drinking absinthe.

The other picture, the real treasure, was a self-portrait of Renoir himself, not yet the Renoir of his mature years, but still the earliest of his self-portraits ever to come to light and the only one in which he is beardless.

The story had caught the art world's attention, and gripping TV specials about it were made in France and Italy. In January of 2015 the *New York Times* Sunday magazine ran a cover story on it with muddy reproductions of the Renoirs even though they were still invisible to the naked eye, thanks to something called the layer amplification method, which is an exciting, spanking-new application of what is known as reflective light technology (as if you really cared).

This illustrated article was the one that Bezzecca's niece had seen. Murky as they were, the photos were good enough for her to recognize them as the pictures that her uncle had told her about so many times. Bezzecca, the sole surviving member of his immediate family, had then come to IRSA with his story, and they had gone to bat for him, assisting him in his pursuit of the paintings, providing advice, and paying for attorneys on both sides of the Atlantic.

The last I'd heard, Bezzecca had lost his claim but, with Esther's help, had taken his argument to an appeals court in Milan.

"I gather something's developed?" I said.

"Yes, we lost. That's where you come in."

"Excuse me? Come in to do what?"

"Didn't I say? I want you to talk to signor Agnello when you're in Milan and work something out with him. You know him, am I right? I heard you're old friends."

"Well, yes, but what do you expect me to be able to do? If the courts have had their say, and if after two years the lawyers haven't been able—"

"Yeah, yeah, but that's the whole idea. You need to work out something informal, something *without* lawyers, and commissions, and precedents, and rules and regulations and especially without judges—God, that mealy-mouthed, nitpicking hypocrite Riccardi, but don't get me started on him—something on a human scale."

"Wow, what a great idea. And that something would be?"

"Well, honestly, Val, that's for you to figure out. I'm only one person. I can't do everything."

I sighed. Loudly.

"Look, Valentino," Esther said. "If you two are such old, good friends, then you should be able to swing him around, get him maybe to show some human decency, you know what I'm saying? Maybe let Sol have the pictures on loan for a while, or even just one of the two. How would that be? You know, like what you did for Mrs. Abrams, so she could live with her Whistler for a few years before she passed on, God rest her. Oh, that was so marvelous! I cried when I heard you pulled it off. I have faith in you, Val. You're a *wonderful* negotiator."

"Esther, you're laying it on too thick now. You *cried* when you heard?"

"Okay, I *almost* cried. Damn near. Sheesh."

"And I am *not* a wonderful negotiator. That was three years ago, and I was lucky, that's all. Froede was an all-around good guy who wanted to do what he could for her, as long as he didn't have to give up the Whistler for good. But I've tried to arrange something like that two different times since then and struck out both times, you know that."

"Are you kidding me? One out of three, after the case has already lost in court? In this business, that's a fantastic average. Besides, Mrs. Abrams was only sixty. Sol Bezzecca is eighty-nine, he's got a bad heart, he's got high blood pressure, he's got an ulcer, he's got one lung, he's got arthritis, and that's only the half of it. The man's a wreck. Even if Agnello made it a lifetime loan, for how long could it be?"

I hesitated. Truthfully, I didn't see much likelihood of this working out. "Would Bezzecca be satisfied with that? A loan?"

"Sure, he would, of course he would. I already raised the idea with him—told him what a terrific negotiator you are—"

"Esther . . ."

"—and you should have seen his eyes light up. Like stars. What, 'Esther'?"

"Never mind. Okay, sure, I'll go see Agnello when I'm in Milan, but—"

"No, stop, I don't want to hear all the reasons why it can't work. If anybody can make it happen, you can, Val."

"Because I'm such a great negotiator."

"Ex-*actly*! But listen, you'll want to talk to Mr. Bezzecca before you go, hear what he has to say. A lovely man, you'll see."

"Can't do it, Esther. I'm on my way there tomorrow."

"*Tomorrow!*"

"Afraid so. First thing in the morning."

She was silent for a few moments. "Ah, listen, Val, what are you doing right now, this evening?"

Well, basically, Esther, once I hang up, my plan is to sit and whine some more to myself, and maybe order up some Thai takeout if I get hungry. "Why?" I asked.

"Listen, Mr. Bezzecca, he's sitting in my office right this minute. I stepped out to make the call. He's waiting for his niece to come and get him, but she won't be here for another hour. So I was thinking, maybe . . ."

". . . I might come over right now."

She could hear the hesitation in my voice. "But don't worry. If you're too busy with packing and things, I'll email you the file. That would give you the hard facts, at least."

But being busy wasn't the problem. I'd been packed for two days, I'd wrapped up any loose ends at work, and I'd already laid out tomorrow's clothes. (Anal personality? Me?) No, the problem was that I'd had two stiff drinks (oops, make that three, counting the one at Bemelmans) in the last couple of hours, and I wasn't sure how much sense I'd be making, or how much sense I'd make of anything Bezzecca told me. Still . . .

"I'll see you in twenty minutes," I said.

Chapter 2

Twenty minutes at most. That was one of the best things about this condo: I could walk just about anywhere I needed to go or even wanted to go. People who haven't been to New York have no idea of how clustered its famous cultural institutions are. Within a twenty-minute walk from where I sat were not only IRSA but the Met itself, the splendid Frick Collection, the Guggenheim Museum, and the country's finest art school, NYU's Institute of Fine Arts. And if music's your thing, just head straight across the park to Lincoln Center and the Metropolitan Opera, or swing left a few blocks to Carnegie Hall. And just a few blocks south of that are Radio City Music Hall, the Museum of Modern Art, and the Broadway theater district. Great restaurants everywhere you turn. A terrific place to enjoy the best in life, the Upper East Side, and all it takes is money, a ton of it. The three-room 1,600-square-foot condo I was staying in, nice but nothing extravagant, had cost my friend Gerry $6,000,000 when he'd bought it two years ago.

IRSA was housed in a donated twenty-two-foot-wide brownstone (as New York townhouses go, that's a biggie), scrunched between two sleek, towering condo buildings on East Seventy-Fourth Street, near Third Avenue. Like most old brownstones, it had an outdoor stone staircase (a "stoop" in New York lingo) leading up to the second of its three floors, although if you went through the door under the steps, in the daylight basement, there was a cute little two-person elevator with an old-fashioned folding gate that would take you upstairs. I climbed the outdoor steps and pressed the buzzer.

"It's me, Esther," I said when a crackle of static indicated that the intercom had come on.

"Good, it's about time, come ahead."

The lock clicked, the door opened, and in I walked, through a little anteroom that had been converted into a receptionist's area, and into what had once been the family parlor but was now Esther's office, an airy, unassuming place with modern furnishings, necessarily narrow but a good sixty feet long. (These skinny little brownstones are a lot deeper than you'd guess from the street.) Alongside one wall was a grouping of easy chairs around a small table, but Esther was sitting behind her desk at the far end of the room, in front of a big bow window that looked out at the pinkish concrete back wall of another giant condo building across a narrow alley. In front of the desk, from one of the two visitor's chairs, an old man creakily pushed himself up as I entered.

Solomon Bezzecca was fragile-looking, all right, but not the wreck that Esther had made him out to be. His eyes were lively and curious, and there was something about him that was unworldly and yet wise at the same time. He looked kind, and guileless, and his smile was unassertive, even a little shy.

I know. That's an awful lot of adjectives for someone you met five seconds ago and haven't even been introduced to, but they all fit, believe me. He wore round, rimless glasses and his white hair, what there was of it, was gauzy and thin, a dandelion puffball that did nothing to hide his scalp.

"Solomon Bezzecca," Esther said from her chair by way of introduction, "meet Valentino Caruso. Val . . . Sol."

"Dr. Caruso," Bezzecca said. "I thank you for coming."

"Sir."

"Sit," Esther commanded, and the two of us obeyed. It was a warm evening for September, but Bezzecca wore a long-sleeved sweater over his shirt and tightly knotted tie, and over that a much-worn suit that was a couple of sizes too small; Esther was in a shabby old cardigan a couple of sizes too large. Me, I had on the jeans and sweatshirt I'd switched to when I'd gotten home.

Bezzecca looked at me with an eager smile. Esther's was no less expectant. As she'd implied, then, this was to be my show. Fortunately I'd thought ahead a little and prepared my first question.

"Mr. Bezzecca, as I'm sure Ms. Lindauer has explained, you've exhausted the legal recourses available to you. At this point, anything I can do is going to be strictly informal. It'll all depend on Mr. Agnello's goodwill, his willingness to—"

"—to do the right thing," Esther cut in, and walloped her desk.

Bezzecca waggled a gentle finger at her. "The right thing? Ah, but doesn't that depend on whose point of view you're looking at it from? The eye of the beholder, no? Why should this gentleman, Mr. Agnello, feel any obligation toward me? Was he a Nazi; did he steal them? He knew nothing about them, and he bought them fair and square. He paid for them, and he paid for the work that got done on them afterward. From his point of view, what does he owe me?"

That may seem like an admirably empathic but not really extraordinary speech to you, but it bowled me over. I'd never heard anything like it from someone in his position. Most people were not so charitable after fighting through two years of court battles to regain looted property that they knew was rightfully theirs—and losing.

Esther didn't agree with him, which was understandable given the amount of time, effort, and—especially—money that IRSA had poured into his cause. "Now you listen to me, Sol," she said bluntly, "Agnello is the holder of stolen property, stolen from your—"

Again the gentle finger-wagging. "I *said*, 'from his point of view.' My own"—and here a soft smile—"is maybe a little different."

That made me laugh. What a likable old guy. "And you're right, Mr. Bezzecca, anything Agnello is going to do or not do is going to be based on how *he* views things. So—what I wanted to ask you—can you give me anything that I might use to help him see things, or at least understand things, the way you see them?"

"I'm not sure I understand."

"Why the pictures are so important to you, what they mean to you."

"Well, I can tell you that to my great-grandfather—"

"No, not to your great-grandfather, but to you. What do you know about them? There must have been stories in the family. I assume you've never actually seen them—"

His eyebrows went up. "Who told you that? Sure, I've seen them. Didn't I live with them from the time I was a baby? Wasn't I right there in my house when they came and took them away?"

"Wait, hold it. I thought they were taken from your great-grandfather's house."

"Yes, that's so—his apartment—but I lived there with him, so it was my house too."

"You lived in Milan? With your *great*-grandfather?"

"That's right. I was born in Milan. You didn't know that?"

"Uh . . . well . . ." The truth was, I'd been more interested in the story of the paintings—their discovery, their restoration, their place in the Renoir *oeuvre*—than in the story of Solomon Bezzecca.

"You see, Dr. Caruso," he said, "my mother and father were killed in a railway accident in 1933, when I was five. My grandparents, both sets of them, immigrated to East Africa years before, to Italian Somaliland, and none of my uncles or aunts in Italy could afford another mouth to feed, which is exactly what I was. That left *nonno* Maurizio. So, could *he* afford me? No, but he took me in all the same; the kindest man I ever knew. For eleven years I lived with him. It was a bad time in Italy, the thirties, the forties, but a happy time for me until they started to . . ." His mild, open expression darkened. The sentence died away as he drifted off into his reminiscences, clearly not happy ones.

"How did he come by the paintings?" I asked softly after a few seconds. "Was he a collector?"

"A collector?" His face cleared and he laughed, an inoffensive little whinny, and gingerly slapped his thigh. "A tailor, he was; he made clothes. And also he mended shoes. He had a little shop not far from the San Siro Hippodrome . . ." He squinted and looked at the ceiling, sorting through ancient remembrances. "We lived above it in two rooms, and those paintings were his pride and joy. Anybody who came to the apartment, he would be shown the pictures. Grandfather's chest would puff out and he would say, 'These were painted by the famous artist Pierre-Auguste Renoir, a personal gift. We were friends, you know.'"

He laughed some more, and I stayed quiet. Good memories now, and I didn't want to put an end to them. "Sometimes he let me help with the shoes. Baths we took in a tin tub in the kitchen. We had a little dog, Solo. It was my job to take him for walks. Sometimes . . ." He blinked and came back to the present, not altogether willingly. "So. How did he come by the Renoirs, you want to know. Just like he said. Renoir gave them to him, that's how."

"You're saying he actually *knew* Renoir?" At first it seemed impossible, but then I thought: *Well, let's see, Renoir died in 1919, and we're talking about the great-grandfather of an eighty-nine-year-old man, so maybe . . .*

"He did, indeed. Oh, I don't imagine they were really friends, the way he liked to claim. More like acquaintances would be my guess. What happened was that, just by chance, he and Renoir had stood next to each other at a workmen's bar one afternoon. And over their espressos they got to talking. What exactly they spoke about . . . that changed a little every time I heard the story—"

"Which was pretty often, I bet," I said with a smile.

He smiled in return. "Not at all, no more than four or five times a week. What came out of that meeting, however, that didn't change: my grandfather agreed to make a suit for him and to mend a pair of boots—the ones Renoir was wearing at the time, the only boots he owned—and Renoir would pay for them with pictures. And that's what happened."

"I see."

But a warning flag had gone up. Renoir had been to Italy only once, in 1882, and then only to Rome and Florence to study the works of Raphael and Titian, the Old Masters he most revered. It was possible, of course, that he'd made an unrecorded side trip to northern Italy, to Milan, but even if he had, by 1882, Impressionism was in; Renoir was a fashionable and successful painter; he could afford to pay for his clothes with cash.

My doubts didn't get by Bezzecca. "You don't believe it?" Behind the round glasses, his eyes were surprised and maybe a little amused.

"No, it's just that I've never heard of Renoir's being in Milan."

It wasn't exactly that I thought he was making things up, but I wondered if he'd gotten confused, or perhaps he was simply repeating one of those family legends that, with enough polishing and retelling through enough generations, become established fact. Still, whatever the facts, the Renoirs were the real thing, no doubt about that, and they'd come to his grandfather *somehow.*

"Milan? No, Milan had nothing to do with it. It was in Paris that they met. A bar on Rue St. Denis."

"Paris." I was lost and getting loster.

"Paris, that's right. In 1864."

"He knew Renoir in *1864?*"

"Don't be so surprised, young man. He was born in 1845."

"Eighteen forty-five? But . . ." I scowled, trying to do a little basic math, which was not one of my fortes in the first place, and which those J&Bs weren't making any easier. "But that means that at the time he took you in, he would have been . . ."

"He was eighty-eight years old—younger than I am now, not so old as all that. He lived to ninety-nine, and if not for—"

Esther, who had quietly gotten up and gone into the anteroom-reception area a few minutes earlier, came stumping back in with a metal tray I'd seen before, a vintage red-and-white beer tray with "*Bierbrouwerij van den Berg*" on the rim and, in the center, a reproduction of Frans Hals's *Laughing Cavalier*, modified to the extent of painting in the cavalier's hidden left hand and putting in it a foaming pewter mug, presumably holding a pint of van den Berg's Best. She'd bought it on eBay years ago. Sitting on it were three black coffees in polystyrene cups, a three-quarters-full, gourd-shaped bottle of Armagnac de Montal VSOP, and three more empty plastic cups.

"I thought we could use these," she said. "Sorry, no brandy snifters. You're gonna have to rough it." She began to pour an inch or so of the golden-brown brandy into each of the cups.

"None for me, thanks," I said, holding her off before she got to mine. I'd had more to drink than was good for me, and I figured I'd be better off getting some caffeine into my system. So I went for straight coffee instead, even though I knew the chances were good that it'd been sitting on a hot plate since eight o'clock that morning.

I was right. I managed to suppress the wince that the first swallow induced, but one was enough. I slid the cup off to the side so I wouldn't make the same mistake again.

While Esther and Bezzecca lifted their brandies to their nostrils, sniffed, took a few appreciative sips, and sighed their pleasure, I thought about what I'd just heard. Historically, the 1864 date did make sense. Renoir, unlike most of the Impressionist pioneers, was not from a rich family, and at that time his own paintings would have been earning him next to nothing. In another fifteen years, he would be a celebrated and fashionable painter, but in 1864 the twenty-three-year-old Renoir was still often forced to decide between buying paints and buying food. Certainly exchanging a couple of paintings that he could dash off in a few days—or maybe already had sitting around unsold—for a decent suit of clothes and a rejuvenated pair of boots that might see him through the winter would have seemed like a good deal.

"I'd like to hear more about your great-grandfather, Mr. Bezzecca," I said.

"Ho-ho, it's some story," said Esther.

So it was, and the association with Renoir wasn't even the most exciting part of it. Maurizio Bezzecca—back even further, in the 1840s, he had been Maurice Lévy—had spent his childhood in a foundlings home in Paris, where he was trained to be a clothes cutter. His apprenticeship to a tailor at eleven didn't work out to either party's satisfaction, and by twelve he was out in the streets on his own, getting into one petty scrape after another with the local gendarmes. In 1858, when he was fourteen, he was adjudged incorrigible and was made to decide between three years on Devil's Island or six years with the Foreign Legion.

Wisely, he chose the Legion, and in it, to the surprise of all, he thrived. In 1859, while stationed in Corsica, he volunteered to join a contingent of Legionnaires that went to fight on the Italian side in the Austro-Sardinian War, known in Italy as the Second Italian War of Independence. The Italians—that is, the Sardinians—were unsuccessful, but young Maurizio received a decoration from the Kingdom of Sardinia for his courage and dedication.

When his term in the Legion was up, he returned to Paris and used his back pay to set up as a tailor. It was then that he got to know Renoir, but in general he couldn't seem to fit in his native country any better than he had before. Inside of two years he'd given up on France, and France seemed to have given up on him. He immigrated to Italy, which suited his nature better, and in 1864 joined Garibaldi's famous and romantically named Hunters of the Alps—*I Cacciatori delle Alpi*—for the brief (and at last successful) Third Italian War of Independence, in the course of which he achieved considerable fame for the extraordinary feat of winning two medals for heroism on a single day, July 21, 1866, at the bloody Battle of Bezzecca.

In the morning, under a devastating cannon barrage by the Austrians against the advancing Italians, the bearers of the "colors," the two flags that served as rallying points for the troops, were both killed in the unrelenting shelling. Maurizio, wounded in the neck, snatched up the two standards from beneath their bodies, and with one in each hand ran, stumbling and bloodied, across the field of battle to a point at which the scattered, directionless regiment was able to regroup around him.

Then, a few hours later, having refused evacuation to the rear to have his wound attended to, he was shot again; this time the ball shattered his knee. Nevertheless, pulling himself along with one hand, he managed to drag one of two comrades almost ten meters to safety, while cannon fire and rifle shots continued to rain down. And then he went back and got the other.

After the war, he was hospitalized for months, although there was nothing much they could do about the ruined knee. Then, on Garibaldi's personal recommendation, at a public ceremony in Milan he was designated as an official Hero of the Risorgimento and was made a citizen of the city and of Italy. It was a lot better than he'd been treated in Paris, and it was then that he changed his name from Lévy to Bezzecca, in honor of the battle that had won him glory. For the rest of his long life, almost eighty more years, he remained happily settled in Milan, where his tailoring and shoe-mending business soon flourished—not least because of his renowned service to the nation— and where he married and raised his family, which eventually included young Solomon.

I could see that Esther was as engrossed as I was, although she must have heard it all before. Bezzecca was an easy man to listen to, speaking slowly and melodiously, and with the barest trace of an unplaceable accent. No, not really an accent, but an oddly appealing, singsong inflection, almost like a lullaby, that was extremely relaxing to listen to; I imagined it was something like the way a kindly, old-country rabbi might relate a Talmudic parable. Not that I've ever heard an old-country rabbi relate a Talmudic parable, or a new-country one either.

It was a bit anesthetizing, in fact, so much so that it was only at this point that I realized I'd taken the conversation off-track with my questions about great-grandpa. Maurizio Bezzecca had been an impressive man, but this wasn't the kind of information—the kind of ammunition—I needed for my encounter with Ulisse Agnello. I waited for Bezzecca to hit a pause at which I could politely interrupt, which wasn't easy because his storytelling was so amazingly smooth and unbroken—no *uh*s or *ah*s or *um*s, or pauses of more than a fraction of a second. It was only when he finally stopped for another taste of brandy that I broke in.

"Mr. Bezzecca, this is truly fascinating—he sounds like an amazing man—but we don't have a lot of time, and we'd better get back to the most important question. As you said, Agnello's not guilty of anything. He bought the pictures fair and square. So then, why should he lend them to you, even for a limited time?"

"Oh, I wouldn't expect him to lend me both of them. That would be too much to ask. But if I could live with just one of them again for a while before the end of my life, even for a *little* while . . ."

I nodded. "That wonderful self-portrait."

He was surprised. "Oh, no, I wouldn't expect him to give that up. It's too valuable. No, I wouldn't ask."

I was surprised too. "You'd settle for the other one? The coffeehouse scene?" For the first time, I felt the burgeoning of a modest sense of hope. I knew Ulisse Agnello and I liked him. An all-around nice guy (if a bit on the unconventional side), he'd been kind to me in the past and I knew that at heart he just wasn't the avaricious type (at least, not by the standards of the commercial art world). I thought that, given the right conditions—insurance, security, and so forth (for all of which IRSA would have to cough up the money)—he might let himself be talked into letting that modest little sketch out of his hands for a while.

"Dr. Caruso, it's not for me to 'settle.' The case has already been settled," Bezzecca rightly pointed out in his dignified way. "Now I depend on signor Agnello's generosity, and on your skills as a mediator, about which Ms. Lindauer has told me so much."

"All right," I said, resisting throwing a nasty look at Esther, "that could make things easier. But still, why should he lend you even that one? Can you tell me if there's some special meaning it has for you?"

To my surprise, his eyes suddenly glistened with tears. "What does it mean to me, a picture of my wonderful old grandfather when he was a handsome, vigorous, young man? The picture that he himself was so proud of and that I saw every day of my life? My friend, what could possibly be more precious to me? To see that dear face, to touch it with my fingers, would be like . . . like . . . ." The glistening eyes brimmed over and were dabbed at with a tissue. "Excuse me, I—" He stopped speaking.

It was a good thing that he did, because it took that moment of silence for me to belatedly take in what he'd been saying. "Wait—you mean that man at the center with a cup of coffee, the guy with the big mustache, that's a picture of your great-grandfather? It's not 'an unidentified young man'?"

"Oh, no, it's Grandfather, all right. I thought that fact was well-known by now . . . ?" He appealed to Esther with a glance.

"I would have thought it was," she said, flinging a look of reproof in my direction.

Hey, people, I thought irritably, *I have my own life to live, you know, and it hasn't been going all that well lately.* "I'm sure it is," is what I actually said. "It's just that, well, I haven't been following the case as closely as I might have, and—"

Bezzecca, good-hearted man that he was, was instantly contrite. "I apologize, Doctor. I shouldn't have said that the way I did. I shouldn't have said it at all. Why should you be following my case? Here we are talking ancient history, and what, you don't have enough to think about in your own life? I'm more grateful than I can say that you're willing to try to help me now."

Esther wasn't so generous. There she sat, guzzling her Armagnac and rolling her eyes at me, presumably for having failed to do my homework. *How the hell could I do my homework,* I threw back at her via mental telegraph, *when I just got this thing dumped in my lap an hour ago?* Not for the first time, I wondered why I was so fond of her.

In reality, though, I did feel guilty. When I'd hesitated during her phone call about taking on the assignment, there was more to it than my doubts about its succeeding. The truth was, I just wasn't that interested in the case. In the paintings themselves, yes; a fabulous discovery. But in Solomon Bezzecca's quest for them . . . not so much.

You see, over time, I'd lost a lot of the sympathy I used to have for the people who come to IRSA for help. With the passing of the years—the decades—the people who actually lived through the terrible suffering of the Holocaust have largely died off and the claimants to their estates have more and more gotten to be two and three generations removed, frequently never even having met their relatives or seen the objects they were now hoping to get their hands on.

But at some point, surely, a moral statute of limitations has to come into play. The wartime looting of art has been going on for millennia, all the way back to Roman times. Where do you finally draw the line and say: "This is as far back as we go in returning art to its 'original' owner"? (Who is the "original" owner of a six-hundred-year-old panel by Jan van Eyck that has been looted or stolen half a dozen times over the centuries?)

And so, when it was that kind of a case, then unless the person or institution that currently owned them was somehow complicit in the original crime or in knowing about it when they bought the objects, I usually didn't care much one way or the other whether or not IRSA's plaintiffs won their suits. And that's what I'd thought Solomon Bezzecca was doing: looking to IRSA and the courts to "recover" something that had never been his in the first place. I'd known he was old enough to be a survivor of the war in Europe, of course, but the idea that he'd actually lived with the paintings had never crossed my mind. I mean, who lives with his *great*-grandfather? But now I knew differently, and the big-headed way I'd written him off made me ashamed.

In fact, now that I thought about it, didn't he even say he'd been there when the Nazis had looted the paintings? My God, what must that have been like? Yet it had floated right by me at the time. Thank you again, Messrs. Justerini & Brooks.

"I guess I'll have a little of that Armagnac, after all," I told Esther unwisely.

She waved a hand at the bottle, palm up. *Help yourself.*

When I did, the fragrances of vanilla and plums, and of brandy that had spent a decade in a French oak barrel rose up so thickly that my eyes watered, but in a lovely way. I sipped, sighed no less appreciatively than they had, nodded my thanks to Esther, and turned inquiringly to Bezzecca.

He blinked back. "Yes, Doctor Caruso?"

This was about the time when I would ordinarily have suggested we switch to given names, but there was a certain formality about him; a sense of propriety and old-fashioned manners that kept me from doing it. Besides, my own sensibilities ran along those lines. I wouldn't have been all that comfortable addressing this venerable man by his first name, even though, as given names go, Solomon has a pretty magisterial ring to it.

Before I could respond to his question, Esther's desk phone rang. She looked at its screen. "Lori," she said. "I should take it."

"My niece," Bezzecca whispered to me with avuncular pride. "Well, technically she's not really my niece; she's my cousin. Technically, so it was explained to me, she's my third cousin, twice removed, my cousin Max's granddaughter; my *third* cousin Max, that would be. You understand how that works? Second cousin, third cousin, once removed, twice removed . . ."

"Not really. Never been able to keep that kind of thing straight."

"Me neither, if I'm going to be honest. But the thing is, there's more than fifty years between us, so to call each other cousins feels funny to us both. So as far as I'm concerned, she's my niece, and as far as she's concerned, I'm her uncle Sol. Problem solved."

An intermittent little clacking sound as he spoke told me he was wearing dentures. And I had noticed a little while ago that his left arm was slightly shrunken and seemingly useless. The sleeve of his suit coat had been shortened to allow for the size difference. And then, when he uncomfortably shifted a little I could see that he was wearing some kind of back brace. Maybe Esther hadn't been exaggerating his health problems after all.

"Yes, Lori," Esther was saying on the phone. "Well, that is something of a problem . . . I know, but . . . oh, yes, that's a perfect idea. Definitely. That's what we'll do. Good. I'll call you back and leave a message."

She hung up. "Okay. Problem: Lori was supposed to be getting here in a couple minutes, but she's stuck in a meeting down at NYU and might not get out for another hour. Now me, I'm due at this event thing in Brooklyn, so I have to boot you two out of here, and lock up, and get going."

She stood up, slipped the cardigan off her shoulders and onto the chair, and pulled the pea-green suit jacket that went with her skirt from the clothes rack behind her.

"So here's the deal. I drop the two of you off at a coffee shop or something down in SoHo or the Village. It'd be on my way to the bridge, close to NYU, and not far from where Lori and Sol each live. That'd simplify things for everybody, wouldn't it?

"Well, everybody but you," she appended, speaking to me. "You'd have to go back uptown to get home, wouldn't you?" A rare foray by Esther into sympathy for anybody other than her clients.

I brushed the concern aside with my hand. "Not to worry, I'll grab a taxi. But let me ask you something, Esther. I'm assuming that the paintings were given some valuation by the courts. Do you remember what they were?"

"Sure. Ten million euros for the portrait, five hundred thou for Sol's picture."

"Eleven . . . whoa!"

"What? You think it's too little? Too much?"

"Too much. By a mile. If they'd been done later in his career, maybe, but at this point Renoir was still learning, still a work in progress. I mean, they're great pictures from what I can tell from the photographs, and historically important, but not *that* great. He hadn't turned into *Renoir* yet, if you know what I mean."

"Darling Val, you know that I will always defer to you in matters of art scholarship, but when it comes to the art *market*, you, my naïve, young friend, are woefully out of touch. Since when does quality have anything to do with it?"

I nodded and laughed. "Yeah, you're right, what do I know?"

Bezzecca's mind was on other things. "What about Eileen's?" he suggested hopefully. "I wouldn't say no to a piece of coconut custard cheesecake. How about you, Dr. Caruso?"

At this point, I wouldn't have said no to a piece of tuna fish custard cheesecake. All I'd eaten since breakfast were those crackers with a little clam dip. If it was edible, I was all for it. "Fine with me."

"All right, it's set then." Esther gave her desk another peremptory whack. "*Vamonos, amigos.*"

The thought that was playing around in my mind—*with* my mind—as we left had nothing to do with anything we'd been talking about. *You'd have to go back uptown to get home,* Esther had said. Well, no, I'd have to go back uptown to get to Gerry's condo. Me, I didn't even have a home.

I had to smile at myself. I was really getting the hang of this self-pity thing.

Chapter 3

"And so we had this little apartment above the tailor shop," Bezzecca was telling me. "The war had been going on a long time—this was 1944—but *nonno* Maurizio and I were getting by well enough, considering the times. The pictures hung on the kitchen wall, along with the framed Hero of the Risorgimento citation and an old patriotic calendar, out of date by sixty years; nothing else. There were only the two rooms; the kitchen and the bedroom, and . . . you have a question?"

"Yes, I'm a little confused," I said. I had asked him to tell me about the day the paintings were taken, and the 1944 date didn't sound right to me. "Didn't the Italian racial laws go into effect long before then?"

"That's right, in 1938."

"But didn't they allow the confiscation of Jewish property by anybody, at will? How did your grandfather manage to keep paintings like that until 1944?"

Bezzecca opened his mouth, but he was drowned out by the racket from a beat-up old moving van badly in need of a new muffler, or any muffler at all, that was slowly backfiring its way along Cleveland Place, a few yards from us. Bezzecca made a perfunctory "can't hear" gesture at his ear and we both returned to our cheesecake.

Eileen's Special Cheesecake is regarded by connoisseurs of such matters as the finest cheesecake bakery in New York (and hence, the world). If you doubt this, you need only read the sign placed in the window: BEST CHEESECAKE IN NEW YORK. We were sitting at one of the two sidewalk tables in front of it, which is generally not a favored location, not only on account of the traffic noise but because the wonderful bakery aromas that enveloped you when you sat indoors were overwhelmed outside by vehicle exhausts, gasoline fumes, cigarette smoke, unwashed passersby, and other big-city fragrances. I had purposely chosen an outdoor table, though; I knew we'd be talking about an unpleasant subject, and I didn't want to spoil the pleasure of the diners inside.

The subject wasn't doing anything for our appetites either, and we picked desultorily at our cupcake-sized mini-cakes—cherry for me, coconut custard for Bezzecca—while the truck limped and stuttered along. Even when it was gone, Bezzecca sat staring at his plate, aimlessly shoving the cake around with the tablespoon he was using to eat it. I waited, regretting that I'd raised this wretched topic with this old and ailing man.

When he began to speak again, he began so softly, with his head still down, that I couldn't make out the first few words. I leaned forward to hear him.

". . . not only *allowed* it but *encouraged* it. And Jews could no longer work in government, in law, in banking, in education. We couldn't go to school anymore, did you know that? At ten years of age I was brought to the front of the class, and sent home, and told never to . . ." He waved a listless hand and offered a sad smile. "Ah, why am I dragging all this up? Ancient history," he said again. "What do you want to know this stuff for?"

"Mr. Bezzecca," I said, "I'm sorry I brought it up at all. I can see it hurts you to talk about it. Why don't we—"

"No, you're right," he said, sitting up a little straighter. "It *should* be talked about, and it doesn't bother me, not really, not anymore." To prove it, he bravely popped a spoonful of custard into his mouth and got it down, although it took visible effort to do it. His point made, he used his napkin to delicately wipe the corner of his mouth, and the spoon was placed back on the plate.

"Now. You asked how it was that my grandfather managed to hold on to his possessions through the Fascist years, until 1944."

"Yes." I was surprised he'd remembered the question. I'd forgotten it myself. But then, he hadn't had three large Scotches; not that I knew of.

"Well, he didn't hold on to his possessions, not all of them. The tailor shop was taken from him—'Aryanized,' as they called it—and was given to a man named Donisolo, the son of some petty functionary in the provincial government."

"But you were still able to live above it? And they let you keep the Renoirs?"

He nodded. "As far as the apartment went, Donisolo now owned that too, but, you see, he himself wasn't a party member; he had nothing against us as Jews. He wasn't a terrible man, really, but when the shop was assigned to him, what was he supposed to do, refuse? He allowed us to stay on upstairs, though. He was entitled to charge us rent, but he didn't, and in exchange we cleaned up the shop in the morning before it opened, and did . . . well, a few other chores. We cleaned his apartment once a week too. Thanks to him, we continued to live in peace."

Oh, yeah, I thought, *a terrific guy, Donisolo.* I was coming more and more to realize, however, what a terrific guy Bezzecca was. Could I have been that understanding toward the man who took over my business without ever paying a cent and "allowed" me to live in my own apartment as long as I cleaned his toilets and did whatever else he didn't want to dirty his "Aryan" hands on? I don't think so.

"And as far as the Renoirs went," Bezzecca went on, "when it came to his personal property my grandfather had been given an exemption from the laws, a very rare thing."

"Because of his service to the country."

33

"Oh, yes, indeed. A Hero of the Risorgimento, a confidant of Garibaldi himself. In Italy, that made him only slightly less inviolable than the pope."

"But not in 1944 anymore."

"No," he said with more sadness than bitterness. "By then the situation had changed."

By then, the war was essentially over, for Italy in particular. Their Balkan campaign had miscarried with tragic results, and the one in North Africa was an utter failure, as was their military incursion into Russia, where more than half their invading soldiers lay dead in the freezing Russian winter. The Allies were in Sicily and heading north, the whole of industrial Italy lay in bombed-out ruins, and the population was sick to death of bombs, and guns, and war, and of *il Duce*'s delusional assertions and decrees, and—especially—of being lorded over by the increasingly detested Nazis. In early June, the Germans fled from Rome and left the city to the American army. Had it happened a few years earlier, to the Italians it would have been an ignominious defeat. Now it was *la liberazione*, and the people of Rome thronged the Piazza Venezia to welcome their liberators.

"Whew," I whispered without meaning to. This was history that I already knew, but I'd never heard it before from the mouth of someone who'd lived it.

"But," he said.

But what was good for Rome was not so good for Milan, which now became the de facto capital of what was left of Italian Fascism, and one of the Fascist groups that bolted north to Milan was the *Banda Koch*, the Koch Gang.

"You've heard of these people?" Bezzecca asked.

I shook my head.

He waved a dismissive hand. "Maybe you're better off not hearing about them."

"No. Please. If you want to tell me."

The Banda Koch, headed by Pietro Koch, the Italian son of a German naval officer, was one of several semiofficial Fascist gangs that enthusiastically devoted itself to hunting down partisans and even more enthusiastically rounding up the few remaining Jews of the city for deportation to the concentration camps of Eastern Europe. And, of course, stealing whatever property of any value they might still possess. Even among similar Fascist groups, they stood out for the stomach-turning brutality and casual killing with which they pursued their tasks.

"Their headquarters," Bezzecca said, sounding distant and removed, like an offstage voice in a play, "and their torture chambers were two blocks from where we lived. The Villa Fossati, it was called, but we learned soon enough to call it the *Villa Triste*." The House of Sadness. He sighed and drifted off into his thoughts again. He removed his glasses and held them a foot in front of his eyes, looking through the lenses at nothing that I could see. "Via Paolo Uccello 17, it was," he murmured, nodding to himself. "Yes."

"And they were the ones who took the painting?" I asked. "Not the Nazis?" I was embarrassed to be pushing him so persistently about two small paintings—two out of the thousands that Renoir had made—when Bezzecca and the rest of Europe had lost so much else, so much more, in that barbaric time. But that's what I was there for, right? If I was going to help him, I needed to know the whole story.

He surfaced. "Yes, that's right," he said mildly, getting his glasses on, one wire earpiece at a time. "They were worse than the Nazis, worse even than the Gestapo."

"Because they were Italian," I guessed.

"No. Because they were worse."

Like the Gestapo, they had come just before dawn. At sixteen, Solomon Bezzecca knew, as did every other Jew in Italy, what it meant to be roused from sleep by the tramp of boots on the stairs in the early morning. It was he who heard them first and shook awake his aged, near-deaf great-grandfather.

Maurizio's mind had dimmed over the years, but he grasped the situation as swiftly as his great-grandson had. Roughly, he grabbed the boy by the arm with suddenly strong fingers. "Go and hide!"

"No!" the boy shot back as the door was thumped, repeatedly, so hard it made the floor shake.

Bezzecca told me this in the simplest manner possible, with no embellishments. There was no "I couldn't leave my grandfather to face them alone," or "It was my duty to try to protect him." In Bezzecca's mind, no explanation was necessary. It was the natural thing to do. Anyone would have done the same.

Right.

"Anyway, where was I supposed to hide?" was all he said.

There were three of them, he told me, two men and a woman, all in black uniforms. (He'd later learned that they were old German police uniforms given by the Nazis to their fawning local militias.)

The woman went immediately to the Renoirs, took them down, and strode out with both of them under one arm. The next time Bezzecca heard anything about them was when his niece Lori told him about the *Times* article.

"They knew exactly what they were and where to find them," Bezzecca said.

"You'd been betrayed," I murmured. "Donisolo?"

He spread his hands. "I don't know. Probably. Don't judge him too severely, Dr. Caruso. The times, for all of us, were . . . difficult."

The two males had manhandled the aged man and the young boy for a while, hoping to learn where Maurizio might have had other treasures stowed, but there was nothing to tell. Maurizio, overcome with an old man's impotent, trembling outrage, took down his gold-framed, beribboned *Eroe del Risorgimento* citation and shook it in their faces. One of them swatted it away with the back of his hand—the glass shattered when it hit the floor—and went on with the questioning, which, as Bezzecca remembered it, had been intense, but, comparatively speaking, not extraordinarily brutal.

The brutal part came later, when the interrogation continued in the Villa Fossati.

"They took us away, *Nonno* in his nightshirt, me in my pajamas. Some of *Nonno's* friends who had been inside it and lived to return had told us about that house," Bezzecca said, "and talked about the bloodstained walls. I'd thought it was, what do you call it, a figure of speech, but . . ."

He shook his head. I didn't press him.

"They treated us very . . . harshly. My arm was pulled out of its socket. My cheekbone was broken. My teeth in front were knocked out. I swallowed half of them."

Thus the dentures and the shrunken arm, I thought, *and maybe the back brace too.* It was hard not to shudder when I imagined what it had been like. A scared, guiltless kid, beaten, tortured . . . and here, just a couple of hours ago, I'd been whining about the rotten day I'd had. Jesus. I really needed to get my priorities straightened out.

"*Nonno* Maurizio, he died in the chair. It didn't take long. They cursed and then women came in—prisoners themselves, I think—and dragged him away over the floor. I saw it."

"How terrible for you both. I'm so sorry."

I would have been happy to drop it there, but Bezzecca was now on automatic pilot, on a wavelength of his own, speaking in a flat, dead monotone unlike anything I'd heard from him before. It was like listening to an actor read from a book, but over the radio, to an audience that might or might not be there.

Later that morning, he said, they had taken him to the train station in Milan, and held him there with hundreds of others. Many, like young Bezzecca, had been hurt; all were frightened, soiled, and bewildered. They were kept in crammed, fetid pens below the public station for what he thought might have been two days and two nights, although he'd been in and out of delirium throughout it. Someone must have taken care of him—given him water, at least, and found a ragged bed-cover to wrap him in, and cleaned him up a little—but he didn't know whom to thank.

On the third morning, everyone was summarily roused and packed into boxcars—the infamous Nazi cattle cars—that were then hoisted to track level and connected to a waiting, huffing locomotive. From there, they would be shipped to someplace more hellish yet, although, fortunately for whatever shreds of peace of mind they had, they couldn't know that then.

"You know what shocked me the most?" he went on in this odd, emotionless, abstracted way. "You'll be surprised. It was when they were loading us onto the train. These were Germans, SS, and they carried long, heavy wooden poles. I suppose they were meant to be used for prodding us if we were too slow about it, and they used them that way, but also they would smash us across the neck or the shoulders with them for no reason at all; not in anger, not to extract information from us, as at the Villa Fossati, or to punish us for some infraction we didn't know about, but for the pleasure of hitting us. Although in truth, they didn't seem to take much pleasure in it, or even interest. It was so . . ." He jerked his head. ". . . *casual.* It seemed to me that they were doing it out of boredom, or because they didn't like the way things were going in general, or for no reason at all other than that they could do it without retribution. I couldn't understand it. I still don't understand it. Why would human beings do such things, Dr. Caruso? They must have had wives and children and mothers and fathers themselves. Did they truly believe that we were *untermenschen,* subhuman? Animals? Even so, why would you treat animals in this way?"

Good thing they were moot questions, because I didn't have any answers for him.

"We were on the train for only a few hours and then stopped in some sort of holding camp—I think we were still in Italy—where hundreds more people were somehow jammed into the cars, impossible as it seemed. More beatings, more cries, more blood, more filth. When not a single person more could be stuffed in, the train started again. We were on it for two more days and nights. We stank, we were sick, we froze—it was December. People clawed at one another to get to the water they brought once a day or to put their faces next to cracks in the wood for a breath of fresh air, cold as it was. People died, many of them . . . many. We stacked them on top of each other like boards at one end of the car. People stole their things. So did I. I was still in my thin pajamas; I took the clothes from one of the corpses."

Another long pause while he rummaged through his thoughts. "It was to Birkenau they took us. And there I learned not to be shocked by anything."

"Birkenau," I repeated dully, while another shiver crawled up my spine. Birkenau was one of the three major subcamps that constituted the most bestial and depraved of all Nazi death camps: Auschwitz.

"I was there until the Russians came and freed us. January 27, 1945. Two months. I know it doesn't sound like much compared to what others went through . . ."

It sounded like an eternity. I tried to imagine him in that freezing, wintry hell, a friendless, solitary sixteen-year-old with a broken-toothed, bashed-in face that had to have made it hard for him to eat (not that there would have been anything that required serious chewing), and a useless arm that would have made him of little value to the work details and thus a candidate for the gas chambers.

I wanted to ask him a thousand questions—How did he manage to survive, on his own like that? Where did he sleep? What did he *do* for those two months?—but I didn't. I wanted not to hear the answers. I was utterly drained. What he must have been feeling was impossible for me to imagine, but whatever it was, it was enough for him too. "I'm a little tired," he said, and from somewhere he dredged up that quiet, implausibly unworldly smile of his. "Would you mind if we stopped there?"

"Not at all," I said, with relief that must have been obvious. And then, on impulse, I laid my hand on his forearm. I'm not much of a toucher. It just doesn't come naturally. I'm lousy at it and it makes me uncomfortable. People sense that and they get uncomfortable too. But Bezzecca left his arm resting on the table, where it was, and I left my hand where it was. I could feel both of the bones in his forearms, as sharp as shins; like a couple of chopsticks wrapped in parchment.

"Mr. Bezzecca," I said earnestly. "I want you to know that I will do everything in my power to get you that picture." As I said it—and meant it—I felt something resonate in my chest. Was this the *mission* I was looking for, the something *important*, the something I deeply cared about? Dropped in my lap just like that, by a phone call from Esther? Well, it might not be the solution to the not-quite-existential crisis I seemed to be going through, but it was sure enough something I had very quickly come to care deeply about.

"I know you will, and I thank you, with all my heart."

"I'm going to try to get Agnello to let you keep it on permanent loan." I cursed myself the instant the words were out of my mouth. I'd let myself get carried away. Talk about unrealistically getting his hopes up.

"A *permanent* loan?" he echoed incredulously. "That would be . . . that would be . . ." He was near to weeping again, and I wasn't so far from it myself.

"That's right," I said, and then, too late, offered a lame qualification, "but don't get your hopes up too high. This sort of thing doesn't happen very often, but since it's just the sketch you're interested in, and he still has the portrait, there might be a chance that he'd be willing."

"Dr. Caruso, please. If it can't be done, it can't be done. Please don't worry yourself. I've lived almost my whole life without it. I guess I can live without it for the rest."

"Truthfully, Mr. Bezzecca—"

"So look, why don't you call me Sol?" he said.

By this time it didn't seem so impolite and I smiled. "And I'm Val."

"Good. Well, you know, Val," he said with a sense of clearing the air, "I think I might get down another bite or two of this—" His eyes filled with life. "Oh, look, here she comes."

He had talked a little about his niece on the ride down from IRSA. A beautiful, intelligent young lady, he'd said, now getting back on her feet after an acrimonious divorce.

I hadn't exactly been on the prowl since my own breakup—no singles bars, no internet dating sites, no checking out every potentially available female I ran into. I just wasn't that interested. Maybe three regrettable dates altogether in the year since Sue and I had separated, all of which were arranged by well-meaning friends, and none of which panned out. But as I was coming to realize, I wasn't dead yet either, and the entry into my life of a beautiful, intelligent young woman got me wondering if maybe, possibly . . . I mean, who knows . . .

His next words stopped that train of thought as suddenly and thoroughly as a bucket of ice water in the face brings you up out of a nice, cozy dream.

"She's a lawyer, you know," was what he'd proudly said. "She teaches law."

Well, that was that. No lady lawyers, thank you very much. I may not always make the wisest decisions in the world, but nobody ever accused me of being a masochist.

But this woman heading toward us looked like nobody's idea of an attorney, a law professor, no less, coming from one of her classes at NYU. She wore sockless old tennis shoes, roomy, comfortable (i.e., baggy, ugly) gray flannel sweatpants, and a light green sweatshirt with *71.24% OF ALL STATISTICS ARE MADE UP* on the front. A backpack was slung over one shoulder by a single strap. Her dark hair was loosely, none too neatly, gathered in the back (by a rubber band, I guessed) to make a ponytail, and as far as I could tell, she wore no makeup at all, not even lipstick. She looked exhausted.

She was pretty enough, though—"beautiful," well, I wouldn't go as far as that—with an appealingly tomboyish look, and now, the moment she caught sight of her uncle, a warm, perfectly lovely smile. White, perfect teeth too. She was glad to see him, there was no doubt about that, and for that alone I liked her.

"Well, hi there, Uncle Sol," she said, bending to loosely drape her arms over his shoulders and graze his forehead with a feathery kiss. "So sorry to hold you up."

"That's all right, my darling. We've been having a very nice chat." He was so happy to have her there that he was practically glowing. "Val—Valentino—Dr. Caruso—this is my grand-niece Lori Bryn. Lori, Dr. Caruso is going to help with the Renoirs."

"Yes, I know. I just talked to Esther." She couldn't have said it any more flatly or disapprovingly, and when she looked at me, her eyes weren't so warm anymore. "Do you mind if I sit down?" she said, and sat without waiting for an answer.

"Nice to meet you, Lori," I said. "Would you care for—"

"I prefer Loren, actually," she said.

Oh boy. I'd known the woman for about two nanoseconds and already she was ticked off at me for something I didn't know I'd done. Hell, this was like being married again. Our relationship, whatever it was, had begun with dismal prospects and had gone downhill from there.

I was irritated by her manner, which was surely intended to be rude, but I held my peace. I didn't want to upset Sol, and besides . . . well, she really was kind of attractive once you got by the sloppy garb and the grooming, or rather the lack thereof.

And so, in a feeble attempt to break the thickening ice with a little wit, I smilingly offered: "I see sartorial standards for profs have changed a bit since I was in school."

"I was taking a class, not teaching a class," she said. "I wasn't aware there were dress requirements." The tone conveyed something along the lines of "We are not amused."

"You're not a law professor?"

"I *am* a law professor. At John Jay." That would be the John Jay College of Criminal Justice up in midtown. "But here at NYU I'm just one more student who flunked the bar the first time around." She turned to Sol. "Uncle Sol, is this really something you want Mr. Caruso to get into? Haven't they all put you through enough?"

"It's *Dr.* Caruso, actually," I said. Payback. Stupid.

"Pardon me, *Doctor* Caruso. Tell me, what would you say the chances are that your dear old *amico* signor Agnello will accede to your proposition?"

"It's not a matter of 'acceding,' and it's not a 'proposition.' The lawyering is over. It's simply—"

"Excuse me, let me make it simpler for you. Why should he do what you're asking him to do?"

Was she *trying* to get under my skin? If so, she was doing a bang-up job. I shot back my answer. "Because regardless of what you think of him from the court cases, he's basically a decent man, that's why. He'll listen to reason."

She laughed—mirthlessly, I need hardly add. "A decent man? So decent he's dragged us—and himself—through hell for two years in order to hold on to something he bought . . . by accident . . . for ninety euros? Something that means nothing to him except the money to come, and that he knows full well is rightfully—"

Sol placed his hand on her wrist. "Lori, dolly, it's enough. I think I'd like to go home now."

"Of course, Uncle Sol." She jumped up, letting him hang on to her arm for support while he ratcheted himself up with little suppressed grunts as his joints unlocked.

He thanked me again, warmly, for my help, reached into an inside jacket pocket, came out with a squeeze-open coin purse, and, with unco-operative fingers, dragged out a crumpled twenty. "I would like to—"

"Not a chance," I said. "This is on me. I enjoyed it."

"Oh, but really, I feel—"

"Forget it, Sol. No dice. You can pay next time."

Loren took him by the arm and dragged him off. "Don't worry about it, Uncle Sol," she said as they moved away. "He can put it on his bill."

Chapter 4

He can put it on his bill?

Was that her problem? She thought—she *assumed*—that I was being paid for this? That I was doing it for money and thus deserving of contempt? A pretty peculiar attitude for a lawyer, if you ask me. In any case, I most definitely was not being paid. In fact, I held no doubts that it'd be costing some of my own money along the way (it always did, somehow), and unless I was misreading my own motivations, I was doing it solely out of altruism.

Well, I was, wasn't I?

But if that was the way she felt about it and she hadn't even bothered to check it out, fine. I wasn't going to chase after her to set her straight. Still, it had been an interesting experience. Frankly, Lori—excuse me, Loren—had been the first female in a very long time to arouse in me, simply on first sight . . . okay, maybe not the "stirring in the loins" beloved by a certain class of writers, but at least a sparking of interest, an intimation of future possibilities.

And inside of two minutes, I had about as many future possibilities as a sardine in a can.

Not that I was interested in them, of course. *C'est la vie*, more fish in the sea. I walked a block to the Spring Street station and caught the Lexington Avenue line uptown. With my alarm set for four in the morning, I intended to be in bed by ten.

Tomorrow, *la bella Italia*, land of my forebears. Where the first thing I planned to do, even before I checked in with the Pinacoteca di Brera, was to put in a call to Ulisse Agnello and test the water to see if there was any hope at all of his letting Sol have that painting for a while.

I doubted it, but best to get it out of the way early, rather than letting it hang over my head.

Ulisse first came into my life when I was twenty-eight years old. I was just getting my BA in art history at CCNY (I was a late bloomer, not having started school until after my stint in the army) and was casting about for something to do in the summer before starting graduate work, when I happened on a printed notice on one of the Art Department bulletin boards.

STUDENTS OF ART! SUMMER IN ITALY!
DO YOU SPEAK FLUENT ENGLISH AND ITALIAN?
YOU WOULD LIKE TO WORK AS AN INTERN IN A MAJOR ART AUCTION HOUSE IN MILAN IN JULY AND/OR AUGUST?
SALARY FROM €2000 TO €3000 EACH MONTH, DEPENDING ON QUALIFICATIONS. IT CANNOT BE COVERED TRANSPORTATION COSTS TO ITALY BUT CAN PROVIDE YOU WITH REASONABLE PRICED LODGING OPTIONS.
BACHELOR'S DEGREE IN ART HISTORY OR RELATED SUBJECT IS REQUIRED, WITH MASTER'S DEGREE FAVORED.
CONTACT SIG. ULISSE AGNELLO, CHIEF APPRAISER
DELL'ACQUA CASA D'ARTE
TELEPHONE: 39 02 879061. YOU MAY TRANSPOSE CHARGES.

The language requirement was no problem—I'd been speaking Italian longer than I'd been speaking English, thanks to my Palermo-born father—so fifteen minutes later I was on the phone to Milan. And ten days after that, having fancy-danced my way around my lack of a master's degree, I was settled into a one-roomer in the Porta Garibaldi district, a ten-minute Metro ride from the auction house.

I took a liking to the lively, often frenetic Agnello from the first, and the feeling must have been mutual, because he not only assigned and supervised my work in the packing and shipping department, but more or less took me under his wing over the next two summers, taking the time from his own busy schedule to help me learn the ins and outs of the entire operation. I'm pretty sure he was thinking of taking me on as an appraiser once I got my master's degree, and for a while there, I was thinking I might like that. But the more I learned about the art auction world, the crazier—and dumber—it got.

When I watched six rows of identical ceramic pizza slices (seventy-two in all; pepperoni, I think) glued onto a blue-painted sheet of plywood go for €250,000, that did it for me. I mean, it was kind of cute, yes; €100 I could see, but a quarter of a million? And the moment it was knocked down, the successful buyer waved, and beamed, and basked in the attention while the audience applauded! Standing next to me at the rear, Ulisse looked over at me, licked his thumb, and pretended to count bills. "Thirty-seven thousand, five hundred," he said with a grin. That was the fifteen percent in commissions Dell'Acqua had just earned from buyer and seller premiums.

Ulisse even tried to look after me off the job, at least once a week inviting me to his apartment for his wife Donatella's *risotto alla milanese con osso buco*, which he had somehow convinced himself was my favorite dish. It wasn't, calf's bone marrow not being among my culinary preferences. Besides, Donatella was that rarity, an Italian housewife who was a truly lousy cook. The less ambitious the meal, the better it was likely to turn out, and *osso buco* was beyond her, let alone real Milanese risotto. I always hoped for something simple, like steak or chicken parmigiana. But four out of five times it was "*os bus*," proudly served.

Nevertheless, Ulisse and Donatella were always jolly, generous hosts who went out of their way to make me feel welcome and at home. Those were happy evenings, filled with laughter, and even the prospect of being faced with Donatella's *os bus* couldn't keep me from looking forward to the next one.

Two hours after my plane touched down at Leonardo da Vinci Airport, I dialed his number and waited. One ring. Two. Three. And then, "*Pronto?*" Friendly but wary, like a store clerk coming to ask if you need help but not so sure he likes your looks. The voice—and the attitude—were instantly recognizable.

"Ulisse, how good to talk to you," I said in Italian. "I'm—"

Apparently, my voice was no less distinctive. "Tino?" he piped. "Tino? *Caro*, you're here in Milan?" Literally, *caro* means "dear," but Italians, especially affectionate, demonstrative ones like Ulisse, use it rather more freely than we do in America.

"I am, Ulisse. I have some work to do at the Pinacoteca di Brera. I just this minute arrived. I'm at the—"

"Hotel Milano Scala. As always, yes?"

"As always, yes," I agreed, touched that he would remember. I'd traveled to Milan only twice in the last decade, and the last time had been four years ago.

"And the first thing the curator from the Metropolitan Museum of Art in New York does is to call me?" Ulisse cried. "Ha-ha, I'm honored!"

Said playfully, but with not even a hint of sarcasm, so now I was feeling guilty. The truth is, until Esther's call yesterday, I hadn't been sure about whether I'd look him up or not. A dozen years ago, Ulisse had been an important figure in my life, and I still thought about him with gratitude and with real affection. But a lot of time had passed since those days, and although we'd gotten together whenever I'd come to this city, our meetings had gotten increasingly stilted.

The thing is, our lives had changed a lot over those dozen years. Back then, while I was working my way toward a master's degree, Ulisse Agnello had been a senior appraiser of paintings at the Dell'Acqua Casa d'Arte, which was a top Milanese auction house. That was then. Now I had a PhD from Yale, while Ulisse had never gotten a degree at all. Now I was an established curator at one of the world's greatest art museums, while Ulisse, almost twenty years my elder, had fallen back on a business that provided advice and artworks to high-end interior decorators. What had happened was that Dell'Acqua had imploded eight or nine years ago under the weight of criminal charges (the CFO and two of the directors had gone to jail), and the firm had had to pull in its horns in a big way.

It had left its tony nineteenth-century quarters in Milan's elegant old Galleria Vittorio Emanuele II for smaller ones in the Porta Nuova district, the city's modern, high-rise business center, a long way, some two miles, from downtown. It had also laid off nearly half of its staff, and another half-dozen of its senior employees, including Ulisse, had resigned on their own, their spirits crushed by the dirty doings of the famous old company they'd loved.

Ulisse had expected to fall easily into another good job, but as with his colleagues his mere association with the firm had made him poison to the other major galleries. He'd managed to find a job as an appraiser at Galleria Amari, a midsized, never very successful house, but they'd folded and reemerged as an import-export warehouse soon afterward, with no place for Ulisse. This new business of his, he'd explained, was the best he could come up with, and a whole lot steadier.

"It's nothing to cry about, Tino," he'd told me when I'd last seen him. "I am still in the world of art. I still have my self-respect, I provide a useful service, and"—a small smile here—"the money I get away with charging . . . I'm ashamed to tell you. It's a step up from Galleria Amari, so much I will say."

"I don't doubt it," I'd said, having some knowledge of what appraisers earned at dubious auction houses like Galleria Amari. But it made for an awkward situation, at least for me. However he described it, it was a comedown from his old position and he knew it. "I still have my self-respect" is not what you say when things are going along surpassingly well. This reversal of status between us had made me uncomfortable. I was embarrassed by it.

I know, I know: Why should it matter? We were still the same people, weren't we? Our shared history was still the same. My debt to him hadn't lessened. Did I like him any less than before? No, not at all. But time happens. The past *passes*. When he asked, as he inevitably would, about what was going on in the international world of art, what was I supposed to ask him about in return? The international world of interior decorating?

"Well, who else would I call first?" I said now, trying to make up for my snootiness, or condescension, or whatever it was. "Listen, I haven't had a chance to congratulate you on that fantastic find of yours. Those Renoirs—"

"Ah, *sciocchezze*." A vigorous but modest disclaimer; in effect, *balderdash*. "It was nothing but luck, Tino, idiot's luck. You know how I found them, don't you?"

"Not really, no. In Hungary—at a flea market, was it?"

"No, I wouldn't call it a flea market," he said, sounding a bit offended. (Interestingly the Italian term is the same as ours, *mercato delle pulci*; no doubt for the same reason.) "More like an art fair, with stalls selling books and paintings and candlesticks and such."

"A flea market," I said.

"All right, a flea market, but the high-class kind, you know? The kind that's geared to buyers who think they're smarter than the dealers, smart enough to recognize a real bargain when they see it. You know what I'm talking about; worthless old books in Latin, middling old paintings with varnish so brown you can hardly see through it, Etruscan coins, mummy beads . . . At one of the stalls, however, a matched pair of seascapes, one above the other on a double easel, caught my eye. The paintings themselves were nothing, student dabblings from the looks of them, but the frames—ah, the frames were just the kind I had on my list at the time; carved, gilded, quite beautiful. So I bought them, and that's the story. Nowadays, when I think how easily I might have missed them—or worse, just thrown the canvases themselves away and kept the frames—I shake all over. They'd have been lost forever."

"But you didn't throw them away, you saved them, and that's what I'm congratulating you on. It took a skilled eye to see there was something under those seascapes, and to realize what it might be."

"What nonsense, Tino. You would have spotted it in two minutes, not taken two years to do it."

"Oh, I doubt very much—"

"Enough. I accept your congratulations with pleasure, but really, you make too much of it."

"I don't think so. Listen, when can we get together?" As I said it, I heard the sincere enthusiasm in my own voice and realized that over and above my mission for Esther and for Sol Bezzecca, I would have regretted it and been ashamed of myself if I'd gone home without having grabbed the chance to see Ulisse again. "I expect to be here all week."

"What about now? It's only six o'clock; the *aperitivo* bars have barely begun serving. Are you free?"

"I'm free, but it's been a long day and I'm afraid I'm not up to *aperitivo*. The sooner I get to bed the happier I'll be."

"Ah, too bad. You'll still be here Tuesday, though? La Scala is doing *Nabucco*. I can get us decent seats."

"That'd be great, I'd love it." We were both opera fans, and La Scala is always on my to-do list when I'm in town.

"Perhaps first meet for *aperitivo* then, what do you say?"

"Yes, could be. Or maybe a late dinner afterward would be better. Umm, listen, there's something I need to talk to you about, and I may as well mention it now. It's about one of the Renoirs, actually. Esther Lindauer at IRSA—"

At the mention of her name I heard a hiss, an intake of breath, and then a deep-throated growl. If eye-rolling made a noise, I suspect I would've been hearing that too. Ulisse is somewhat high-strung, which is, of course, another way of saying he's easily unstrung. Bringing up Esther so soon had been a mistake; I should have known better.

"Look," I said hastily, "I know that IRSA has been giving you a hard time on them for a couple of years now—"

"Hah!" As if to say "a hard time" didn't even come close. "Will she never take no for an answer, that woman, even from a judge? No, three judges! Is this to go on forever? Tino . . . !" He'd gotten himself really agitated now.

"No, Ulisse, don't get yourself excited. The legal battles are over and done. You've won. The Renoirs are yours . . . period. There's no argument there."

"Ah," he said, and he sounded calmer. As always, he was almost as easy to settle down as he was to flare up. But a shadow of misgiving still remained. "Then what is there to talk about?"

"Well, this would be something strictly informal, just the two of us. All I want is to present an idea—"

"I am not interested in hearing any more ideas from a woman who—"

"No, no, *my* idea, not Esther's. If you don't like it, that's the end of it, I promise. And if you don't want even to hear it, just tell me now, and *that* will be the end of it. You'll hear no more about it from me."

"I *don't* want to hear about it. What is there that hasn't already been talked into the ground?"

"Say no more. If that's the way you feel, then consider it—"

"But inasmuch as it's you who's asking, *carissimo* Tino, I will listen."
(*Carissimo* is like *caro*, only more so.) Whew, I'd been gambling on that.
He'd had me scared there for a minute. "All right, then," he said, "what
is this idea of yours?"

The question caught me off guard. My presentation, if you can call
it that, was still at a pretty rough stage. I'd assumed I'd have at least until
tomorrow to prepare it. Still, I did the best I could. Ulisse said not a
word for the entire time it took, not an observation, not a query, not
even an argued point. When I was done, a long silence, broken only by
his breathing, ensued. *Bad signs,* I thought. I'd muffed it. I'd been stupid. *Why hadn't I put it off to tomorrow?* I asked myself. I should have—

My imaginary voice was so loud and Ulisse's real one so soft that
when he finally responded I didn't hear what he was saying.

"I'm sorry, what?"

"Give him the sketch on permanent loan . . ." he was musing. "I
am not averse to this idea, Tino."

I was stunned. "Are you serious? You'd do that? Ulisse . . . I . . .
I . . ."

"Tino, against signor Bezzecca I have nothing. I believe he is a
gentleman, an honorable man—something that cannot necessarily be
said of his several lawyers."

"Well, they *are* lawyers." A small attempt at humor to relieve the
remaining sense of tension, but Ulisse didn't respond.

"And his grandfather was a very great man, you know, one of the
last true heroes of the *Risorgimento.* They were both terribly wronged.
No one can deny that." He paused. "Tino, may I ask you something?
When you learned that I was fighting this man, this good man, over his
grandfather's paintings, that I didn't return them to him the minute I
learned what they were, did it surprise you that I would do such a thing?
Were you—are you—disappointed in me?"

"Truthfully, Ulisse, I guess I was, a little," I said uneasily.

Actually, it was more complicated than that. When I'd first heard that the man who'd discovered the Renoirs was my old pal Ulisse, I'd been surprised, yes, naturally, but not surprised *at* him. At that time, remember, I'd assumed that this Solomon Bezzecca person was some thirty-year-old sixth cousin, four times removed, who was just jumping at the chance to make a quick few million bucks.

But that had all changed once I met Sol and heard him out. Ulisse must surely have known the true story early on, though, and it grieved and disappointed me to know that a man that I liked and admired *hadn't* willingly turned them over to Sol the minute he'd learned what they were, these two paintings for which he'd paid €90. The two frames, which were the reason he'd bought them? They could have stayed with him. From my point of view, that would have been a just settlement and I sure wished Ulisse had proposed it himself.

All this had been bubbling away in the back of my mind, marring my considerable pleasure in seeing him again. This was an opportunity to unburden myself and I did, telling him honestly what I'd been feeling. I held the phone away from my ear while I did, knowing that an explosion of temper and/or self-justification was due any second. But I was wrong. He took it on the chin for a good two minutes without interruption. I had to tell him I was finished before he said anything.

"You have to understand, Tino. When signor Bezzecca first came forward, I had no idea who he was. I'd done my research on the paintings. I'd established that there was no record of anyone's having searched for them before—no record of them at all, for that matter—and that signor Bezzecca, despite his name, was not an Italian but an American. And so I thought he was a . . . a . . ."

"*Una sanguisuga,*" I said. The word means *leech*, but its literal translation packs more punch: *bloodsucker*. It also rolls off the tongue more pleasurably, what with that second *s* being pronounced like a *z*.

I really couldn't argue with what he'd said so far. It was exactly what I'd thought at first. "But then, when you learned that he had a real case,"

I said, "that he was a gentleman, an honorable man, you kept on fighting. That's the part that surprises me. I'm sorry, Ulisse, it doesn't sound like you, like the man I know."

"And do you think I'm proud of myself? Tino, I had no choice! By that time I'd invested an enormous amount of money in researching the paintings, and then in having them analyzed and evaluated. I was already drowning in debt. The banks would shut their doors when they saw me coming. Winning those paintings and putting them up for sale—what other way was there to get out of the hole I'd made for myself? I tell you in all seriousness, *caro*, I had suicide on my mind if the case went against me."

"I can understand that," I said. I knew he was looking for more than that from me, some expression of reassurance, or of sympathy at the least, and I did sympathize with his situation, but the words stuck in my throat. I was thinking about Sol and what he'd been through. I was silent.

Still, it was good enough for him. "Thank you, my friend," he said. "And so now I would like to make some amends to him if it's at all possible. If a loan can be arranged, he shall have his painting."

"That's terrific, Ulisse," I said, warming to him again. "You have no idea how much joy this will bring to that man. I'll call him as soon as we're done talking. Or maybe *you'd* like to. I can give you his—"

"Not so fast, Tino. *If* it can be arranged, I said. There will be conditions. Obstacles. Others to be considered."

"Of course. Security, insurance, so many things. IRSA will take care of them all." This would come as news to Esther, but I knew my Esther Lindauer, and I didn't have a doubt in the world that she'd come through.

"Yes, yes, but other conditions."

"I'm sure they can be taken care of too," I said, my voice rising along with the excitement I was feeling. Never in a million years would I have expected this.

"I'm not so sure we *can* take care of them, Tino." Ulisse was sounding grave now. "It's not only up to me."

"Ah, the bureaucracy. Regulations. Red tape."

"No. Regulations, I can deal with."

This was beginning to take on an ominous tinge, and my hopes were taking a downturn. "Well, then, what's the problem, exactly?" I asked quietly.

"The problem, you see," he said with resignation tinged with annoyance—this was something he didn't really want to get into—"is . . ." For a thin, narrow-chested guy, he could produce theatrically long, loud sighs, one of which he emitted now. ". . . is that I don't exactly own them."

Chapter 5

It took a second for me to process that. *"What?"*

"Well, I own them in the technical sense, you understand," he amended. "But a decision like this is not entirely mine to make. You see?" he finished brightly.

"No, I don't see. What the hell does that mean, Ulisse—not *entirely?*"

"Do you happen to be free tomorrow morning, Tino?"

"Sure. I don't have anything at the Brera till eleven."

"Excellent. You remember Camparino?"

"The café? Of course."

"Could you meet me there at nine?"

"Absolutely. It's not even a ten-minute walk."

"Good. I'll keep you in suspense until then, if you don't mind. I think this will work out, my friend, but don't get your hopes up too much yet. There's work to be done."

But that final admonition didn't make that much of a dent in my optimism. When we hung up a few minutes later I was picturing Sol's reaction if this were actually to work out, and my heart was thumping away.

-ఞ-

Half an hour later, despite what I'd told Ulisse, I went out to *aperitivo* on my own.

In the guidebooks, *aperitivo* is often described as the Italian version of the American happy hour, which it isn't (no cut-rate drinks or snacks), or the Italian version of Spain's *tapas*, which it also isn't (no platters of little goodies that you order one by one, and no hopping from one establishment to another; you stay put). It is also not a synonym for *aperitif*, the drink. What it is, is a sort of sit-down, predinner dinner. You pay a fixed price—maybe €5 at an inexpensive bar or restaurant, on up to €20 or €25 at an elite hotel. What you get at the €5 joint is a glass of jug wine and access to a buffet of snacks—maybe peanuts, olives, and potato chips. At the fancier places, it's top-of-the-line wine or liquor, and an amazingly wide, constantly changing array of elegant bruschetta, focaccia, seafood, pastas, and superior cheeses and meats.

You're welcome to spend two or three hours over it but the idea isn't to make a full meal of it; it's expected that one glass of whatever you order entitles you to one self-filled plate of food. If you want to get yourself another plateful, you're supposed to order another glass, and if you don't, well, it's frowned upon . . . but not very hard. Nobody gets lectured or kicked out for filling his plate too high or too many times, as I learned from experience a decade ago, when I was a reasonably but not exactly overpaid apprentice at Ulisse's auction house. In fairness to the restaurant or bar, if I planned to make *aperitivo* my dinner, I always satisfied my moral guidelines by paying for that second glass. But the third trip to the buffet, if there was a third trip—that was generally on the house. I figured that at least they broke even on me that way, even if there wasn't much profit in my custom.

So why had I turned down Ulisse's offer to join me in this pleasant experience? Well, I liked the man enormously, but he did have an eccentricity or two, or five. Obsessive-compulsive disorder, I suppose the shrinks would call it. In general, these little tics made him that much more unusual and interesting. They certainly didn't bother me—not when he counted steps aloud whenever he went upstairs (but not downstairs), and if the total turned out to be an odd number, he had to step back down to take the last one again so that he wound up with an even number. Or when, if he bumped his right elbow while walking, say, he then had to bump the left one to even things out—sometimes doing it more than once until he'd gotten the pressure "equalized."

But what did drive me up the wall at *aperitivo* was his need, when eating bite-sized bits of finger food, to put two of the same treats in his mouth at the same time, one tucked into the left cheek like a chaw of tobacco, and the other into the right. This was followed by some behind-the-scenes (thank goodness) shifting of them until he got them set to his satisfaction. Only then could he start chomping, two chomps on the left, two on the right—you could tell from the angle of his mouth which side was in use—until he was ready for the next input. Throughout the whole thing I would find myself counting chomps to make sure they came out right: the same number of alternate double-chomps on each side, and an even-numbered grand total. They always did, but after three such sessions I was practically a nutcase myself.

Fortunately, these particular quirks did not apply to knife-and-fork food, so I was always happy to dine with him, to drink with him, to see an opera with him, but *aperitivo*? Never again, not in this lifetime.

Nevertheless, the custom had been an important part of my expat existence eleven and twelve years ago for social reasons as well as culinary ones, especially during the second summer when I'd had a wonderful Italian girlfriend named Allegra. I remembered with real warmth those evenings of laughter, and lively camaraderie, and new (if temporary) friendships.

It wasn't until after that time that I'd married Sue, who had come with me on a subsequent trip to Italy, but we hadn't done *aperitivo*. Her mother had been a long-standing alcoholic, and Sue was uncomfortable in places where there was a lot of alcohol-lubricated prattling going on.

So what did I want to do, here in Milan, on this solitary evening of my first full day as an officially certified single man after seven years? Well, what else?

I remembered that via Fiori Chiari, only a few minutes' walk from the hotel, had been *the* street for lively bars and restaurants, and it was there I headed.

And what do you know, it still was. I could hear the voices of laughing men and women from half a block away on via Madonnina. Once I turned into via Fiori Chiari I saw that it had been pedestrianized since my day, and now outdoor tables flowed from just about every restaurant, most of them filled too, with seemingly carefree young people. *Aperitivo* was at its peak, and everyone was having a good time, just as I remembered. As I walked the street, I got a couple of waves from diners who beckoned to me with smiles and gestures, pointing out open seats at their tables. One of them came from a dark-haired Italian beauty with black, smoldering eyes. It all couldn't have been more alluring, more inviting.

I was miserable. Those bursting free spirits of theirs made me feel as if I were twice as old as they were. And, as a little reflection told me, I *was*. That dark-haired beauty with the enticing eyes? She couldn't have been much more than eighteen. In the ten years since I'd been here, the drinkers and diners who populated via Fiori Chiari were the same age they'd always been.

But I wasn't.

I turned around and headed back down the street. At the foot of it, the very first restaurant, Torre di Pisa, looked like something that had wound up on this particular street by accident and had never quite gotten to belonging. Through the windows I saw that it was quiet and two-thirds empty, that the walls were dark wood, and that the largely unoccupied waiters were in their fifties and sixties, wearing black vests and black bow ties over white shirts, with towels over their forearms.

It was staid, conventional, even a little melancholy. A perfect fit for my frame of mind.

I went in, ordered a small carafe of the house red wine—a Barolo, I think—to go with a bowl of minestrone and a basket of crusty bread, and then *cacio e pepe*, the simplest, starkest spaghetti dish you can get: pasta, pepper, Pecorino Romano cheese, a little butter, and that's it. "Stark" seemed right for my mood, but it turned out to be tasty enough, as it always is when the chef knows what he's doing, so that I devoured it with pleasure, adding a glass of the house white about halfway through. To my surprise, it was Loren I found myself thinking about while I consumed my solitary pasta in this sober, quiet place.

Well, maybe I wasn't so surprised. I was a grown man. I'd been through two marriages. I knew that the mind and the emotions weren't always on the same track. Just because I'd concluded inside my head that Loren wasn't the woman for me, that didn't mean that what I was feeling inside my stomach would go along. And what I was feeling about her in my stomach was a certain fluttery sensation that didn't bode well for a sensible, rational outcome.

What was it about her that had reached me so, from the moment I first saw her last night? She was snooty, she was rude, she was a slob, she wasn't all *that* great-looking . . . and yet, whatever it was, I was having a hard time getting her out of my mind (and my stomach). Chemistry? Love at first sight? Did I even believe in that?

Nah.

So why did I find myself thinking that maybe I ought to call Esther at IRSA and ask her to come up with some subtle way of letting Loren know that I wasn't helping Sol for pay? I debated with myself about that for a while but decided against it. It felt too contrived. I wanted Loren to find out, sure, but it had to happen naturally, not because I engineered it. I thought there was a good chance of its occurring on its own, but if it wasn't in the cards, so be it. This was all in my head anyway and very clearly not a two-way street. It was probably some kind of temporary fixation thing, an early rebound effect from getting divorced, which, after all, had happened that very morning. It would pass, the hell with her.

Unless, of course, it was all part of some grand cosmic plan. Then I might have to reconsider my thinking.

The food was rustic and hearty, and so was the wine, but they failed to do anything for my state of mind. I walked back to the Hotel Milano Scala in a funk. Too much wine, maybe. Tomorrow would be better. Maybe I'd call Esther about Loren after all. Esther knew how to be subtle when it was required.

Chapter 6

The Café Camparino is one of those rare places that manages to be both a tourist attraction and an "in" place for cosmopolites. Its appeal lies partly in its genteel and belle époque ambience—it's been there for a hundred and fifty years, under one name or another—and partly in its history; it is reputed to be the birthplace of Campari liqueur, which would surely be the official drink of Milan if Milan had an official drink, and in the late 1800s it was a haunt for the celebrity-watchers of the day, the place to go if you wanted to catch a peek at Giuseppe Verdi and Arturo Toscanini with their heads together over coffee after a performance of *Rigoletto* or *La Traviata* at nearby La Scala.

Mostly, though, it is its location that keeps its tables filled. It stands at the foot of the Galleria Vittorio Emanuele II, Milan's glass-roofed, muraled, splendiferous old shopping arcade, and opens directly onto the vast Piazza del Duomo, always filled with people who have come to goggle at the great multispired, many-buttressed Milan Cathedral, the largest church in Italy. (Yeah, okay, Saint Peter's is bigger, but Saint Peter's is not in Italy; it's in the sovereign State of Vatican City. Ha.)

The cathedral is especially notable for being coated with thousands of sculptures—yes, literally, over three thousand of them, stuck into every possible cranny in its façade and even on its roof. Up there are statues of just about every cultural and religious icon from Anastasia and Basilissa, the first Italian (i.e., Roman) saints, to Primo Carnera, the first (and last) Italian world heavyweight boxing champion. As art, they're mostly pretty dreadful, and the cathedral itself—the Duomo—as a whole has had mixed reviews over the centuries. Myself, I'd never made up my mind whether I agreed more with Mark Twain ("a wonder . . . grand, solemn, and vast") and Percy Bysshe Shelley ("sublime"), or Oscar Wilde ("monstrous and inartistic") and John Ruskin ("barbarous . . . detestable . . . utterly vile . . .").

On the whole, speaking as an art guy, I guess I'd have to go along more with the Wilde-Ruskin contingent, but I do have to say, it's still a stunning thing to see. And the six hundred years of almost continuous labor that went into building it . . . astonishing. To add its own fascinating touch of incongruity this morning, the carillon was ringing out gloriously with the Beatles' "Yesterday"—and very harmoniously too.

I'd arrived early and had taken one of the patio tables. While I was sitting there being suitably astonished by it all, I spotted Ulisse coming across the piazza. Even at nine o'clock in the morning, it was swarming with people, mostly in groups being herded by Mary Poppins–like ladies with yellow or red umbrellas, but Ulisse's outfit, rather an, ah, distinctive one, was hard to miss. It was exactly the sort of thing he'd been wearing ten years ago: black fedora, black velour blazer, and long white silk scarf looped around his neck and hanging down his back—none of which were exactly standard Italian fashion accessories, either now or ten years ago, or thirty years ago, but they suited him perfectly. He would have fit just fine on the stage at La Scala as one of the cheerfully starving artists from *La Bohème*. I suspected that when he unwound the scarf there would be the familiar black string bolo tie at his collar, probably the only one in *la Repubblica Italia*.

He spotted me when I waved and adjusted his course to head in my direction. His gait was curious too. Ulisse didn't simply walk or stroll. He scurried, he scampered—but he did it in his own dainty, squirrely way—and I was pleased to see that this morning he seemed to be as lively as ever. He'd be about sixty these days, getting on in years. As he got closer I saw that he was remarkably unchanged. There were rather distinguished-looking wings of gray at his temples now, but the rest of his curly—make that *frizzy*—hair was almost as glossy and jet-black as ever. I smiled to see that he still had a single, cheeky little tendril poking artfully down on his forehead, a couple of inches to the left of center. His mustache had grayed to pepper-and-salt now, but it was as narrow and perfectly sculpted as ever, a 1930s matinee-idol mustache, an Errol Flynn mustache, a Ronald Colman mustache.

This is not to suggest that he was handsome. He was a jumpy, herky-jerky little guy, more along the lines of Charlie Chaplin than Errol Flynn. There was, to be truthful, always a faint air of the ridiculous—the charmingly ridiculous—that hung about Ulisse, and it wasn't only those obsessive-compulsive tics. Once, one of the auction-house bidders who showed up fairly regularly, mostly at those creepy sell-offs of dead celebrities' possessions, came looking for him but couldn't remember his name. "The funny little man," she prompted me, and then, with a twirl of her fingers, "with that funny little mustache."

Ulisse Agnello in a nutshell.

Now he bustled to my table, arms spread wide—he was a natural hugger—but he remembered that I wasn't, and so he offered his hand instead. I passed that up and hugged him anyway (what the hell), and he accepted happily. A round of amiable, masculine backslapping followed. Then came the handshake, warm on both sides.

"What will you have?" I asked as he sat down. "I'm going to have another caffè latte myself."

"Thank you. For me, an espresso."

I caught the attention of a nearby black-tied waiter, who hurried to the table, but not to me.

"Signor Agnello! How good to see you! What may I bring you?"

This was really grating because the guy had sure made a point of doing his best to ignore me earlier.

"Thank you, Carlo, it's good to be here, as always. I hope you're well. For my good friend, another caffè latte, and I will have *un caffè*." In Italy, that meant an espresso.

Carlo bobbed respectfully and hurried off. Ulisse delicately set his homburg on an empty chair, and an attaché case beside it. The white scarf was unwound, and yes, under it was the bolo tie. I was pleased. Then we looked at each other across the table.

"So," he said.

"So."

In other words, a little amicable chitchat, a little catching up with each other, was called for. I talked about my divorce and Ulisse surprised me by saying that he too was now a divorced man.

"I'm sorry to hear that," I said, but the truth is, I was ready to stand up and cheer. No more homemade *os bus*, now or ever again!

By the time the coffee arrived a few minutes later, the small talk had been pretty much wrapped up. There was a cup of cigarette-sized packets of sugar on the table and Ulisse tore one open and poured half the contents into his tiny cup. Then he tore open a second and did the same: one half of each packet. His need for symmetry and balance met, he drank half of it, not bothering to put the cup down before tipping his head back again, swallowing the rest, and setting the cup in its saucer with a let's-get-down-to-business clink.

"So," he said again and took up last night's conversation where it had left off. "What exactly did I mean when I said that I didn't exactly own the paintings—that was the question?"

"That was the question."

He nodded. *"Allora . . ."*

Allora is what Italians use where we would throw in a "well." Literally, it means "so" or "then," but in practice it has about as much intrinsic meaning as "well" does, which is to say, none. It's a filler, a placeholder that buys you a little time to put in order what you're about to say. Ulisse took a good five seconds to do that, and then he got started, speaking slowly for him.

By the time the first trial was over, he explained, he was in over his head financially. The forensic evaluations by the lab in Florence and the scholarly ones by the Louvre had set him back some, but they were nothing compared to the legal costs that went along with the trial. The decision had gone in his favor, of course, but then IRSA immediately appealed it and a new trial, probably even more expensive, was scheduled. "I was desperate," he said. "My attorneys were willing to negotiate their fees, but not willing to wait for them until I was able to sell the paintings."

"Understandable," I said.

"What I needed was another two hundred thousand euros, but the legitimate lending institutions, the banks, the finance companies, would have nothing more to do with me."

"They'd advanced you too much already, was that it?"

"That, and also I had no more collateral to offer. My home, my business—virtually everything I owned—all of that would go to them if I couldn't repay what I'd already borrowed."

"But what about the paintings themselves? You couldn't use those? Aren't they expected to bring more than ten million euros?"

"Yes, they are . . . to the person who sells them. But if the decision went against me, I wouldn't have *been* that person. Besides, as you well know, there is nothing less predictable than the proceeds from a sale of art. No, the regular lenders, and you can't blame them, wanted no part of it."

By now I thought I could see where he was headed. "And so you went to a nonlegitimate lender," I said. "The Mafia."

"The Mafia!" he exploded. "Certainly not! You've been watching too much television. This is Milan, not Palermo." His hand shot to his mouth. "Oh, I'm sorry, Tino. Your father, he was from Palermo. I intended no offense."

I laughed. "None taken, Ulisse. Please. Go ahead."

"And so I went to an old friend of mine who sometimes makes loans to his friends who cannot get them otherwise . . . for one reason or another, you know."

No, I didn't know and I didn't ask.

"Tino, this is strictly between us, yes?"

"Of course."

"Then I may as well tell you that the friend of whom I speak is Benvenuto Castelnuovo."

"Ah," I said.

He was disappointed. "You don't know the name? Really? He's quite famous. His flagship store is here in Milan, on via Monte Napoleone."

"Sorry, I don't know Castelnuovo, but I do know via Monte Napoleone. I gather he's a big fish in the fashion world."

"Very. Mostly he designs rather avant-garde men's styles. The fashion media are quite taken with him, but I must say his productions are a bit too, ah, audacious for my tastes. Brazen, even."

"Which explains why the fashion media love him, obviously," I said with a smile.

"Be that as it may, he came through for me when the banks wouldn't. He agreed to accept a share in the sale of the paintings as collateral. For which he lent me the two hundred thousand euros I needed. Without it, I don't see how I could have successfully fought the case."

"Well, I'm glad it worked out for you, but what would have happened if you'd lost? You couldn't forfeit the collateral to him because you wouldn't have owned it anymore, right? How was that going to work?"

"I probably shouldn't have called it 'collateral,' Tino. It didn't work that way. If I lost, then I'd owe him nothing. He was taking a big gamble."

"I'll say he was, but of course you *have* won your case. So how much of a share in any sale will he be getting? If the details aren't private, I mean."

"Nothing about this is private from you, Tino. Twenty percent."

That sat me up straight. "And you *agreed*?" I tried not to sound too amazed, but it was one hell of a loan fee, not twenty percent of the *loan*, which would have been bad enough—€40,000, not exactly what you'd call a trifle—but twenty percent of the value of the *paintings*. If they really did sell for ten and a half million, that would come to—

Ulisse read what I was thinking. "Two million one hundred thousand euros," he said. "And yes, I agreed. Gratefully." He set his mouth. "Happily!"

But he didn't look happy. He was rubbing his hand up and down his pants leg, maintaining eye contact with me; the kind of locked-in, slightly crazed glare that meant something along the lines of "go ahead, tell me what I *should* have done, just try it."

Well, I wasn't about to do that, but I could sure think it: You, my friend, have been the victim of the Mother of all Loan Sharks. It means you now owe the lender more than *ten times* the amount of the loan—extortion by any definition. Other than the fact that this guy wouldn't whack Ulisse (one hoped) if he failed to deliver, his terms out-mafia-ed the Mafia's. Still, it wasn't for me to say anything, so I kept my mouth shut. And after all, as he'd rightly said, what other options had he had? He'd done what he'd had to do. But the other guy—he'd bled Ulisse unmercifully. I stood by my assessment: loan shark.

The atmosphere had gotten a little strained. I tried to ease it. "Well, in any case, you did win . . ." I raised my cup in congratulation. "So it's all moot. Everything has worked out."

Ulisse was still a little uptight. "Tino, I didn't tell you all this to entertain you, you know, but because you need to be aware of it."

I frowned, not liking the sound of that. "Why do I need to be aware of it?"

"Because Benvenuto has to agree to anything concerning the disposition of the paintings. It's in our contract. That sketch can't be lent out, or sold for that matter, unless he gives his consent."

Those obstacles and conditions Ulisse had tossed about so airily the previous evening were beginning to take shape. "And you think he might not?"

"No," he said thoughtfully, "I think he'll agree if it's properly explained to him. But he has to be asked. Naturally."

Yes, naturally, but now there were a few doubts flitting around my mind. "I hope you're right, but . . . well, let me put it this way: Why should *he* agree to it? This was purely an investment for him, wasn't it? Why agree to lend a painting out for nothing when you could be selling it for a lot of money?"

"If it was the self-portrait we were talking about, he wouldn't, oh, no—and, frankly, neither would I. But it's the café sketch, is it not, and relatively speaking, this is a drop in the bucket." *Una goccia nell'oceano* is what he said. To the Italians, who have more of a natural bent for extravagance in their metaphors than we do, it's a drop in the ocean, not a drop in some lousy bucket.

"Five hundred thousand euros," I said. "That's some drop."

"It is that, yes. And now that you mention selling it, mm, ah . . ."

Up went the warning flags; another little glitch was winging its way to Café Camparino.

". . . there is one more little point that I need to mention, one more factor to be addressed. The fact is, we have signed contracts for both paintings to be auctioned next month at Montefiore Arte, here in Milan." He cleared his throat, very gently. "In, ah, a little over two weeks, actually. October 9."

I sat back with a sigh of my own, perplexed and frustrated. "Well, if that's the case, then why the hell are we even talking about it?"

"Because—now don't be so touchy, Tino, I'm only trying to help— we're talking about it because I think that Giulietta—Giulietta Barone, the *amministratore delegato*"—the CEO—"of Montefiore, will be open to removing the sketch from the sale, even though the catalogs have already gone out."

"Because it's just *una goccia nell'oceano*?" I said, smiling.

"Precisely. There has been a wonderful show of interest in the auction, but, as you might expect, it has centered on the self-portrait." He leaned forward and placed his hand on mine. "I have high hopes, Tino. I'll do my best, I can promise you that."

"Thank you, Ulisse. Um, would there be anybody else we need to—"

"No, no, just those two."

"I'm glad to hear it. You'll be presenting the idea of the loan to them, then? Soon, I hope?"

He leaned back and responded with one of his cunning, jaunty little smiles, accompanied by a certain glitter in his eye that meant he'd been keeping something up his sleeve, which he was extremely fond of doing. And then dumping it on you like a truckload of bricks.

Which he did now. "No, *you* will."

I blinked. "*Me*? When?"

He savored the moment, his eyes bright. "Would now be soon enough?"

Chapter 7

"Now . . . ?" I laughed, more out of disbelief than anything else, but then I saw that he'd meant it. "You mean you've already gotten them together for this? On a Saturday morning?"

"No, Tino, *carissimo*, not for this. You're not *that* important. But now that the case has been settled, a number of items need to be clarified between Benvenuto and me, and we also need to straighten out a few of the auction details with Montefiore—with Giulietta. And now," he appended, "also to hear from you. After we talked last night, I took the liberty of putting you on the agenda. I also called the two of them, Benvenuto and Giulietta, to tell them a little about you. To prepare them, you know."

"Ulisse," I said, embarrassed about my show of annoyance a couple of minutes earlier, "you've really gone to a lot of trouble for me—"

"And for signor Bezzecca."

"For which I can't thank you enough. All I can say—"

Whatever it was, it was summarily dismissed with a shrug and a wave of his hand. He then produced a sheaf of paper, twelve or fifteen pages in all, from the attaché case. "Here, I had a copy made for you as well."

I hefted it. "That's a lot of agenda."

"The agenda's only the first page. The rest is the paperwork from Montefiore, with all the usual denials of liability for everything they can possibly think of; you know how that works. No need for you to bother with any of that." His eyebrows drew together. "Tino, this hasn't upset you, has it? I thought it would be a pleasant surprise."

I laughed again, although I shook my head at the same time. "It's a surprise, all right. Whew, I haven't really prepared anything."

"What is there to prepare? Say to them what you said to me last night. You convinced *me*, didn't you?" He leaned across the table to give my shoulder a reassuring shake.

"I guess I did, at that," I said, and then, after a couple of beats: "Only what exactly did I say?" I wasn't kidding, either. I don't do well with jet lag. A six-time-zone change generally takes me a couple of days to find my stride again.

"Oh, it will come to you, I have no doubt." He glanced at his watch.

"Should we get going?" I asked. My nerves were jumping now and I didn't want to sit anymore. I needed action.

"No, no, we have time. It's only a ten-minute walk. There's time for another coffee, if you like. But listen, there'll be one other person there that I have to tell you about. He doesn't have any formal say in this, but if anyone is likely to disrupt things, it's Dante."

"And who is Dante?" I had the distinct feeling that things were starting to pile up on me. It didn't feel good. Motioning to Carlo, I asked him to bring us a couple more espressos. I know, I know. More caffeine—brilliant, just what you need when your stomach is already clenching like a sea anemone that you've poked with a finger.

"Dante's our restorer. He's been working—"

"Wait a minute, I thought the paintings had already been restored. By the lab in Florence."

"Oh, no, they didn't restore them. They examined them, that's all, and they did it entirely with noninvasive techniques; infrared and such. The seascapes were still there when they were finished, still intact. Dante has been working for some time now at removing them and doing any further repair work that's needed. They're more than a century and a half old, after all."

Ah, that explained why those layer-amplified X-ray photos were still the only ones out there.

"Dante, you said? Would that be Dante Zampa?"

"Yes. You know him?"

"I've heard about him."

There was something in my voice, or maybe it was the use of "about" instead of "of," that had given away what I was thinking, because Ulisse immediately got nervous. His knee began to bounce, a sure sign with him. Now we were both worked up.

"You don't think he's a good choice? I've been out to his workshop to see them many times. Every week, almost. The work he's doing seems wonderful to me, so meticulous and faithful to the original art." He was biting his lip as he spoke. "Of course, I can't claim your expertise in that end of things, so it might be that I didn't—"

"Hold on, Ulisse, relax. I didn't say he wasn't a good choice. He's got a top-notch reputation in the field. Some very good museums use him."

These weren't outright lies, but they weren't exactly the whole truth, either. Zampa had the technical tools, all right, and he did have a good reputation, generally speaking, but there were some people, admittedly a minority, but one that included me, who had some serious reservations about him. Art restoration, in its simplest terms, consists ideally of returning a damaged or timeworn painting to its original condition *to the extent possible*—without getting too inventive or imaginative about it; in other words, cleaning or removing varnish that has "browned" the painting's appearance or repairing flaking or blistered paint, patching holes and cracks, perhaps retouching small areas where bits of paint have been damaged or fallen away.

Zampa was indeed very good at all this. If he stopped there I'd have thought him a fine choice for the Renoirs. But he was somewhat of a reversion to the now deplored eighteenth- and nineteenth-century restorers who went further and "improved" the pictures they worked on. Pictures were not merely cleaned and retouched, they were altered, reworked to suit the restorer's view of what they *ought* to look like; that is, what they must have looked like, in his opinion, on the day they were painted. The result had been the irreversible ruin of the many, many works that had fallen into their hands.

The reason is partly that restoring a degraded artwork to what we think it originally looked like not only involves a lot of guesswork, but the very notion of what essentially defines a Renoir as a Renoir, or a Rembrandt as a Rembrandt shifts with the times, sometimes markedly. This is the reason so many nineteenth- and early-twentieth-century forgeries, famously successful when they were made, look so inept, so wrong, to our (supposedly) more educated eyes.

Well, Zampa wasn't as bad as all that, but he was inclined in that direction. He made colors that seemed to me brighter than they'd probably been a hundred or two hundred or three hundred years ago, when they were created. He got rid of *pentimenti*, the ghosts of earlier tries that the artist himself had overpainted but which had bled through the newer paint to become visible with time. Why would he do that? Because they offended his sense of what the original finished painting *should* look like. But what was lost was the precious visualization of the artist's mind at work.

And so I did regret hearing that he'd been given the Renoirs to work on. I should add that nowadays reputable restorers—and Zampa was surely one—no longer did their retouching of painted areas directly on the painted surface, but on a thin layer of "isolating varnish" that had been applied over it after it was cleaned. Also, the pigments they use are soluble in mineral spirits, one of the mildest of solvents. These precautions ensure that failed restorations can later be removed without damaging the artist's original work.

No one had ever called Ulisse unperceptive or called me very good at prevaricating; he sensed my unease at once. "But you don't approve," he said, growing increasingly distressed.

"Ulisse—"

"Don't say you do. I know you, I can see it in your eyes; I can hear it in your voice." He smiled. "I know you, *caro*, better than you think."

"Look," I said, "it's got nothing to do with his competence or reliability. It's just that I've heard from people that he's not the easiest man in the world to work with, that's all."

Actually, I'd heard a lot about him. In fact, he was something of a legend in New York museum circles. Everybody who knew him had stories about him. He'd spent two years in New York as a visiting lecturer at NYU's Institute of Fine Arts. That's the one that sits right across Fifth Avenue from the Met, so naturally he spent a lot of time on my side of the street, and a lot of my colleagues got to know him. This was a couple of years before I was hired, so everything I knew about him was hearsay, but it was remarkably consistent.

The overriding impression I got from my older colleagues was that, in addition to being an extremely skilled restorer, he was witty, intelligent, and perceptive . . . and really hard to take, which was probably because he found others so hard to take. If ever a man was created *not* to teach, it was Zampa. He was brutal—caustic, derisive, mocking— toward any student who didn't meet his standards, and since his standards were impossibly high for anyone who wasn't lucky enough to be Dante Zampa, it made for a lot of unhappy students.

On top of that, he was notoriously unreliable—lazy and inconstant—when it came to trifling administrative matters like returning phone calls, showing up at staff meetings, being in his office during office hours, turning in forms, and the like.

By the close of his second year at the institute, the complaints, outrage, and tears that had flowed from his students (and a few from his colleagues) had offset his very obvious talents to the extent that he was not offered a renewal for a third year. When he was called into the director's office to hear this news along with some gentle, well-meant criticism, his response, so the story goes, was "I know you people imagine how rewarding it must be to be a genius, but what you don't realize is how hard that makes it to put up with the cretins you have to deal with in a place like this." Upon which he resigned on the spot and walked out, instead of waiting for the end of the school year, as he was contracted to do. Apocryphal? Maybe, but everybody I knew believed it.

And I remembered a framed placard that hung proudly in the office of a fellow curator:

> *Only take the time to peer behind the false humbuggery of the art world, and you will find the real humbuggery.*
>
> *—Dante Zampa*

She'd even gotten Zampa to sign the thing.

"And since you're not the easiest man in the world to work with, either—" I continued.

Ulisse's hand flew to his heart. "I? Not the easiest . . . ?"

"I'm kidding, Ulisse," I said promptly and not entirely truthfully. "All I mean is, from everything I've heard, he's not too fond of the human race."

"Oh, no, Tino. He loves the human race. It's people he can't stand."

When I laughed, he said: "I'd like to be able to take credit for that, but in fact it was Dante I heard it from. He said it about himself."

"So at least he has a sense of humor. That's something, anyway."

"Yes, but was he joking? Well, we'd better get started, Tino. We're meeting on via Monte Napoleone, at Benvenuto's store. Are you ready to present your case?"

"No," I said.

"Ha-ha," said Ulisse.

Chapter 8

Milan's via Monte Napoleone is one of a handful of streets in the world—Fifth Avenue in Manhattan, Beverly Hills' Rodeo Drive, Rome's via Condotti, London's Bond Street, Paris's rue du Faubourg-St. Honoré are some of the others—on which the titans of the fashion world stand cheek-by-jowl. Looking for something from Dior? Here you are. Prefer Hermès? Right next door. And if you're really into comparison-shopping, on via Monte Napoleone as on the rest of them, it's but a few steps to the nearest Prada, Gucci, Pucci, Vuitton, Versace, or Armani.

Architecturally, though, via Monte Napoleone, all two blocks of it—five hundred yards in all—stands out from the crowd in that so many of the shops occupy the ground floors in rows of handsome, immaculately maintained palazzos. Or at least that's the way they're usually described, and to our American eyes that's what they look like. But in reality, most of them have the same function today that they did two hundred years ago when they were constructed and Milan was the capital of the Napoleonic Italian Republic: they are apartment buildings for the wealthy, the main difference being that they are even more expensive now than they were then.

And the street-level shops were even more expensive than they'd been when I'd been in Milan last. No surprise there; what *wasn't* more expensive than it'd been four years ago? Still, you had to shake your head. We stopped for a moment to look in the window of Dolce & Gabbana, the first of the biggies that you come to if you're approaching from the south. The display was of men's backpacks—at €2,000 a pop.

"I guess I'll stick with L.L.Bean," I said with a sigh, and did indeed accompany it with a shake of my head.

Ulisse mimed a shudder. "I can't imagine buying a backpack at *any* price. The last time I was in the mountains was in 2002. And even then, it wasn't my idea."

That was enough window-shopping for us, and while we walked up the famous street, Ulisse filled me in with thumbnail bios of the two people I was about to meet in addition to Zampa.

Benvenuto Castelnuovo: The all-important lender of Ulisse's two hundred thousand euros, and the celebrated avant-garde men's fashion designer. His creations at the Milan Fashion Week the previous spring had featured men's resort wear that consisted of nothing but studded leather straps of varying thicknesses and, where it was absolutely necessary to avoid charges of indecency, brushed leather pouches.

"Not a skiwear designer, I'm guessing," I said.

"The spring show features summer wear, Tino. At the fall show a few weeks ago he went in more for faux furs in pastel colors. Unfortunately for him, his creations were more lampooned than admired, but that's an old story. As usual, Benvenuto himself was one of the most photographed celebrities attending."

"Why was that?"

"Because Benvenuto Castelnuovo is . . . unique."

When I asked him how he was unique, all he said was: "You shall see."

Giulietta Barone: Divorced, forty-nine-year-old CEO of Montefiore Arte, the art auction house that would be handling the paintings, and daughter of the man who had founded it thirty years before as a hole-in-the-wall antiques shop catering to tourists. Under Giulietta's fifteen-year leadership, it had morphed into a robust challenger to long-time reigning Italian champions Finarte and Semenzato. Giulietta had accomplished this by spearheading an aggressive, expensive advertising campaign to associate the house with sports cars and sex. Considering that this is Italy we're talking about, it would have been hard to come up with an approach that was any more run-of-the-mill and clichéd than that, but for a fine-art auction house? That was unheard of and was met with early disparagement. However Giulietta's campaign was funny and peppy, it poked sly fun at itself and at the art world in general, and somehow it had succeeded. The only major bump in the road to fame came when unauthorized clips of Steve McQueen in *Bullitt* had brought on not one suit but two (from McQueen's estate and from Warner Brothers), both of which had been settled out of court at reputedly astronomical costs. Despite these setbacks, Montefiore had steadily moved up in the auction world to its current status.

"Hey, you like her, don't you?" I asked, just a little archly.

"Oh, yes, she's very nice. You'll like her too."

"No, I mean *really* like her." I accompanied this with a playful eyebrow waggle.

His own eyebrows shot halfway up his forehead. "Now what did I say that would make you think such a thing?"

"Oh, just a feeling. I thought I heard a sort of proprietary tone when you talked about her, an affectionate kind—"

"Ridiculous. I said I *liked* her. I like chocolate too. I like you. I like—"

"Also, you went out of your way to mention that she was divorced—"

"I didn't go 'out of my way' to mention it. I simply mentioned it. I was telling you about her."

"You told me about Benvenuto too, but I didn't hear you say anything about his marital status. Or Zampa's either. You didn't bother to specify their ages, for that matter."

When he didn't come up with a response to that other than one of his put-upon sighs, I probed a little more. "Ulisse, by any chance, are you and Giulietta, umm . . . ?"

He finally gave in and laughed. "No, I wouldn't say we're as far along as *umm* yet, but who knows what the future might hold?"

"Well, I hope it holds something good for you, old friend. It'd be—*urk!*"

"Watch out!" He had grabbed my arm and jerked me back as I was about to step off the curb to cross a narrow alley a few yards shy of the Benvenuto Castelnuovo boutique. An instant later, there was a screech and then the eardrum-shattering gunning of an engine as a motorcycle lurched into a spectacular skidding turn on via Monte Napoleone, anchored by the rider's extended, booted foot, and then pulled expertly into the alley in front of us.

This wasn't just any old motorcycle, either. I admit, I don't know much about motorcycles but what had just roared by two feet from my toes was as different from Italy's friendly, omnipresent, putt-putting Vespas as a ninety-pound Doberman was from a cocker spaniel puppy. It wasn't that big, really, but it was as sleek as sleek could be, slim and tear-shaped, tapered toward the back, and looking like something ready to launch from the Starship *Enterprise*. It was all black and gold, and the equally sleek rider was dressed to match in black leathers with gold detailing and a gold helmet with an opaque black visor. On the sidewalk several people gave thumbs-up signals and laughed. Someone applauded.

Ulisse was laughing at me as I stared after the thing. "Now you know why the photographers love him."

"You're kidding me. That was him? Castelnuovo?"

He nodded. "Our host for the meeting. He has his own parking space behind the shop."

"Does he always travel like that?"

"Here in the city, I have not seen otherwise. He has three of them, all racing motorcycles, and all fitted with muffled exhaust systems so as not to break the noise regulations. He's very proud of them."

I shook my head. "If that was muffled, I'd hate to be around one that wasn't. So tell me, does he also always dress to match the colors of his bike?"

I'd meant it as a moot question, a joke, but Ulisse's response was "Yes, I believe so."

All I could do was shake my head. Again.

When we entered the spacious shop, Ulisse was familiarly greeted by a few of the sales staff, all male. I was greatly relieved to see that they were wearing suits and ties, like any other salesmen on via Monte Napoleone, and not studded leather straps and pouches. There were only a few customers in the place, and they were checking out the socks and shirts, which looked like your basic, ordinary socks and shirts. The three capacious, ankle-length fake fur coats, one pink, one mauve, and one turquoise, that were thrown over the shoulders of mannequins set up on revolving platforms weren't even getting any lookers.

"Slow day on the sales floor," I said quietly as we stood, taking in the place.

"Oh, yes, well, those over-the-top haute-couture creations of his don't ever really sell very well." He waved his hand toward the window to take in the other famous shops along the street. "None of them do, really. The last time one ever sees them is the first time, on the runway.

You never run into a normal person actually wearing one of them on the street, isn't that so?"

"Would you *want* to?" I said with a laugh, thinking about running into crowds of "normal" men decked out in Benvenuto Castelnuovo resort wear.

"As with all of them," Ulisse said, "Benvenuto does it for the publicity and the notoriety, and the envy of his peers. Even more than most, he enjoys raising eyebrows."

"Well, that fits," I said, thinking about his attention-grabbing arrival a few minutes ago. "But how the heck does he make the living he must make from selling shirts and socks? I'm thinking the rent on this place has to cost a fortune."

"A large fortune. But then, he has a number of other business interests that would seem to bring him income."

"Such as making wildly profitable loans, you mean?"

Ulisse received this friendly barb with a slight grimace, probably thinking about the two-plus million euros he was going to have to turn over to Castelnuovo from the eventual sale of the Renoirs. Then he put an arm over my shoulder and pulled me a little closer to indicate I was about to receive something in strictest confidence. "Now, you must never tell him I told you this, but the greater part of his fortune comes from the chain of camping villages and mobile home parks he owns, the second largest in Italy."

It struck me as so incongruous that I was laughing as we came to the meeting room door. The celebrated fashionista, the idol of the paparazzi, the enigmatic, gold-and-black figure who had rocketed down via Monte Napoleone on the flashy motorcycle to park behind his flashy boutique, was in actuality the owner of a string of trailer parks?

"It's not a matter for laughing," Ulisse said severely. "It's a sore point with him."

I straightened my mouth. "Ulisse," I said, "you know me. I will be the soul of discretion."

"Oh, yes," he said, with the lift of just one of his eyebrows, "especially when you want something."

"Well, yes, there is that," I allowed, and pressed down the handle of the door.

Chapter 9

There was only one person in the room, a massive, slope-shouldered, glowering man wearing a beat-up corduroy blazer covered with spills of ash and even a few burn marks, in addition to the occasional dab of paint or varnish. He got up to shake hands with us, even though he didn't look that crazy about it. But then, shaking hands in Italy, especially in business interactions, is a given, the equivalent of a casual "Hey, how ya doin'?" in the States. If you ever do business in Italy (and if you're a male), you'd better warm up those handshaking muscles first because you're going to be doing a lot of it: when you arrive for a meeting, when you depart, when anybody else arrives, and when anybody else departs. This holds even if you last saw the other person yesterday and the interaction is two minutes long. In Italy, it's practically a law.

The man, as I assumed, turned out to be the restorer Dante Zampa, who made an arresting appearance with his high, wide forehead, marked widow's peak, and heavy-lidded eyes with black bags under them that made him look as if he hadn't slept for a week. Most notably, he had just about the most sour, cynical, sarcastic face I'd ever seen. I'm not talking about an *expression* here, something that comes and goes. I'm talking about an ingrained, permanent set to his features that indicated he was greatly disappointed in the human race, but more or less resigned, or at least indifferent, to its inadequacies, and perhaps even wearily amused by them.

You may have noticed that I'm extremely good at quick, shoot-from-the-hip character analyses. This is not to say that they always turn out to be accurate. But I honestly think that in Zampa's case, the same impressions would have come through loud and clear, and just as fast, to anyone, even without having heard all those stories about him.

There were bottles of mineral water and glasses on the oval conference table, but Ulisse went to a narrow table along one wall and got himself a bottle of *limonata* from the row of soft drinks and liqueurs that was on it, and I·followed suit.

"So where is everyone?" Zampa said sulkily as we took seats across from him. "I don't have all day, I have a lot of work to do."

"Such as finally finishing up those Renoirs for us?" Ulisse asked lightly. "Please, don't let us stop you." A twinkling glance in my direction told me that I was witnessing a performance: *See? Intimidating he may be, but Ulisse Agnello knows how to stand up to him.*

Zampa threw him a disgusted look. "Listen, if what you wanted was a quick, slapdash job, you should have gone to a cut-rate hack, not the consummate craftsman of his era."

Now Ulisse looked openly at me with a smile. "Humble, isn't he?"

"I *am* humble," Zampa shot back. "I'm every bit as humble as the level of my talent allows me to be." From somewhere inside his jacket he produced a slim, crooked *sigaro Toscano* (Remember those black cheroots that Clint Eastwood chewed on in those old spaghetti Westerns? Like that), or rather half of one, which is the way they're often smoked here. That explained the ashes and burns on his jacket. I noticed now that the first two fingers of his right hand were stained almost the same rich brown as the cigars.

"One thing the world could use more of," he went on, to no one in particular, "is *more* geniuses with a sense of humility." He stopped to light the cigar with an arrowlike blast from a torch lighter, creating an artful pause before finishing up with what I thought was a pretty good zinger, given the circumstances: "There are hardly any of us left these days."

A feebly dismissive laugh was the best that Ulisse could come up with. He was outgunned and he knew it. As for Zampa, he was definitely living up to expectations.

At this point, our attention was diverted to the opening of the door, and in pranced a soft, peppy-looking gentleman, forcing us all to clamber out of our chairs for another round of handshaking.

"Ah, Benvenuto, *ciao*," said Ulisse, looking relieved to have him there, and then, more formally, "Signor Castelnuovo, may I present my good friend *dottor* Valentino Caruso."

There's an old expression about being bowled over by . . . well, I can't remember by what, but whatever it is, you could have bowled me over with it. This—*this* mincing, pink-cheeked, middle-aged dandy was the Darth Vader–like rider who had rocketed by me on his sinister chopper a few minutes ago? Incredible. And the thing was, he didn't look any more like an avant-garde fashion meister than he did like a biker. Or a trailer park mogul, for that matter. And *especially* not like a loan shark.

What he looked like was the starchy maître d' who greets you at your everyday, ultra-ultra-expensive French restaurant in midtown Manhattan: cheerfully fussy and distantly polite ("You have a reservation, *m'sieu*?"), but not terribly excited about seeing you and already looking over your shoulder in hopes that there might be somebody more important back there, even perchance an honest-to-God celebrity. Small-featured and sort of squinchy-faced, but with pouchy, chipmunklike cheeks, he was wearing a dark, almost invisibly pinstriped suit that fitted his pudgy body beautifully—perfectly—the way Cary Grant's suits used to sit so elegantly on him, the way no suit had ever fitted me or ever would.

Like any proper maître d' he had on a hand-tied bow tie, but this one, rather than being black, was a lively mint green with tiny white polka dots. His blindingly white shirt was so stiffly starched that his neck was chafed at the collar line. As contemporary fashion demanded, only the top button of his two-button suit was fastened, and I caught a glimpse of suspenders that matched the bow tie, polka dots and all. The cheerful colors and the perky twin peaks of the knot under his softening chin added to the affable appearance he conveyed. As with that Fifty-Seventh Street French maître d', though, there was something slightly put-on about it, as if it might not be something that came naturally. I felt as if I were watching an actor in a play.

There you are: another profound five-second character analysis. A wonderful gift to have, wouldn't you agree?

"Ah," he said, "the clever fellow who can't wait to deprive us of our hard-earned profits." He said it lightly and with a cool smile, but it made me nervous anyway.

"Only temporarily," I replied with equal lightness, "and only a little part of them."

"Una goccia nell'oceano," sang Ulisse.

"Oh-ho-ho, I wouldn't say that" was Castelnuovo's merry reply. I couldn't make out what he was thinking, which way he was leaning.

We were in the act of sitting back down when we heard a tinkly, toy-piano version of the third-act quartet from *Rigoletto*. Ulisse pulled a phone from the inside pocket of his jacket and looked at the screen. "I'd better take this."

"Perhaps I can save us all some time while we wait," said Benvenuto when Ulisse made his exit, cell phone to his ear. He clasped his hands on the table and turned directly to me with that pinched, pouchy smile. *This is not going to be good,* I thought. On the outside, I thought I was putting up a good front, but inside I wilted.

"*Dottor* Caruso, I feel it's only fair to tell you that you are going to have a harder time with me than you did with your friend Ulisse. This proposal of yours . . . really—"

He was interrupted by Ulisse's frowning return. "I'm afraid I have some bad news. That was Giulietta. She was in an accident on the way to the ferry. Her residence is in Bellagio," he interjected for my benefit. "She has an apartment at the Villa Serbelloni. On Lake Como."

"She's all right?" Castelnuovo asked. "She's not hurt?"

Zampa, not very interested in Giulietta's condition, went to get himself a pastry from the side table.

"Yes, a broken finger, that's all. She was calling from the hospital to let us know."

"So she's not going to be here," Zampa grumped.

"Well, no," Ulisse replied, returning to his place at the table. "As I said, she's still in Bellagio."

"Fine. Then there's no point in my hanging around, is there?"

It was Castelnuovo who responded, rather prissily. "Not as far as I'm concerned, Dante. To be honest, I can't imagine what you're doing here in the first place."

Zampa darkened and opened his mouth to speak, but Ulisse jumped in before a bolt of fire could shoot forth. "Dante is here because Giulietta requested his presence, Benvenuto."

"Yes, and after all, if signora Barone requests it," Zampa said, heavy on the sarcasm, "it must be done, must it not?" This was accompanied by a look at Ulisse suggesting that his not-quite-umm relationship with Barone was general knowledge.

"So what are we expected to do now?" Castelnuovo asked Ulisse.

"Well, there's Tino's request pertaining to the sketch. Perhaps—"

"Yes, we were talking about that when you came in," Castelnuovo said. "I was telling him that I am not inclined to agree to it."

Ulisse seemed genuinely surprised. "You're not? Benvenuto, I can't believe you mean it. Surely you don't deny that signor Bezzecca suffered grievous wrongs? Surely—"

"Yes, but not committed by us. Why should we pay for what the Fascists did in 1944? Were you even born yet? I wasn't." Castelnuovo had a strange way of speaking. His tone seemed always to be the same. Everything he said sounded sprightly and upbeat, but also a little strained. If I hadn't heard the words themselves, I might have thought he was talking up his creations at the next Fashion Week.

"That's all true," Ulisse said, "but we have an opportunity, by making a small sacrifice—"

"And when I think of all the trouble that sorry old man made for us . . ." Benvenuto shook his head back and forth. "No, I don't think so. I'm sorry." Sung out as cheerfully as ever.

Ulisse threw his hands in the air and sank back in his chair with a cold, frustrated "I'm very surprised at you, signore."

I felt as defeated as Ulisse looked, but I had to give it a try of my own. "Signore," I said respectfully, "I understand perfectly why you would feel that way and I sympathize, but would you give me a chance, ten minutes, no more, to present my case—his case—before you decide?"

"That's fair," he surprised me by saying. "All right, I'll listen to what you have to say."

Good enough. "Thank you." I geared myself up to wow him. "I really appreciate the chance to—"

"But with Giulietta's absence today, we're going to have to meet again in the next day or two anyway. Wouldn't it be better to wait until then, so you don't have to go through it again for Giulietta? She'll have to agree to take the picture out of the auction."

"Giulietta again," Zampa muttered, fastening the clasps on his briefcase.

"Yes, Giulietta again, and once again at her request, you are cordially invited, Dante."

"Cordially commanded is what you mean," Zampa grumbled.

"So, then," Ulisse said brightly, "is everybody available tomorrow morning? I realize it's an imposition, a Sunday, but . . ."

A predictably cheery nod of assent from Castelnuovo, a predictably aggrieved one from Zampa.

Ulisse raised a forefinger. "There is a small problem, though," he ventured. "Giulietta has asked if it would be possible for us to meet in Bellagio, rather than here. Because of her hand."

"That's almost two hours each way!" exploded Zampa. "There goes my entire day! Oh, why did I ever agree to submit myself to these heartless inhumanities?" He finished by lowering his head to rest his brow on his fingertips, the tragedian's classic pose of consternation.

He was overdoing it to get a laugh, and it was well-done enough at least to get a smile out of me, but it got Ulisse's dander up, or maybe he was still proving to me that he could handle Zampa. "She has been willing to make a two-hour drive here for our convenience more than once, Dante. I don't think it's asking too much of us to return the favor, considering her accident."

"Accident," he said sarcastically. "Tell us, how does her *accident* stop her from coming here? She broke her finger, not her leg. Does she walk on her hands? And what about Montefiore? Is she staying away from her work there as well, because of a broken finger?"

This was ignored all around. "Ten o'clock tomorrow, then," said Ulisse, "if there are no serious objections. At the Serbelloni. If you ask at the desk they will tell you where we are to meet."

Once Zampa had slunk out, Castelnuovo stood up, waving his hand in front of his face to clear away the smoke. "I don't know why I don't forbid that man's cigars in here," he said.

"Neither do I. Why don't you?" asked Ulisse.

"And provoke one of his explosions? No, it's not worth it. Better to simply hold my breath for an hour or two. Gentlemen, I need to straighten out something with my manager in the shop. Ulisse, shall we hold off the rest of our conversation until tomorrow? *Dottor* Caruso, it's been a pleasure. I look forward to seeing you then."

"Looks like Castelnuovo might not go along with it, after all," I said to Ulisse as we got to the sidewalk outside.

"Oh, I wouldn't say that. I think we can bring him around. We'll just have to see, I suppose."

"Right," I said moodily. I was feeling a little deflated. Things weren't sounding too promising.

"Listen, Tino, would you be able to find your own way to Bellagio tomorrow? I'm off to Lugano later today for an Arts Council event— lots of carousing and working the crowd and that sort of thing, and I expect it will run late, so I'll probably stay over at the Splendide and drive to Bellagio from there in morning. It's not a long drive, but Milan would be considerably out of the way, so if you could possibly—"

"Absolutely. Don't give it a thought. I wouldn't expect you to cart me around anyway. I'll catch a train. Done it before. It's a pleasant ride. I'll enjoy it." We shook hands. "Well, I'm off to the Brera. Time to go earn my salary."

Chapter 10

The Pinacoteca di Brera—the Brera Art Gallery (Brera is a district in Milan)—owes its existence to the looting proclivities of Napoleon Bonaparte even more than the Louvre does. While there's no shortage of Napoleonic booty in the Louvre, it did start off as a gallery to showcase the collection of Louis XIV, who had recently given up residence in the building to move the royal court to Versailles. The Brera, on the other hand, was explicitly created to house the enormous hoard of looted art that the Little Corporal had brought back to his newly created (and short-lived) Italian Republic from his various campaigns in Europe and Egypt. Even today, two hundred years later, it is those works, by Titian, Botticelli, Raphael, Caravaggio, and the like, that make up the bulk of its masterpieces.

Fittingly, in the center of the great courtyard through which one passes to enter the building, there stands upon a pedestal a bronze statue of Napoleon Bonaparte cast in 1811 as *Napoleon as Mars the Peacemaker.* It's intended as a tribute to the museum's great benefactor, of course, but today it draws more smirks than approbation. For one thing, it's a really *big* statue, well over life-sized, and it kind of hits you in the face when you walk into the courtyard, and he's totally naked except for what strikes one as a precariously small fig leaf. For whatever reason, some nude statues simply look nuder than others, and this is definitely among the nudiest. That's one reason. The other is that on his outstretched right palm is a tiny winged figure meant to be Nike, the Greek goddess of victory. Since the opening of *Peter Pan* on the London stage in 1904, however, people, and even some guidebooks, have taken to referring to the statue as "Napoleon and Tinker Bell," which has an undeniable aptness but does nothing for its dignity.

Still, I gave it my usual nod of appreciation in passing (artistically speaking, it's worth seeing, expertly cast from an earlier marble sculpture by Canova, and a handsome work of sculpture in its own right, but once you've gotten "Tinker Bell" into your head, just try getting it out).

I was early for my meeting, the first session of the coordinating committee for the upcoming *Treasures of the Brera* tour, so I took the opportunity to stroll through the galleries for the first time in four years. They are pretty much arranged chronologically, and, as I usually do out of respect for my fellow curators, I took them in in the order they intended, starting with the early Italian galleries—Bellini, Carpaccio, Vivarini, Mantegna, et al. They are genuine masters, all of them, but in the fourteenth and fifteenth centuries, European art was overwhelmingly religious, which meant scene after scene of crucifixions and martyrdoms, and the bodies of fiendishly slaughtered saints. Frankly speaking, they make my skin crawl.

I know that, as an art curator myself, I'm not supposed to make value judgments like that about an important period in the history of Western art, but I don't see how I can help it. I don't see it as a value judgment at all, but as a matter of taste, and how am I supposed to do anything about that? You know how people like to say, "I don't know a lot about art, but I know what I like"? Well, I *do* know a lot about art, but I also know what I like, and they don't always match.

I stopped in only a couple of these rooms, when the stoic, depressed guards sitting near the doorways made me feel guilty about sprinting on through without even a glance at the works they spend their lives overseeing. This happens to me in museums all the time, so I did now what I always do, taking a few moments to pause before some painting I really didn't want to look at and nodding, wisely and appreciatively, in hopes that the guard might feel less inconsequential. And then hurrying on to, and through, the next gallery, until I reached the paintings to which I was looking forward.

No, not the Impressionists—there are no galleries dedicated to that bunch here—but my other favorites, the Dutch and Flemish artists of the seventeenth and early eighteenth centuries. At the Brera they are in three small rooms, and walking into them was like coming out of a dark tunnel into a green and sunlit meadow. Here, in galleries 31, 32, and 33, the only dead bodies in sight were those of fish, and deer, and fowl, artfully arranged on sideboards or kitchen tables, and the gaunt, somber faces of the pious gave way to the jolly, plump, pink-cheeked burghers of Rubens and Hals.

Aahh.

For twenty minutes I stood basking in their sunny glow (and, yes, nodding wisely and approvingly, but wholly for my own benefit). I could have stayed longer, but eleven o'clock was coming up and I was expected in the boardroom. It took some considerable wandering to find the room—the Brera, a onetime palace, is vast—so that I wound up being the last to arrive.

There were fifteen people around the kayak-shaped table, which would have been a lot for a meeting like this by American standards, but was pretty typical over here. In the States, most museums are privately run (the federal government owns only two: the National Gallery and the Smithsonian), but in Europe, museums are usually government institutions, so a lot of political types want in on the act, which doesn't make getting things done go any faster. As in all countries, Italian government officials also have a tendency to be windy. This, I thought, was going to be a grind.

Other than James Bradburne, the Brera's famously unconventional director (among other things, here he is, the head of one of Italy's greatest museums, and the guy's a Brit), I knew none of them, and Bradburne left after a brief welcome, leaving me the only stranger in a room full of people who all seemed to know one another, many of whom were eyeing me with expressions ranging from innocent curiosity to downright skepticism.

This is an old story with me. The thing is, you see, I've learned from hard experience that I make an underwhelming first impression at meetings with trustees, or boards of directors, or wealthy patrons, or other VIPs in the art world.

My problem is, I don't look like anybody's idea of an art curator, let alone an art curator at one of the world's great museums. When meeting a curator, people seem to expect either a patrician blue-blood oozing erudition and sophistication, or a brusque, preoccupied academic with deeper, more important things on his mind. And actually—let's be honest here—as generalizations go, there's some justification for it. What I bring to mind on first impression, so they tell me, is a "wiseguy," a mob enforcer. I'm five eleven, but being thick-shouldered, and broad across the chest, and not having much to show in the way of neck, I seem shorter to people. One former girlfriend with a penchant for similes told me I was built like a tugboat. ("But a very nice-looking tugboat.") Then there's my hair, which comes down to an almost straight-across hairline that is admittedly pretty low on my forehand, and I have a ferocious five o'clock shadow to go along with it.

A couple of years ago, in an effort to look more like a curator, I started getting better haircuts, taking a second daily shave at noon, and buying a couple of thousand-dollar Hugo Boss suits at Bloomingdale's, but the result (based on an unscientific but convincing poll) was that now I looked like a slick, sharp mob *consigliere.* Better than an enforcer, I guess, but not really the look I was aiming for. So I gave up and went back to one shave a day, to my old barber in Queens, and to off-the-rack sport coats from Macy's. I was wearing one today. By now I'd gotten so used to having this effect on people that I was untroubled by it and, inside of twenty minutes or so, as expected, it dissipated, or at least the perceptible aspects of it did. The committee chair, a Brera senior curator whose name I didn't get, was a formal, efficient woman who got us down to business in a hurry, and the civic dignitaries, thank goodness, were content to offer a brief platitude for the record now and then, and leave the nitty-gritty to us museum types. By eleven thirty, half of them had left and we were able to do some real work.

There was a lot involved, especially for me, as the representative of the first museum on the tour. I had already been working with the other museums—in Boston, Chicago, Cleveland, and Los Angeles—for several weeks, and I had brought with me their "facilities reports," in which they'd specified the preparations they proposed to have in place for the exhibition: lighting, humidity, fire suppressants, anti-intrusion devices, and so on. These were all actually responses to earlier conditions set by the Brera, and the Brera would now make additional, highly specific requests of each museum, which would then respond with their alterations, and on and on.

It's a long process. This one would take a little over two years before it opened in America.

It's also enormously expensive, and although the basic division of costs had long ago been standardized by the international museum community, a lot of specifics had to be worked out.

And last but definitely not least, assuming you're a person of refinement, culture, and discrimination (you know, like me), it's boring as hell. So if it's all right with you, I'll skip the risk management and insurance details, and all the logistical and packing minutiae, and just tell you that we worked through lunch, set up the next few meetings, and closed things down at two thirty.

Among the few civic officials who stuck it out was a tall, stout, handsome man in his sixties with merry, intelligent eyes and an impeccably manicured, silver-and-gray Vandyke beard, the kind with a distinct, separate mustache above it. A pair of wire-rimmed reading glasses sat low on his nose, giving him an inescapably bookish look. He'd made some useful suggestions during the session, and his friendly smiles in my direction made it obvious that he knew me, but he looked entirely unfamiliar to me, even when I mentally took off his glasses and removed his beard. And now, as the room cleared and I got up, he was on his way around the table in my direction, coming to renew our acquaintance. His was one of the many names I didn't remember from the introductions at the start, so I geared up my ambiguous "How are you? It's good to see you again" routine—awkward at best, but better than "Who the hell are you again?"

"So you're Tino Caruso," he said. Ah, so he didn't know me, after all, not personally. "And I, I am Adriano Riccardi." He stood there, looking expectantly at me, as if I ought to know *him*.

"Umm . . ." was the best I could do for an uncomfortable few seconds and then I remembered that Esther had mentioned his name. "Yes, of course, you were the judge in Solomon Bezzecca's appeal."

"Just one of three," he said. "The Court of Appeal functions as a tribunal. But yes, I hereby admit it, I did serve as chief judge."

A little defensive (in an amiable way), but completely understandable. I'm afraid my tone had been a bit accusatory. In my mind's eye, I realized only now, I'd pictured the man who'd denied Sol's appeal as crabbed, and pinched, and mean-spirited; certainly nothing like this hearty, convivial character with the rich, booming voice. Put an apron on him, and with his ruddy cheeks and that nineteenth-century beard, he could have been the jolly, aproned pubkeeper at the Crown and Anchor in some newly gentrified old town in the Cotswolds.

I smiled and shook his hand for the second time that day. "I apologize for sounding a little hostile there, signor *giudice*." Mister judge—that's the way you address judges here, no exceptions unless given an exemption by His Honor himself. "Sol's a friend of mine"—I was surprised to hear myself say this, and mean it too; I don't usually make friends that fast—"and the decision was a terrible blow to him. So I guess I'd been thinking of you as the enemy. That was wrong of me. I'm sure you did your job and did it well."

"I hope so. I hope we all did. The decision was unanimous, you know."

"Ah."

"Yes. Well. I understand that you're hoping to get signor Agnello to agree to lending your signor Bezzecca the picture of his grandfather."

"How do you happen to know that, signor *giudice*? I was hoping there wouldn't be any publicity."

"As far as I know, there hasn't been, but Esther Lindauer—despite our courtroom battles, Esther is an old and dear friend . . ."

I came dangerously near letting out a bark of startled laughter. *Old and dear friend?* I'd heard her use Riccardi's name only once, and that was in the warmly affectionate phrase "that mealy-mouthed, nitpicking hypocrite Riccardi." Or maybe, on second thought, it was affectionate. Esther could be like that.

". . . and she told me about it yesterday, when I spoke with her about a completely different matter. In any case, I simply wanted to wish you luck with it. I mean that sincerely, and if there is any way I can help, please call on me." He held out his card.

Talk about stunners. I was too astonished to take the card. After denying Sol's plea for the painting when it counted, *now* he wanted to help me get it for him?

"I don't understand. You think he *should* have the painting?"

"The sketch, oh, yes. Nothing would please me more."

I continued to goggle at him. "But . . . but . . ."

"But if I feel that way, why did I vote to award the two paintings to signor Agnello?" He was smiling as he spoke. "Would that be your question?"

"That's my question." Only now did I think to take the card that was still in his outstretched hand.

"You know," he said, "forgive me if I state the obvious, but the jurist's obligation, in both our countries, in any civilized country, is to apply the law as he understands it, not to do what he personally believes to be the right thing, wouldn't you agree? A judge who is ever and always happy with the outcomes of his juridical findings is in my opinion a poor jurist."

"Sure, I can see how that makes a lot of sense, but let me get this straight. Are you saying that, in this case, the law was properly applied, but that it didn't result in—"

"The right thing? No, that's not what I'm saying. I believe our restitution laws are just and fair. I support them."

I shook my head. "You just lost me again. I—"

"Are you free for a late lunch, *dottore*? I know a nice little place not too far from here. A brisk ten-minute walk. Nothing fancy, but good Italian food."

"Couldn't ask for more," I said. "Let's go." *Andiamo.*

"Let's start at the beginning," he said as we left the museum and walked past Napoleon's muscled, gleaming backside out to via Brera. "I assume you do know that there are some fundamental differences in the way our two countries—their legal systems—address the competing rights of the original owners of art and good-faith purchasers, yes?"

"Yes, I think I know what you mean. American law leans very much toward the rights of the original owner, while Italian courts—European courts, in general—tend to favor the good-faith purchaser."

The good-faith purchaser. This was the generalized entity that Sol had been describing when talking about Ulisse: a person who'd innocently bought a stolen or looted work of art from a legitimate seller; he'd had no way of knowing the work had ever been stolen, and in Ulisse's particular case, he hadn't even known what he was buying.

"Correct. And you—permit me another assumption—you are inclined to take the American point of view. Would I be right there?"

"Of course. The same way I feel safe in assuming that you're inclined to take the Italian point of view."

He inclined his head and laughed. "True."

"But look, signor *giudice*—"

"Adriano, Tino."

"But look, Adriano, I make no claims as a legal scholar, far from it, but it seems to me that a victim of something as brutal as Nazi looting during the Holocaust, like Sol—"

"A victim of brutal Italian looting, I'm sorry to say."

"—a victim of Italian looting, then, has suffered a whole lot more than this perfectly honest good-faith buyer would suffer from the loss of the money he spent to buy the object, which is all he *would* lose. Doesn't the original owner have more claim to the object, on the basis of simple moral probity?"

"Well, he certainly has a claim, but so does the completely innocent purchaser, who by the way—when it's paintings that are in question—has usually invested a *very* great deal more than your friend Ulisse."

"I understand that, and he should certainly be reimbursed for the amount he spent, but the object itself should—"

"And nothing more? Just ninety euros?"

"Well, any other losses or expenses he might have had; cleaning, restoring, shipping—"

"And what about future losses? The lost opportunity of realizing a profit by selling the object? Should he be compensated for that? And if so, how?"

This was an area that I didn't feel very secure in, so I took some time to think. After which I hedged. "I can't see how a general answer would apply. I think he *should* be compensated, yes, but the amount . . . that would need to be left to the court, based on the circumstances. Case by case."

"Very good. That's the way our courts see it too. But now let me turn things around. What about doing it the other way? Awarding the object in question to the purchaser, but compensating the original owner for *his* loss?"

"Compensating him with what, money? It's the *painting* that means something to him. But the purchaser, all he's got invested in it is what he spent on it. Money."

"Oh, I'd say it's the painting that means something to both of them."

"Sometimes, sure. Unfortunately, it's a zero-sum game, though, isn't it? One of them gets the painting, one of them doesn't get the painting. There's no way to split the difference."

"Not unless you're King Solomon," Adriano said, smiling.

Unsurprisingly Adriano's idea of a brisk walk turned out to be my idea of an energetic jog, during which I looked wistfully at every restaurant we passed, hoping it was where we were headed, but the ten-minute walk ran a good twenty minutes, even at Adriano's ridiculous pace, before we finally stopped at an unprepossessing restaurant on via Ceresio. Trattoria da Mario, it was called, and if that isn't the commonest restaurant name in Italy, I'm sure it's right up there. The place was simple and modern, and busy, with aproned waiters scurrying about.

But the second we came through the door, one of them dashed up to us, wiping his hands on the towel at his waist, and without a word to him or from him, but only a respectful half-bow to Adriano, led us through the buzzing room and into a smaller one that held only a few tables, none of them occupied.

"Do you like seafood?" Adriano asked me as we followed along.

"Love it."

"Pasta?"

"Who doesn't love pasta?"

"Good, good, a man after my own heart."

Once we'd been shown to our table, Adriano and the waiter—his name was Livio—put their heads together for a hushed discussion, with Livio nodding his approval and taking notes as it went along and then bustling off with his pad as we sat down.

Well, you might at least have consulted me, was my petty reaction, but Adriano did everything with such happy good humor that it didn't last. Besides, I knew we'd get a better meal than if I'd ordered. I had no doubt that he'd also slipped the waiter his credit card, which meant that I had already lost the obligatory dispute at the end about who would pay—but what good manners demanded was that I vigorously dispute it all the same before giving in and accepting. This was pretty much the way things worked over here. Next time, I'd be buying.

Livio was soon back, and three platters were laid on the table: pickled octopus chunks, paper-thin filets of pickled anchovies, and a mixed grill of fried whole sardines, calamari, small whole octopuses, and inch-long shrimp—heads, legs, and all, that amounted to no more than a tangy, briny crunch or two. There was a crusty loaf in a straw basket along with them. No wine was offered (this was probably Adriano's preference; it was still the workday), but there were bottles of mineral water.

Adriano, as I'd imagined, was a hearty, enthusiastic eater. I was no match for him, but I wasn't any slouch either, so for some minutes there wasn't much in the way of meaningful conversation. I admit that I kept my distance from those baby octopuses with their soft, sacklike heads, but other than those, I gave the judge a reasonable run for his money, and we both helped ourselves to seconds (thirds for Adriano), passing the platters amicably back and forth. It was a lot of food and I assumed that was our lunch. I was about to suggest espressos to finish the meal off when Livio showed up again with more bread, and with two fragrant, ample plates of *spaghetti con vongole*. I was stuffed, but the pasta really was delicious and the two of us got down to eating again.

People up here in Milan eat their pasta differently than the way they do down south. As a kid, I learned to do it the Sicilian way, twirling my fork against the bowl of a tablespoon to get the pasta wound around the tines, and sticking a napkin the size of a tablecloth down my collar to keep my shirt clean. I still think that's the most efficient way to eat spaghetti, but in good company I go along with local etiquette. In this particular case, that meant following Adriano's lead, using not a spoon but the raised rim of the plate as a base for spaghetti-twirling (the plates are designed for this purpose). And, instead of sticking the corner of the napkin down my neck, I did as he did, holding it in my free hand throughout, in front of my chest, ever ready, I suppose, to catch a falling droplet, or to dab away at my chin. I still find this silly-looking and uncomfortable. It did not, however, stop either of us from chomping the stuff down.

But appetites are finite—even the judge's—and we soon slowed and started talking again.

"Now then, Tino," he began, "you were talking about 'moral probity,' yes? Justice. And that is an important part of our legal framework too, just as it is in yours. But if we relied wholly on it as an underpinning, how could things ever be settled, particularly in Europe with its centuries—its millennia—of wars and looting, *especially* in the world of art?"

"Well, sure, that's a good point. There aren't many major artworks going back any length of time that haven't been stolen or looted over the years, most of them more than once. If title could never again be transferred because of that, how could any would-be buyer ever feel secure? People would be coming out of the woodwork contesting every purchase."

"Yes, exactly, now you've got it! And so here in Italy, we put our faith in an overriding qualification, so to speak: an individual who acquires property from someone who is not its *bona fide* owner *can* acquire ownership of it—if it was acquired in good faith *and* if he can show some valid instrument or detailed record of the transaction."

"And Ulisse had one?"

"Yes, a detailed—and well-documented—receipt from the market at which he bought the paintings. The court was fully satisfied."

"And what about Sol? He must have had something too, some kind of evidence in order to have his claim, his suit, considered."

"Of course, although we, unlike certain of our European neighbors, have never demanded incontestable *proof* of ownership from Holocaust victims like signor Bezzecca—how could they be expected to have it? But we do require reasonable evidence of prior possession."

"And I'm trying to imagine what it was, but I can't come up with anything."

"It was a small thing, a little object of solely sentimental worth that a kindly neighbor found and saved for him, along with other mementos. When the war ended, he was able to return it to him."

Adriano's mouth relaxed into a wistful smile. "A photo taken in what is obviously a kitchen in a modest apartment. There is old Grandfather Maurizio, beribboned and bemedaled, as erect and regal as if the kitchen chair he sat in was a throne. He wears the simple green uniform of the *Garibaldini*, the Hunters of the Alps. At his side, standing no less rigidly, is a boy of nine or ten, his head no higher than the top of the old man's head. On the wall behind them is a citation, its printing not legible in the photograph, but identified from its ornamentations by the court-appointed documents-examiner as a Hero of the Risorgimento proclamation—a very rare object. Also a small calendar. And *also*—"

I took an easy guess. "Two small paintings."

He nodded. "Easily recognizable as signor Agnello's two Renoirs."

"And that was good enough for you."

"That was good enough for us."

"But not good enough to award him the paintings."

He spread his hands. "I was acting as a judge; I followed the law. Now I am not acting as a judge; I follow my instincts, my heart. I mean what I said, Tino. If there is any way I can help you get that loan for him, you just let me know."

"That's terrific, Adriano. I just might do that."

Adriano had his second and last swallow of the espresso that Livio had brought us without our asking and looked at me with twinkling eyes. "Within the law, of course."

After our lunch Adriano went off to his meeting and I headed back down via Ceresio in the general direction of the Hotel Milano Scala. Never having been on this street before today, I didn't know exactly where to turn off to get to the hotel, so when I came to via Fiori Chiari—the opposite end from which I'd gotten onto it last night—I turned up it because I did know how to get to the hotel from there.

The sky had clouded over during lunch and now a light rain was floating down, more like a dull, gray mist, really, but wet enough so that

Chapter 11

I had told Ulisse yesterday that I would take the train to Bellagio, that I remembered it as a pleasant ride and I expected to enjoy it. It was, and I did: a relaxing hour and a half on a near-silent, super-clean, red-and-white, commuter-style train. (The old-time European trains of vintage movies, with their romantic compartments like little drawing rooms, each with its own door to the outside, are, regrettably, a vanishing breed.) My notes for what I wanted to say at the meeting were on my lap but I'd spent more than an hour tweaking and rehearsing them over breakfast before leaving, and so mostly I just watched Italy glide by.

Italy, as everyone knows, is shaped like a boot. Lake Como, to continue the sartorial metaphor, is shaped like a pair of pants, with the village of Como at the left ankle and Lecco at the right. To the north where the legs join the body, there is Varenna on the right hip and Tremezzina on the left. Bellagio—and this has provoked much low humor through the years—is right smack in the crotch, surrounded by water (the legs) on two sides. To get to Bellagio, one takes a fifteen-minute ferry from Varenna, and this is what I did, arriving well in time for the meeting.

La perla del Lago di Como, the pearl of Lake Como, is what they call Bellagio, and it deserves the name, a truly lovely lakefront village with winding, quaint old streets in the town center, and along the lake, villas that are among the grandest of the grand. And always in sight from everywhere, sky-blue Lake Como itself.

Until recently, those were the elements that brought in the tourists. Now, what beckons them in increasing swarms is the opportunity of bumping into the Hollywood nobility of the day on the crowded streets. A magazine stand at the ferry dock prominently displayed a newspaper called—in English—*Celebrity Sightings*. And there, smiling (or scowling) back at me from the front page, were Robert De Niro, George Clooney, Helen Mirren, and Brad Pitt, all spotted in the neighborhood "disguised" with sunglasses and looking variously happy (De Niro), furtive (Pitt), or annoyed (Clooney, Mirren). And those are just the ones I recognized.

The Grand Hotel Villa Serbelloni, a five-minute walk along lakefront via Roma from the ferry dock, is the premier hotel here, a palatial, nineteenth-century, neoclassical edifice with yellow stucco walls and bright red-tile roofs. It sits on a pretty promontory all its own, amid impossibly neat Italian-style gardens, and fronted by patios planted with palm trees and set out with round dining tables. It was at one of these tables, under an awning, that the little group was assembled for our meeting.

Except that, as with yesterday, only three of the four were present—but this time the missing party was Ulisse.

After ten minutes of small talk and desultory toying with the coffee and pastries that had been carried out from the hotel by a three-man parade of smooth, seasoned waiters (were they actually walking in step, or was that my imagination?) in pristine white waistcoats, Giulietta Barone finally jumped up. "This is ridiculous," she announced. "I'm going to call him. For God's sake." She stepped away from the table, pulling a phone out of her shoulder bag as she went. The last three fingers of her left hand were taped together, the only sign of the previous day's misfortune, which was what had made today's meeting necessary. They didn't seem to bother her.

She was an imposing, self-assured woman with graying brown hair that was cut short in pert layers—what I think is referred to as a pixie cut, and very pixieish it was. In my opinion it didn't suit her; too sassy, too cute. Giulietta was not cute. I'm not saying she wasn't a good-looking woman. She was, but in a severe sort of way. A little scary, in fact. Decked out in the right costume, she would have made a terrific dominatrix, or more charitably, I suppose, a judge—not a jolly judge like Adriano, but the sternly righteous kind you did *not* want running the show if you happened to be the defendant in a criminal case. I couldn't help wondering how the flighty, erratic Ulisse was going to handle her, should their relationship develop beyond the umm stage.

In five minutes she was back to tell us that she had four numbers for him and hadn't gotten hold of him on any of them. She'd left irritated with him; she'd come back worried. "This isn't like him at all. I can't imagine—"

"Oh, I'm sure he'll be here before long," Castelnuovo said, and suggested that, since I'd already filled Ulisse in about the loan I was hoping for, I might as well make my pitch to Castelnuovo himself and Giulietta while we awaited his arrival. "The stage is yours, Valentino."

Treating Bezzecca's request as a time-filler while they waited for something else to happen (something more important) seemed like the least promising way to go about it that I could imagine. My heart sank at the idea, but I didn't see that I had much choice. I had another gulp of coffee to rev up my failing spirits, leaned earnestly across the table, and prepared to give it my all. I managed to get five words out ("Solomon Bezzecca is the most—") before Zampa interrupted:

"Look, I don't give a shit about the old fart. I don't give a shit about lending it out. I don't have anything to *do* with lending it out. So if somebody would just tell me what I'm doing here, I can deal with it and get the hell out, and let you work out your own problems. Maybe I can still get something useful out of the day instead of wasting my time with you people."

111

Gracious as ever, signor Zampa. A man with a gift for never missing an opportunity to offend. But he was so bald-faced, and out front, and reliably consistent about it that there was something almost endearing about him. Unless, of course, you were on the receiving end.

"You know, Dante," Castelnuovo said with a purse-mouthed smile, "a little tact now and then might help things along, don't you think so? Make things a little smoother, I mean." Delivered in very near his usual amicable, slightly vacant manner, as if he were merely trying to be helpful, but a certain rigidity around his mouth made it clear that he was well and truly fed up with the Great Restorer.

"Oh, *tact*?" was Zampa's retort. "Yes, I know all about tact. The art of saying 'nice doggie' until you can find a big enough rock. No, thank you. I don't believe in it."

"You are here," Giulietta said stiffly, "because I require some straightforward answers from you—explicit answers, not runarounds."

"My dear Giulietta," Zampa said, "I may have a character deficiency or two—I am human, after all, so I suppose it's at least theoretically possible—but giving runaround answers to questions? That is not something I've ever been accused of."

"Oh, really? Then why is it that every time I ask you one simple question, one vital question, a question that absolutely *requires* answering well in advance of the auction, so that I have time, if necessary, to amend the—"

Zampa had lowered his chin to his chest and was making snoring sounds. "Hey, Giulietta, do you mind if I go get some lunch in the hotel while you get to the point?"

She scowled at him. "When are you going to be finished with the damn paintings?" She was almost shouting. "Can you tell me that?"

"I see. And you want a specific, explicit answer to this vital question of yours, not some vague generality, that's what you're asking for?"

"*Yes*, damn it!"

"All right, then," Zampa said tranquilly. He drew himself up, folded his hands on the table with measured precision, and looked levelly at her. "No."

A beat passed while she glowered down at the tabletop. Then, without raising her eyes, she uttered a low, menacing, "No, what?"

"No, I cannot tell you when I'm going to be finished with them. Is that explicit enough for you?"

"Damn you, Dante. I don't know why we ever . . ." Not having much success with him, she appealed to Castelnuovo and to me. "How can I be expected to put up an auction if this . . . this man can't tell me whether or not the items are going to be ready?"

"Oh, is *that* what you want to know?" Zampa said innocently. "Why didn't you say so? In that case the answer is yes."

"Yes . . . what?" she said through clenched teeth.

"Yes, they'll be ready."

Eyes dangerously narrowed, she peered at him. "By October 9?"

"That's the auction date, isn't it?"

"What about the week before, so we can have them ready for a preview?"

"Hard to say. It's possible."

Giulietta turned suddenly and surprisingly to me. "*Dottor* Caruso, you're an expert, a specialist in this kind of thing. Tell me: If you gave a restorer, even a skilled, experienced, dedicated, famous *craftsman*—two pictures that had been painted over, not very big pictures, not very old pictures, and hired him to clean them up, how long would you expect it to take? A week? A month? What about *two* months, and counting?"

And now Zampa finally took a shot at me. "Yes, *signor specialista*, tell us, how long? And while you're telling us that, why not also tell us, what is this great number of paintings you've restored?"

His questions were flung at me in a tone every bit as belligerent as the words implied. I pushed my chair back from the table, in effect backing away from him, and held up my hands to indicate that I was staying out of this. Anyway, why pick on me? What did I do?

Zampa snorted and turned away; apparently, I wasn't worth scrapping with. "I'm going. Thank you all for a delightful morning. *Ciao.*"

"Well, really . . ." began Castelnuovo as we watched Zampa stomp off.

But Giulietta was steaming, and with Zampa out of reach, I got the brunt of it. "So, Valentino, what's your answer? How long should it take?"

I was irritated at being put on a spot that I had no interest in being on. Defending Dante Zampa was not at the top of my priority list at the moment. I was also bothered by her high-handed and condescending tone and manner. However, unlike Zampa, I was a firm believer in tact, and since Sol had little chance of getting his painting without Giulietta's cooperation, I managed not to show it when I answered her. At least I hoped I hadn't.

"Well, in the first place, Giulietta, 'cleaning up' a picture that's been painted over is easy enough to say, but it can be a tricky job, and extremely risky if you're not ultracareful. For example—"

She sighed—loudly—and looked around, as if expecting help from Castelnuovo, but no such thing was forthcoming from that quarter, so her attention went back to me. "I thought it was a simple question," she said rather crossly to me. "'How long should it take?' I wasn't looking for a lecture."

Too late, lady, you shouldn't have asked. "Think about it for a minute. How do you come up with a solvent that'll dissolve the top layer but not in the least harm the pigments underneath, particularly when both layers are done in the same medium: oils, in this case, that alone probably took a lot of experimenting before he came up with just the right mix. And then, the work itself: you can't just slop on your solvent with a brush, you see, not even the thinnest sable artist's brush you can find. You have to dab it on, millimeter by millimeter, with a cotton swab, under a binocular stereo microscope."

"Really," said Castelnuovo with seeming interest, but I had my doubts. From what I'd seen of the man so far, he was perpetually bright-eyed and credulous. Like Porky Pig, you know? Only without Porky's lovable purity of heart. With Castelnuovo, it was hard to escape the feeling that it was all put on, that he was trying to manipulate you.

As for Giulietta, she didn't even bother to pretend interest. She had Zampa's guarantee that he'd finish in time for the auction and that was probably as much as she could expect. I could tell she was sorry she'd ever pinned me down about this, but these were things an auction house CEO really ought to be familiar with, and it wouldn't hurt her to learn about them. Besides, I love talking about this stuff.

"And believe me, when what's underneath is a newly discovered work by one of the greats, you do it *very* carefully, which means very *slowly*. Sometimes you have to use a scalpel to slice away the overlying paint, which, as you can imagine, requires nerves of steel, as well as a supremely steady hand. I wouldn't try it for a million bucks. On an Andy Warhol, maybe, but on a Renoir? Not a chance. So, honestly, if Zampa's been at it two months, I'd say that doesn't sound overly long to me. And I haven't even mentioned the work that he had to do *between* the overpainting and the underpainting—that is, the varnish that Renoir originally applied, and which by now has surely darkened. That's got to be dealt with too—more solvent detective work. And don't forget that a lot of this involves fluids—not only solvents, but varnish, shellac, the paints themselves. And you have to give fluids time to dry. Oil paint, for example, is one of the most . . ."

I'd gotten a good head of steam going, so I probably didn't realize how I'd been droning on, but Giulietta let me know by brusquely and loudly answering her cell phone when it played a few bars of something I didn't recognize. "Yes, I can," she yelled into it. "Tell him I'll be right there. Yes . . . yes . . . definitely. Right there." She put away the phone and stood up. "I have to go, gentlemen. Obviously Ulisse isn't going to be able to find time for us today, so we're not going to resolve anything anyway. We do have yet to straighten out a few important matters concerning the auction, though, Benvenuto . . ."

Such as whether or not it's going to include the sketch, I thought, but I was reluctant to say anything. I was pretty sure I'd already worn out my welcome. Giulietta had feared a lecture, and that was what she'd gotten. All I could do now was hope for another chance, at a more propitious moment, to make my pitch again, but it wasn't looking good. I'd already had two supposedly propitious chances and had yet to get out more than five words.

". . . for which we require Ulisse's input. Look, I'll be going into Milan most days this week." Out came the cell phone again, its screen to be studied for a moment. "Benvenuto, will you be available at two o'clock on Tuesday? The sooner we get this taken care of, the better."

He nodded. "Yes. We can meet at the shop."

"No, let's do it at Montefiore. I'll let Ulisse know, if I ever get hold of him. All right, I think we can conclude here."

"Excellent," said Castelnuovo enthusiastically, even clapping his hands together. But then his face fell, if only for an instant. "Oh . . . wait, not yet, Giulietta. We haven't heard from *dottor* Caruso yet."

It took her a few seconds to remember what and to whom he was referring. "Oh, yes, the . . . Bezzecca matter again." The little hitch in the middle told me she'd caught herself barely in time before saying "the damned Bezzecca matter" or worse. But now she smiled at me. "Valentino, I really must run now. Would it be imposing too much to ask you to join us on Tuesday and tell us about it then?"

"Of course. That'll be fine."

Better than fine, really. I'd flinched when Castelnuovo had brought it up. They were both itching to leave. I didn't have Ulisse with me for moral support, and I'd already talked too damn much anyway.

Conditions were not exactly encouraging for trying to win them over to Sol's point of view. Tuesday would be better; I'd try to get my pitch in early when everybody was still fresh and nobody was mad at anybody else yet.

And so the meeting at the Serbelloni came to its unsettled end. The question of the loan remained unresolved.

And, really, where the hell was Ulisse? Giulietta was right. This just wasn't like him. I remembered him at Dell'Acqua as being a bit of a martinet with his staff when it came to promptness, and faithfully holding himself to his own standards. "Punctuality is the politeness of princes," he would sometimes intone when informing us of an upcoming meeting or event. None of us ever did understand what exactly it meant, but we all got the message: *Don't. Be. Late.*

And so, yes, I was really starting to worry.

Chapter 12

I caught the ferry back to Varenna, bought a mortadella *panino* for lunch from a glassed-in display at the little train station's hole-in-the-wall bar, and took it out onto the platform to chomp down on while I waited for the 1:10 to Milan. I had just tossed the wrapping into a trash can when the train, prompt to the minute, glided to a stop in front of me and I happened to see Dante Zampa stomping toward it, head down, hands thrust into his pockets, and his usual *keep-the-hell-away-from-me-you-peasant* look on his face. Engaging him was the last thing I wanted to do, so I ducked behind a ticket-vending machine to watch him board, then climbed in two cars behind him.

The ride back wasn't as relaxing as the trip out had been. I spent most of it reviewing the aborted meeting, trying to see if there were any clues to be gleaned from it as to which way Benvenuto and Giulietta were leaning, but got nowhere. They were both impossible to read. Yes, even for an accomplished reader of character like myself.

I was continuing to worry that something had happened to Ulisse. I just couldn't see him purposely skipping the meeting without letting *me* know; he knew how much Sol's loan mattered to me. I tried his cell phone number a few times during the ride—the only number I had for him now that he was no longer at Dell'Acqua—to no avail. If I hadn't gotten hold of him by evening, I'd call 1-1-2, Italy's version of 9-1-1. And if they were reluctant to help, which they well might be—after all, he'd barely been gone a day—I'd get on the phone myself to all the hospitals between Lugano and Bellagio and Milan. Yes, and give Giulietta a call too to see if she'd had any better luck.

Practically the minute the train arrived back in Milan at the Porta Garibaldi terminal, my plan to keep clear of Zampa fizzled. I was on my way to switch to one of the local Metro lines when I heard my name called from behind me.

"*Ehi, dottor* Caruso?"

The mordant, world-weary voice was perhaps a little less mordant than usual, but unpleasantly recognizable and impossible to pretend to ignore. I turned and dredged up a surprised smile. "Why, signor Zampa, hello. Did we come in on the same train?"

"It looks like it. Listen, Tino, got a minute?"

He was now speaking fluent New York English, so I answered with the same. "You bet. What's up?"

"Look, Tino . . ." His head hung down. ". . . all right if I call you Tino?"

"Of course."

"Thanks." He tapped his chest with the flat of his hand. "Dante."

Now what the hell was this about? If I were in the hunt for a new friend, which I wasn't, it certainly wouldn't be this unlovable curmudgeon.

"I just wanted to thank you," he blurted. "And to apologize." He looked not only embarrassed, but embarrassed to be embarrassed. He was uncomfortable, and he was making me uncomfortable.

"For what and what?"

"I ran into Benvenuto on the ferry. He told me what you said to them after I left, about how much work goes into restoring those paintings. Well, I guess it actually made an impression on them—on him, anyway—and I appreciate it very much, and I, well, I just wanted you to know, you know?"

119

"You're more than welcome, but it surprised me when they said they'd never heard any of that from you. I wondered why not."

He hunched his shoulders. "You don't understand. These people drive me up the wall. They don't know a damn thing about art, which I could understand, but they don't even *want* to know. Oh, Ulisse, he's all right, but the other two . . . I start to explain something, and their eyes glaze over. They don't care about what I'm doing, or why, and they don't care about Renoir either. All they want is for me to get the hell finished so they can cash out. Even Giulietta, who you'd think would . . . well, you heard her for yourself this morning."

"I sympathize," I said, and I did. "I can see why they might strain your patience a little when you try to explain things, but—"

"Patience? It's not my patience that's the problem. I'm the most patient man you ever met, ask anybody. What I *am*, however, is a man of honor, and as such I refuse to engage in a battle of intellect with unarmed antagonists."

Funny, yes, but I'd begun to wonder if, *à la* Oscar Wilde, he kept a sizable stack of epigrams in his head, ready to pull one out the second an opportunity arose. All the same, it did make me ease up and laugh. "Anyway, I hope what I told them does make a difference."

"Ho, ho, not much chance of that, but still I wanted to say thanks."

"You couldn't be more welcome. And what was it you wanted to apologize for?"

He dropped his eyes. "I guess I was a little rude to you this morning, that's what for. I had no right."

A *little* rude, did he say? Still, I appreciated his saying anything about it. "It's nice of you to mention it, but no problem. Forget it."

"Good." He cleared his throat. "Well. So. Listen, I have my car right outside on the piazza. Can I give you a ride? Where are you staying, downtown?"

"Yes, thanks, but I was on my way out to the Fiera district. I can catch the M2 from here."

"But that's where I live, Fiera, where my workshop is. Not out of my way at all. Come on, it's no trouble. Be faster than the M2. And the company, needless to say, will be much better."

"Well . . ." When I hesitated, he tugged on my sleeve. "Come on, come on, let's get out of here."

His car was a modest little blue Fiat, fairly new, in decent condition, but with the back seat strewn with art supplies. More was on the front passenger seat—bottles of rectified mineral spirits and Venetian turpentine (quality products both) and a bundle of small wooden stretcher bars standing on their ends. (Stretcher bars, as their name implies, are used in the mounting of canvases to keep them from sagging or shrinking, and to stabilize their frames.)

"Just toss all that junk in back," he said with an indifferent wave as we got in, and I loaded it—with care—wedging things into relatively safe niches in the piles that were already there.

"Where exactly are you headed?" he asked as he got the car started.

"Via Paolo Uccello, near the corner of via Monte Bianco."

"Ah, San Siro alla Vepra. Hey, I congratulate you. A beautiful little church. With all the mammoth cathedrals in this damn city, hardly anybody bothers with it, and that's a shame. It's only the apse that's still standing, you know, but it's well worth visiting. The murals—fifteenth-century Lombardian works—are . . . yes, what?"

"Well, it's not the church that I wanted to see. It's the . . . it's the building next to it, a house. If it's still standing."

His mouth stiffened. He dragged one of his skinny half-cigars from out of a jacket pocket and jammed it angrily between his teeth. "The Villa Fossati," he said under his breath. "*Villa Triste*. Christ, wouldn't you know it."

The likelihood of this kind of response was why I'd shied away from saying its name a moment earlier. It was the building in which Sol had been tortured and his grandfather killed by the Banda Koch, the Italian Fascist militia group. I'd assumed that today's Italians might find it a sensitive subject, and as far as Zampa was concerned, it seemed I was right.

"You can't go inside, you know," he said, and then, sardonically: "Not even with a MilanoCard."

"Ah." I had hoped (although that's not quite the right word) that the interior might have been preserved for visitors as a memorial, a reminder, and I was sorry—and relieved—to learn that it hadn't been— sorry because I'd felt in some obscure way that I needed to go there for Sol's sake, relieved because I'd dreaded doing it. "I didn't intend to go in," I lied. "I just wanted to look at it. To get at least some sense of what it must have felt like, I guess."

"Fine." We drove in silence for two or three minutes, and then, abruptly, he said: "Why, for God's sake?"

I told him the horrific story of what they had done there on that early morning in 1944 to young Solomon and his aged, much-honored grandfather Maurizio Bezzecca, *Eroe del Risorgimento*. When I got to the end of it, he sat for a moment, and then, with a long sigh, he closed his eyes and laid his head against the steering wheel.

"Christ," he said. "People."

A good ten seconds passed with nothing further from him. "And so I just needed to look at the place, Dante," I said to reopen communication. "I really can't explain why."

"Sure, I understand. Right." But it was another few seconds before he leaned back from the wheel and gazed past me out the side window. "So there it is," he said without expression. "You wanted to look? Look. Nothing special, is it?"

We had parked at the curb a sidewalk's width from a shoulder-high brick wall topped with glazed red terracotta tiles, behind which was a nineteenth-century, mustard-colored, two-story house, with a simple balcony—more an ornament than a usable space—above the front door. He was right, nothing special, a plain, comfortable family residence like dozens of others in the neighborhood. Even the graffiti on the wall looked no different from what was scrawled on all the other walls in front of all the other houses.

But two marble plaques on the wall here distinguished this particular one from all the others. They were too far away for me to read, but the funereal marble wreath atop one and the agonized head in profiled bas-relief on the other made it clear that this was the place, all right.

I was suddenly drained. This pleasant, ordinary house, so normal, so commonplace—

"There was barbed wire around it in those days," Zampa was saying distantly. "There were five separate torture chambers set up in the basement. The walls—"

"Were splattered with blood. I know, he told me."

"Yes, but did you also know that it became an entertainment center of sorts? That people well-connected to the *fascisti*, famous people, in fact—movie stars, writers—came here for the entertainment value of watching the interrogations?"

"No, I didn't know that. To tell you the truth, I wish I still didn't know it. Dante, how come you know so much about the place? It all happened before you were born. Is the history of it well-known, then?"

"Not really. It's not hidden, not suppressed. There have been books written about it, even a movie, I think, but, you know, it's not something people especially want to remember, so they try to make themselves forget. Or they pretend to forget. Or they really do forget."

"Hard to blame them."

"True, but then, you know the old saying about learning from history."

I nodded. "That not learning it condemns us to repeat it."

"Nope, that's a new one on me. Good one." The unlit cigar was still between his teeth, and now he took it out of his mouth. "The one I was thinking of is that what we learn from history is that people never learn from history. Hegel, I believe."

I was more than ready for some light relief, and I smiled appreciatively. I was thinking that maybe I could learn to like the guy, after all.

With one hand he wedged the cigar back into the corner of his mouth, and with the other he reached for the ignition key. "You've had enough of this, haven't you?" he said, taking in the villa with a sweep of his arm. "God knows, I know I have. Where can I drop you? I can have you back in Brera in ten minutes. Or we could stop for an afternoon *caffè*. What would you say to that?" He had perked up considerably now.

"That'd be great to do a little later, but you know what I'd really like right now, if it's no trouble?"

"Speak, and it shall be yours, assuming it's at all feasible." He was almost smiling.

"You said your place was nearby?"

"Via Taddeo Gaddi, practically around the corner."

"Well, I was wondering if you'd let me . . ."

When he realized where this was going, he began to shake his head no, but I plowed on anyway. ". . . come up for a few minutes. I would dearly love to see the Renoirs. The photos are all X-ray-type stuff. They barely give you an idea of what you're looking at. And as for the colors—"

"Ah, Tino, I'm sorry, really, but at this stage things are a mess. Give me a couple of weeks—"

"I don't have a couple of weeks."

"Look, I'm sorry. I never let anyone see my work in an unfinished state. No exceptions. A craftsman's privilege."

"Dante, Ulisse told me he showed up at your studio practically every week to see how you were coming." I usually don't press that hard and that blatantly about anything, but I really wanted to see those pictures—especially the sketch.

"Well, yes," he admitted, "but that's different. He has a right. He *owns* them, he's the one who's commissioning me, but I regretted it every time. That's when he starts with his inane questions. 'I heard that even the experts can't tell the difference between acrylics and oil paints. Why don't you use acrylics for those little spots? Wouldn't that be faster?' Can you believe it? You would think that a man like that would have some understanding—"

"Ulisse's extremely impressed with your work, by the way," I interrupted, resorting to shameless flattery. "He said what you've done with them has been absolutely terrific, the best he's ever seen. How can I not want to see them myself after that?"

"He did, did he? Well, you know, I think quite a lot of Ulisse too." Pregnant pause. "Not as much as he does, of course."

"Dante," I said, laughing, "I can promise you won't get any dumb questions from me. If you want, I will swear to keep my mouth shut altogether. I will simply look, and I will be content. On my honor. And then we can go get that coffee."

And around he finally came. "Oh, what the hell," he said with a long-suffering sigh, and got the car started again. "Into the breach!"

I had the impression that, underneath all the sarcasm and clearly genuine reluctance, he was eager to show off his work to somebody who knew enough to really appreciate it.

Via Taddeo Gaddi was a modest street of 1960s three-story apartment buildings on one side, some of them with eateries or small neighborhood shops on the ground floor—a hardware store, sewing supplies, a laundry, other mom & pops. The entire opposite side of the street was taken up by a stark, concrete monolith of a building—a cosmetics factory, Dante said—that was surrounded by a stark, six-foot-high, concrete wall made marginally less monolithic by the introduction of vertical breaks, six or eight inches wide, every hundred feet or so; wide enough to add a little visual diversity, but not enough to let any industrial beauty supply spies squeeze through.

On second thought, "stark" is probably the wrong word for that wall. Once maybe, but not any longer. Throughout Italy, the idea of a public wall lacking graffiti seems to offend the sensitivities of the urban arts community, which is never long in dealing with the challenge, and so it had in this case—very thoroughly.

We parked in front of an open-air, blue-collar café, and Dante turned to me with a look that was probably as free of sarcasm as his face ever got, although there wasn't much he could do about that liver-lipped, constitutionally sneering mouth and those cynical, heavy-lidded eyes of his.

"I'm glad you told me Bezzecca's story, Tino. I don't have any say in whether they'll lend the painting or not, you understand that, but I'd like you to know, for what it's worth, that I've changed—that is, *you've* changed—my mind about the old guy. I would really love to see him have that sketch for as long as he wants. You're right, I wasn't even alive when they took him to the villa and then shipped him off to the con-centration camp, but I'm Italian; it was Italians who made that happen."

It was a long speech, and he'd spoken it with straightforward pas-sion, obviously something he wasn't used to doing, and it had taken the steam out of him. He stared for a moment at his hands on the wheel, muttered something unintelligible, and when he looked at me again, the ironic half-smile was back in place. "As long as he doesn't go to extremes," he said, straightening up. "I'd say that not living beyond ninety would be the decent thing to do, in consideration of Ulisse's kindness."

Chapter 13

The entrance to Dante's apartment—actually two apartments; he had the upper two floors of the building, plus a storeroom at the rear of the ground floor—was between the café and a small optician's shop, both probably catering to the factory employees. Today being Sunday, the factory was closed, as was the shop. The café was open, but only a couple of tables were occupied. Two aproned waiters stood smoking and chatting in the doorway. They waved at Dante, who granted them a cursory nod.

Beside the door to the building was a blackened, easy-to-miss brass plate with two engraved lines:

D. ZAMPA
RESTAURATORE DELLA PITTURA

I couldn't imagine that it had ever brought him a scrap of new business (who wanders down an out-of-the-way little neighborhood street like this looking for a painting restorer?) but I suppose it served as confirmation to new customers that they had found the place, and the man, that they were looking for. Below the plate was an even smaller keypad.

With his finger halfway to it, he paused. "It's up a flight of stairs. I have another entrance in back, with an elevator. If you'd—"

"This is fine."

Shrug. Onward continued the finger, and five numbers were slowly punched in. He was so measured and deliberate about it that I pretty much couldn't avoid seeing the first four: 2-0-1-4. I looked away, feeling as if I were snooping. Once inside, in a cramped foyer, we faced a narrow, two-flight stairway with a landing between the flights. "The Renoirs are in here," Dante told me as we reached the landing. "This is my studio. I live above, but sometimes, when the work's going well and I keep at it through the night, I catch a nap down here."

There was another keypad beside this door and this time I watched more closely as he worked it. Now I wanted to see if someone could actually get the whole combination just by standing next to him. And I could, easy as pie: 2-0-1-4-8. The same number as on the street-level pad, then, or close enough not to matter.

Not for the first time, I shook my head at the lack of care people gave their works of art. And not only *people*, but museums, famous museums. Off the top of my head, I could give you examples of cultural treasures and art objects successfully stolen from museums not because ingenious thieves had evaded the motion detectors and heat sensors by rappelling down from the skylights with ropes and pulleys (although that has most assuredly happened, and not just in the movies), but simply because the place was wide open. Somebody had neglected to turn on the alarm system, or it was getting its monthly servicing, or it had never been installed in the first place, or it just didn't work right from Day One, and someday, darn it, they were going to have to do something about it: everything from the theft of the priceless (and I mean *literally*) solid gold Aztec and Mayan masks taken from Mexico City's National Museum of Anthropology in 1985 to the three-quarters-of-a-million-dollar heist from the National Civil War Museum in 2016, and plenty more in between.

I had seen for myself that Dante was not the kind of man who took kindly to advice, but there were those Renoirs to think about.

"Um, Dante," I said gingerly, as he turned the door handle, "you might want to be a little more careful with those keypads when there are people around. I couldn't help seeing your combination."

He paused in opening the door and scowled at me, working the still-unlit cigar from one side of his mouth to the other without using his hands. "You couldn't help it, huh? So what is it?"

I told him.

"That's right. Damn." Surprised? Maybe. Concerned? Not a bit.

All the same, I pushed ahead. "You know, I wonder how many other people know that combination. You just might want to change it. In fact, maybe change it periodically. Once a week, for example?" Commenting that it might also be better not to have the same combination on both doors seemed as if it would be overdoing it. Another time, maybe.

He nodded, placidly enough. "Yeah, I know I should."

Obviously he wouldn't be following through on that anytime soon. Dante had a long-standing reputation for procrastinating. When it came to anything other than his work itself—returning phone calls or emails, paying bills, remembering to show up for social events (once, famously, when he was the guest of honor)—he had a hard time forcing himself to get around to it, and often didn't, short of legal persuasion.

Still, I couldn't help giving it one more little nudge. "It only takes a minute, you know. You just do it yourself, and it's done."

"Yeah, but then I have to remember the new combination. It took me long enough to get this one to stick in my mind." He opened the door into an airy, high-ceilinged room that took up the entire floor, except for a tiny kitchen and bathroom in one corner. The place reeked of turpentine and looked like every artist's and art conservator's workshop that I've ever been in: in two words, a mess. Photos and sketches and daubed color trials were pinned or taped helter-skelter to the walls; on the paint-spattered floor were scrunched-up disposable gloves, dried-out brushes, and crumpled sheets of newsprint that had been used to test pigments or finishes or to clean paintbrushes. A spectacularly unmade cot was wedged into a corner.

There was a freestanding easel off to one side that held a cloth-covered painting, and two worktables, a spanking clean one against the wall, with a fancy electrified binocular microscope mounted above it, and another, larger, L-shaped table in the middle of the room, smeared and splotched with paints (I recognized some of the colors from his sport coat). The longer arm of the L was loaded with crushed, half-squeezed-out tubes of paint, cans and jars of varnishes, resins, solvents, linseed oil, mineral spirits, and other accouterments of the job, along with several white porcelain flower vases holding various sizes of brushes, mostly upside down.

The shorter side of the L held only a second draped painting, smaller than the other one and clipped to a table easel.

"Is that it?" I asked. "The sketch?"

"You want to look at that one first?"

"Please," I said. I could see that he was eager to show me the self-portrait, the more important and ambitious of the two, and the one that must have required more meticulous work from him, but I couldn't help myself. It was the sketch I couldn't wait to see. The portrait would hold.

"I still have a little to do on it," he told me as I approached the table, "but the painting itself is finished. The varnish just went on a little while ago, so best not to touch it."

"Okay, sure."

I lifted the cloth and folded it over the back of the easel, surprised to find myself holding my breath and even keeping my eyes averted until I could take it all in without obstruction, like a kid torturing himself by putting off the pleasure of really, seriously looking at the shiny, wonderful, prayed-for new bike that astoundingly now stood in front of the Christmas tree. It brought home what a really big deal this thing had become for me.

I exhaled the breath, took a step back, folded my arms, and looked down at it. The picture itself, as expected, wasn't really anything special, a simple, workmanlike, utterly unflamboyant café scene, probably painted from life and tossed off in a couple of hours, much like a hundred, maybe a thousand other perfectly competent French café scenes from the mid-nineteenth century, and a long way from the best of them. And yet I couldn't remember the last time a painting had thrilled me like this. I was electrified. Here he was, in person, Sol's great-grandfather, the heroic Maurizio Bezzecca, in the full flower of his young manhood, virile, broad-shouldered, bearded, and handsome, taking his ease in a humble café. By God, I thought, whatever it took to get Giulietta's and Benvenuto's blessing for the loan—begging, badgering, reasoning, threatening, whatever—I would do it. I was damn near ready to just grab the thing and run right now, if that was the only way.

"So what do you think?" Dante asked with uncharacteristic reticence. He was standing beside me at the table, scowling down at the painting, his hands clasped behind him.

I very nearly started on a disquisition about the painting before I realized that he wanted to know what I thought of *his* work, not Renoir's. "It looks terrific, Dante; you've done a great job."

I wasn't lying, either. This time around, at least, he seemed to have stuck with restoration, not reinvention, possibly because the picture had been in good physical shape in the first place and didn't need a lot of work. I'd read that it had been done mostly in drab browns, and grays, and greens, and—thankfully—that's what they still were, dull and rather flat. I was pleased and a little surprised to see that Dante hadn't taken it upon himself to brighten things up to match the joyful, brilliant colors that had become Renoir's trademark and indeed a trademark of Impressionism as a whole.

"I really appreciate that from someone like you, Tino," he said, puffing up a little. "It was trickier than you might think." He really did seem pleased, even relieved, at the good grade. "Now. Let me make us a couple of espressos—I have a great machine—and we can admire it in comfort. I want to show you some of the problems I had to deal with."

"I'd like that," I said as he retreated to the mini-kitchen and I pulled a chair up close to the table, absorbed in the picture before I even hit the seat. Bezzecca, apparently a bigger man than I'd imagined, was the central figure in it, reading a newspaper, with a cup of coffee in front of him and a clay pipe in his hand, but there were others as well. At a table behind him two men were playing cards and sharing a bottle of wine. And off to the side, a slatternly woman sat drowsing over her glass of absinthe. All of this done in those same somber hues.

If you're familiar with Renoir's work, then you've probably been scratching your head. Flat? Drab? Dull? *Somber?* Pierre-Auguste Renoir, the acclaimed master of joyous, opulent, light-filled scenes and plump, pretty, incandescent pink nudes? *Seriously?*

Well, yes. Like many another creative artists, Renoir evolved through one phase after another—"periods," in artspeak—throughout his life. As a child, he was an apprentice in a porcelain factory, painting miniature versions of Boucher's and Watteau's frothy, immensely popular pictures on vases and table services. (Actually, he'd started out as a singer, even studying for a time with the great Charles Gounod, but by the time he was thirteen his family could no longer afford to pay for lessons, and he was apprenticed to the porcelain maker.) Four years later—this would have been 1858—he was without a job when a new mechanical production method was developed that could do what he did, a lot more cheaply if not anywhere near as well. And not at all coincidentally, it was in 1858, only a few weeks later, that his first known painting on canvas appeared, a wreath of roses, much like the designs he'd been painting on flowerpots for the previous four years.

He had committed himself to being an independent artist by then, and in those early years—Impressionism had yet to be born—he followed a well-trodden artist's path, imitating other painters, bouncing from one school of painting to another, and just generally trying to find his own métier. At this initial stage, it was the work of his older contemporary Manet that influenced him the most, and Manet's approach showed in this sketch: the muted, conventional colors; the relative lack of tonal variation (and thus the flatness); the rather inelegant composition, driving home the point that it was meant to be life as life was, rather than having been arranged for symmetry and balance, as the traditions of the Academy demanded.

And still, touches of the Impressionist-master-in-the-making could be seen: a delicate, feathery brush stroke . . .

"Huh," I said aloud. "That's interesting."

"What is?" Dante called from the kitchen. I could hear the heated water beginning to hiss through the powdery coffee.

"Come have a look, will you? Bring a magnifying glass. This is . . . interesting."

"High-power? Low-power?"

"Low-power's fine."

"Sure. The coffee's ready. I'll bring that too."

In my dreams, I am invariably a coward, never a hero, and this one was no exception. I was a child again, in my old schoolyard, and another kid, someone I didn't know, was knuckling me in the shoulder, the forehead, trying to get me to fight, but I was too frightened to take him on. He was smaller than I was, but a real tough guy, wiry and coarse, with a scarred, grown-up face to prove it. It was one of those dreams where I knew I was dreaming, and I somehow understood that if I could just lie down flat on the ground I would get out of it.

I tried it and it worked. The bully was gone, and the dream splintered into fragments that faded and then vanished altogether, leaving me lying there, relieved and thankful. But lying where? I was on my stomach, on a hard, gritty surface that rolled and tilted. The deck of a ship? I pressed the palms of my hands against it to keep from rolling off. My eyes wouldn't open. I floated off into another murky dream, but a peaceful one involving horses, the beautiful blue, and red, and chestnut horses of Franz Marc come to life . . .

But the bully was back, jabbing at my shoulder. I was more annoyed than frightened this time and tried to shake off the prodding fingers. "What the hell—"

"Thank God, I thought he killed you!"

My eyes popped open, producing a bolt of real agony. It was as if a pair of knives—serrated ones—had been thrust through them and deep into my brain. My eyes promptly clamped shut on their own, but not before I took in where I was, and it wasn't on a ship. I was on the floor of Dante's studio and Dante was on his knees at my shoulder, leaning over me.

"I thought he *killed* you, Tino."

"I heard you," I said, my eyes still closed.

"Are you all right?"

"I don't know. What happened?"

"What hap—? You don't remember?"

"If I remembered, would I be asking you?"

"He hit you! Hard! With the gun! Twice! You were just sitting there looking at the painting. But you *must* have heard him—you started to get up and turn around when he came in . . . Tino, you *really* don't remember?"

"Damn it, Dante . . . !"

It was silly, I know, but he was annoying the hell out of me. I'd opened my eyes again, making sure to do it slowly this time, and that jagged shock of pain hadn't come back, but my eyes ached and my head felt as if it was being whacked with a mallet with every beat of my pulse. I was dizzy and sick to my stomach too, on the verge of throwing up. I realized that my ears had been ringing—clanging was more like it— since I'd come out of that first dream. I was having a hard time putting two coherent thoughts together, let alone any of Dante's disjointed, agitated yammerings. I managed to lift my head and raise myself up on my elbows despite another billow of nausea, thinking that maybe being able to see him talk would help.

"And he shot at me!" he was shouting, two feet from my face. "I tried to stop him, I did, I confronted him and he *shot* at me! He could have killed me."

"Uh," I said, "whoa," able at least to sense that I was supposed to say something. And then, inanely, "He missed you, then." I motioned him off. "Dante, back away a little, will you?"

"Well, yes, sure, he missed me, of course he missed me, thank God, but Tino, he took the painting! He took *both* paintings! He just grabbed them! I don't know what to do." He had backed off a foot and now he was rocking wretchedly back and forth on his knees, that cynical, supercilious veneer of his having cracked and dropped away the way a plaster mold falls off under a hammer and chisel, to reveal the newly made bronze sculpture inside. In Dante's case, what was inside was a shocked, uncertain, defenseless man.

"Did you see what he looked like?" I asked. In my fuzzy state of affairs, it seemed like a helpful, supportive thing to say.

"How could I see what he looked like? He was wearing a . . . one of those masks, what do you call them, uh, uh, *passamontagna*—a ski mask."

At this point I still wasn't making much sense of what he was telling me, but then bits and scraps and snippets of memory began to snap back into place: meeting up with him at the train station, the stop at Villa Fossati, the chance to finally see the café sketch . . . and that was it. I had no memory of anyone's coming into the room, let alone hitting me, but my throbbing, aching head assured me that it had indeed happened. Waking up with my face on the floor was pretty good evidence too.

"How did he get in?" I asked. "Wasn't the alarm system turned on? It must have been somebody who knew the codes."

He just stared dimly at me from his knees, his mouth open, his jaw working. ". . . Somebody who . . . ?"

"Did you call 1-1-2?" I'd actually remembered the Italian version of 9-1-1. A good sign; my mind was functioning again.

"No, it just happened, don't you understand, just this minute. The second he ran downstairs I came right over to you." He jumped up. "But the police, yes, of course, the police! Right away. And I'll get an ambulance for you."

"I don't need an ambulance." This was sheer, silly bravado. I had no idea of whether I did or didn't. I sure wasn't feeling too great.

"But you're bleeding, Tino; you're all bloody. Look at your face!" He uttered a pallid little giggle at that.

Even as he said it, I realized that the right side of my head had a gluey, slippery feel to it. An exploration with my fingers confirmed that it was coated with blood, still wet. I had sat up by now, and looking down at the front of my shirt I saw a messy pattern of bloody spots and splatters. It all seemed to have come from a single wound—to my forehead, above and just to the right of my right eye. The blood was still welling out of it. Strangely, it was the one part of my head that didn't hurt. Yet. I pressed a couple of wadded Kleenex to it.

"You are too," I mumbled.

"I'm what?"

"Bleeding." I pointed. "Your hip." When he'd gotten up I'd seen that the left leg of his pants had a saucer-sized, spreading splotch of bright blood on it. And the cloth had a rip in it. It looked like the guy with the gun hadn't missed him after all.

Dante stared. "My God, he did shoot me! I never felt it—I still don't feel anything."

Calling 1-1-2 was forgotten as he fumbled with his belt and trousers and anxiously pulled down the waistband of his shorts for a closer look. He had to twist around to see the wound clearly, and when he did, he sucked in a quavery, pathetic gasp. "Oh, Tino, look what he did to me!"

He'd been shot, all right. Sort of. Luckily for him, the bullet had caught him at an angle, resulting in a tangential graze rather than a straight-on perforation.

I recognized it for what it was because I'd seen one like it before. When I was eight or nine, I had a friend named Sal, whose father was a homicide detective out of the Sixtieth Precinct in Coney Island. Well, Pop came home one day with a bullet graze to his forearm. Sal promptly got a few of his street pals together and offered to bring us up to his apartment to let us see his father's bullet wound—for half a dollar apiece. We all jumped at the chance.

Detective Maglio was a good guy about it, actually peeling back the dressing so we could see it up close, and enthralling us with an exciting if dubious story about the ferocious firefight in which he'd come by it. Whether he got to share in the box office receipts ($2.50) that Sal collected I never did learn. What I did learn was what a bullet graze looked like. And there was no mistaking that that was what Dante had.

Dante's was at the top of his hip, maybe four inches long and on a diagonal slant, a greasy, bloodless furrow shaped like a stretched-out teardrop for most of the way. But at the bottom end, the rearward end, the bullet had dug in a few millimeters deeper, creating a bloody, inch-long channel before continuing on its way. It wasn't pretty, but it didn't look like anything that some antibiotic ointment and a few stitches couldn't put right. However, the sight of blood (of *his* blood) seemed to unman him entirely. He looked astounded and utterly helpless. And sick. His sallow, yellow complexion was now closer to gray. "But how—but . . ."

I could see it was time for me to take charge, but I just didn't have it in me even to get up off the floor. I did make it to a sitting position, but there I had to stay, with my head between my knees for fear of keeling over again. "You'd better make that call now, Dante," I prompted gently. "And I guess I'll take that ambulance after all. We can both use one."

"Yes, yes . . ." But first, understandably, he limped pitifully toward the kitchen for a dish towel to press to his hip.

I must have passed out again, because I never saw him get there. The next time I was aware of anything, a couple of carabinieri and a two-man ambulance crew were in the room, squabbling over which of them would get me. Apparently the ambulance people had laid claim first, because I was already on a hospital stretcher that had been set on the floor. Some kind of apparatus around my head prevented me from moving it. That was scary; it meant they were worried that I might have a brain injury. And why wouldn't they be? I was too. I'd been knocked silly, I'd been slipping in and out of consciousness ever since, and I was dopey, and slow, and my head hurt; a lot, and it wasn't getting any better.

"Can you give me anything for pain?" I asked the ambulance guys. I had to ask it twice because the first time it had come out as barely more than a whisper.

One of them was about twenty, the other a grizzled veteran. "Better not to," the old one said. "Looks like you've had a concussion, and they'll want to do some tests before they give you anything. Don't worry, we'll have you there in five minutes and they'll get you started right away."

That brought some more objections from the carabinieri, but the medics appeared to have the moral authority here and they asserted it—"You can talk to him at the hospital, as soon as the doctors permit"—and it was down the elevator in back, and into the ambulance I went. Behind me, I heard Dante's piteous whine: "Hey, come on, what about me? I've been shot!" And then, while my stretcher was being clamped down in the ambulance, in he came and was given possession of the stretcher-bed across from me. I half expected the carabinieri to crowd in with us, but they didn't. Well, they had their own car, and I supposed they knew where the hospital was.

As the ambulance got going, the younger attendant worked on stanching my bleeding, the older one on Dante.

"This one is going to need to be stitched up."

"This one too."

I couldn't tell which attendant was which, but I figured it didn't make any difference. That struck me as funny enough to make me laugh, which also scared me.

"Hey, Tino—" Dante said while we both were being cleaned up and bandaged.

"Don't talk, please," said the older attendant.

"Why not?" Dante said bravely. "It's a mere flesh wound. I'm fine."

"Yes, but I'm not so sure about your friend."

Oh, great. Thanks, pal, love your bedside manner.

"Ah," Dante sighed to the roof, "the jackbooted tyranny of the petty functionary in full measure."

Lame as it was, at least he was trying to become Dante Zampa again. But I noted he said it in English so that the two jackbooted tyrants wouldn't know what he was saying.

"Screw you, Jack," the attendant working on him said equably. Also in English, not bothering to look up from his bandaging.

Chapter 14

At the hospital, Dante was deposited in a wheelchair and hauled off in one direction, while I was taken off in another on a gurney. Once in what I took to be the emergency room, I was put through a battery of questions and demands by an insistent but patient doctor, or at any rate a middle-aged man in a white coat. "Tell me where you are." "Tell me how you got here." "Are you seeing flashing lights?" "What day is this?" "What time would you say it is right now? No, don't look at your watch." "What's the last thing you remember before waking up on the floor?"

That last one stopped me because I couldn't remember the last thing I remembered. "Let's see," I said slowly. "I have no memory of being hit—"

"No, that's not surprising," I was told. "Retrograde amnesia: ninety-nine times out of a hundred a concussion will produce it. What I'm trying to find out now is how far back in time it goes. So . . . do you remember entering the building with signor Zampa?"

"Uhh . . . yes!" I said, although a moment before I hadn't. "We went up a flight of stairs, then into the studio . . ." Now I was faltering a little, although pieces were beginning to come back. The doctor continued to be patient, encouraging me with minute nods of his head. ". . . I sat down to look at one of the pictures . . ."

"Can you tell me what it was a picture of?"

"No, I . . ." Again, a memory came filtering through the murk. "Yes! I can! It was the café scene, and I . . . I . . ." But that was it; that was the last thing I remembered. I shook my head. "Nothing after that."

"That's all right," the doctor said. "Not bad at all. Sometimes people lose entire days."

But it didn't feel fine to me. *You're forgetting something important,* something was telling me. *You need to try to remember.* But trying did no good, and I shook my head again. "That's it. Will any of it come back in time, or is it gone for good?"

"Impossible to say. Sometimes it does, sometimes it doesn't. Retrograde amnesia," he said again. "You never know."

After the questioning, the head restraint was removed and they sat me up. Good signs, I hoped. I was then prodded and poked, repeatedly made to stand up and sit down, my strength was tested ("Press against my fist. Now do it with the other hand."), and my eyes were checked, rechecked, and checked again. Other things too, but my memory is hazy here. Early on, I remember, my head was stitched up by another doctor.

"I'm Doctor Fannucci," I was told by the young woman wielding needle and thread alongside my eye. "The skin was split open by one of the blows. It happens. And you've got some moderate contusions to go with that, which is hardly surprising. There was a blow to the back of your head too, but no bleeding. We'll do a scan or two to see what's going on inside there, but from your behavioral responses I'm guessing there's been no brain bleed."

"How many stitches?" I asked. My forehead had been anesthetized, so I was feeling nothing there, but the rest of my head still ached mightily, although the pounding sensation had stopped, and the clanking in my ears had diminished to a tolerable drone. My jaw and neck had now joined in the aching, though.

"Oh, twenty or thirty, somewhere in there."

"Thirty stitches? Well, I'm glad it's nothing serious, but I guess it's farewell to my chaste and unflawed beauty." I know: pretty dopey, but you really have to take my condition into account, or maybe you just had to be there.

Either way, she went along with it. "Not at all. I like to put those little babies in r-r-e-e-a-a-l-l-y close together, that's all. Makes a *lovely* scar. It'll give you that dangerous, mysterious look we females go for. You'll be sexier than ever." She leaned close to whisper. "Keep this to yourself, but I'm not really a doctor, you know."

My eyes had been closed, but I opened them up at that. "You're—"

"Well, I *am* a doctor," she amended, "but only temporarily, while I finish up my diploma at the *scuola estetica*. That's my true calling: *estetista*."

That made me laugh, gingerly. An *estetista* is a beautician. I closed my eyes, and let her finish up her needlework.

After that, they glided me into one of those giant, noisy cans—I'm not sure if it was for an MRI or a CT scan—during which I dozed some more.

When they slid me out of it a nurse gave me a paper cup holding a fizzy dose of Efferalgan, which you drink like Alka-Seltzer but is actually Tylenol—acetaminophen, that is. Then, while I was still sitting up with the help of the gurney's adjustable frame, Dr. Fannucci came by to tell me that the lab report indicated I'd had a concussion, all right, no doubt about that, but that it looked as if no permanent damage had been done. Most important, there was no sign of brain bleed.

"Thank you, doctor," I said, relieved.

"All in all, I wouldn't worry about it too much. Just don't overdo it for a while, that's all. In five or six days, you can have your own doctor remove the stitches."

However, given that I'd lost consciousness several times and been woozy and intermittently confused as well, she thought it would be a good idea if I stayed in the hospital overnight so they could keep an eye on me. If I didn't like the idea of staying, she'd have me released now and I could talk to the carabinieri, who, she told me, had finished with Dante and were now waiting downstairs to interrogate me.

"It's up to you," she said, "but personally, I don't think that's a good idea for you right now."

"Personally, neither do I."

"Personally, I think you should be resting quietly for a while."

"Personally, so do I."

"I'll take care of the paperwork. Good night, signor Caruso, and good luck."

"Thank you, doctor, and good luck to you in what I know will be a wonderful career as an *estetista*."

A few minutes later, after I was installed in room 402, with a wrap-around-bandaged head and in crisp hospital pajamas (not, happily, one of those demoralizing open-in-the-back gowns so familiar to hospital patients in America), a new doctor appeared. I could tell at first glance that he was not a subscriber to Dr. Fannucci's brand of upbeat patient engagement. Bearded, worn, and in his fifties, he walked into the room with a cursory knuckle-rap on the open door and a harried, dubious *Dear-God-what-next* expression on his face.

"My name is Dr. Bakshi," he said, then stood silently beside my bed somberly studying my chart and occasionally *tsk*-ing or talking to himself. "Grade three concussion . . ." he murmured as he read down the page, ". . . contusions . . . abrasions." He was gravely shaking his head as he hung the chart back on the bed. All this made me feel really good, as you can imagine.

"A concussion is not to be taken lightly, signor Caruso. The brain is delicate. Yours has been jarred, and shaken, and wobbled. That is never a good thing, my friend, no, no, no, no, no."

Jarred and shaken. My brain was starting to feel like a martini in a James Bond movie. And *wobbled*. I imagined it sloshing around inside my skull like a jellyfish in a bell jar that's been set on a roll. "I understand," I said meekly.

"You are here to rest, and that is exactly what you must do. Do not hesitate to call the nurse. I will look in on you, and I will be available throughout the night. Oh, these *lights* . . ." He looked up at them accusingly. "Oh, my goodness, they must be made not so bright." He went to a wall switch and turned them down to his satisfaction, leaving what had been a relatively pleasant, welcoming room dim and sterile. It also made me realize that it was getting dark outside. This had been going on for a long time; the excitement at Dante's studio had been about two in the afternoon, so a good five hours had passed. It seemed like two. I had a lot of gaps.

"Do you have any questions?" he asked. "Is there anything you need?"

"Is it possible to get something to read? Some magazines? Italian ones would be fine."

He was shocked. "No, no, you do not understand. *Mental* rest as well as physical. This is essential, Mr. Caruso. No reading, no watching television, no *thinking*, nothing at all requiring mental effort."

"Is there nothing at all I can do to pass the time?"

"You can rest. That is what you can do. Do you have any other questions?"

Yeah, I thought, *how do I get Dr. Fannucci back?*

"No," I said. *"Molte grazie, dottore."*

Room 402 contained two beds, but the other one was empty, so there was no fellow occupant to interfere with my following Dr. Bakshi's orders: Rest. Sleep.

Hospital staff was another matter, however. I was awakened at 10:00 p.m. by a pair of nurses to make sure I was sleeping all right.

"You woke me up out of a sound sleep to see if I was sleeping all right?" I asked ungratefully; it had taken me a long time to fall asleep. "What did you think I was doing?"

"We needed to make sure it was a normal state of sleep and not unconsciousness," said one of the nurses, taking no offense. "A coma."

"Or death," the other supplied cheerfully. "That's always a consideration in a case like yours."

That shut me up, and I was Mr. Cooperative on the next one, at 1:00 a.m., but it threw me entirely out of sleep mode. I was done for the night, I knew that, but I wasn't feeling too bad. It had been something like ten hours since that dose of acetaminophen, but my head wasn't hurting much anymore. I rolled it from side to side to see what happened: nothing; couldn't even feel my brain sloshing around. I was starting to get hungry too, and steadier inside, no longer nauseated. These were all welcome signs. I would indeed be checking myself out of the hospital as early in the morning as the rules permitted. In fact, now that I thought about it, if I got into my clothes right now, maybe—

As suddenly—and painfully—as a dislocated joint slips back into place, a host of dislocated memories slipped back into their own places, shoving far into the background the self-centered concerns that had totally absorbed me for the last twelve hours: not until this minute had I given a further thought to where Ulisse was and what might have happened to him . . . to the theft of the pictures . . . to Sol and how he was going to take the news.

I knew that the loss of the two Renoirs would show up in the media, but it wouldn't be huge international news outside of the art world (if they had been stolen from a major museum or gallery, that would be a different story), so I doubted that Sol would come across it, not yet, anyway, but I anticipated that Lori—pardon me, *Loren*—would, and

I didn't want her to be the one to tell him about it. Or even Esther at IRSA, who would certainly learn of it, and probably before the day was done. No, telling him was my responsibility.

There was a clock on my bedside table. 1:10 a.m. 7:10 p.m. in New York, as good a time as any to get hold of him. So, despite dreading the conversation, I climbed down out of bed (no sign of vertigo when I stood, unsupported, on my bare feet; another positive sign), located my telephone on a bureau, sat down, in the dark, in one of the room's two metal and faux leather chairs, dialed his number, and sat back and waited while the phone went through its transatlantic booping and cheeping. I half expected Dr. Bakshi to poke his head through the door and waggle a cautionary finger at me, but I was secure in the knowledge that, unlike TV, reading, and thinking, he had issued no specific proscription against use of the telephone.

To my surprise, it was Loren who answered. "Hello?"

"Good evening, may I speak with Mr. Bezzecca, please?" Given our not-so-smooth encounter at the cheesecake place, I didn't think it would help matters if I announced myself.

But she wouldn't let me get away with it. "May I tell him who's . . . this is Val Caruso, isn't it?"

It was the first time she'd called me "Val." At Eileen's Cheesecake it had been "Mr." or "Doctor," and very coldly enunciated, at that. Aha, had Sol or Esther perhaps convinced her that I was one of the good guys? The possibility provided me with a ridiculous little tick of pleasure. Was I still hoping something might come of our relationship, then? Apparently so.

"That's right, Loren. Something's happened at this end that I need to tell him about."

"Oh, I'm glad you got me on the line. I need to talk to you too. I . . . oh, damn. You're not going to be giving him good news, are you? I can tell from your voice. Agnello turned you down?"

"No, it's not that; he's in favor of the loan, but there are some complications, some *big* complications, and . . . well, look, the main thing is, the sketch—both paintings, in fact—they've been stolen."

"What?" I heard a clunk, followed by the creak of leather, and guessed that she'd set down a glass or a cup on a table and had sunk into a chair beside it. "Val, I follow every scrap of news about—"

"It only happened yesterday—not even twelve hours ago, really. It wouldn't be in the news yet."

"Oh, no." Then a doleful sigh, and then, "What happened?"

"Loren, no offense, but if you'd let me tell Sol about it first, I'd feel better about it."

"Look, we just got here from the Forty-Second Street library, on my way back from John Jay. Quick stop at Chipotle for dinner, and now he's in the kitchen fixing up his world-famous bread pudding for dessert, which means he won't be out for twenty minutes, minimum, so he's occupied at the moment, but I'm sitting here with ten or fifteen minutes to spare, just having some coffee and Oreos to tide me over, so you might as well—"

"Okay, all right. Here's the story—as much of it as I know."

"You were actually there when it happened?" she said once I'd gotten into it.

"In spirit and in body, yes, but not in mind. I was off in la-la land at the time. The first thing they—that is, he—did was to coldcock me. I never saw it coming, I never saw the guy, I never saw anything. One minute I'm looking at the sketch, and the next one I'm lying on my face on the floor, bleeding like hell. The—"

I heard her sharp intake of breath. "My God! Val, are you all *right?*"

I admit it, it was just the kind of heartwarming reaction I'd been shooting for with that shamefully unnecessary "bleeding like hell." The "lying on my face" touch wasn't strictly required either; I thought of them as mood enhancers, you might say. And from there I milked the situation for every ounce of compassion I could. Disgraceful, I know, but there I was with my head newly stitched up and still oozing blood through the bandage, in a darkened hospital room in a foreign city, far, far from home, all alone, with no one there who really cared . . . I mean, jeez, poor me.

Nonetheless, inexcusable. It didn't take more than a matter of a minute or two before guilt and self-reproach caught up with me and I cut it off. "Seriously, I'm fine. Really. I'm just here in the hospital overnight. They'll be checking me out in a few hours. Okay?"

She took it as the change of subject it was meant to be. "Okay, back to the painting, I'm really worried about how Uncle Sol is going to react to this. I'm afraid the loss of—"

"No, stop," I said. "Now that I think about it, it's way too early to call it a loss. It just happened. The police have barely gotten started. In fact, I wouldn't be calling about it at all, not at this point, except that I don't want him—or you—to read about it somewhere and imagine the worst."

"I'm not sure I'm following you. They've both been stolen. Nobody knows where they are. You were practically killed. How much worse did you have in mind?"

"Stolen, yes, but I honestly believe the chances of getting them back are good. I'm not talking about tomorrow or next week—"

"Or next month, or next year," she added glumly.

"No, I didn't say that. 'Weeks,' would be my prediction." This was a statistical average based on the vast number of cases with which I have been directly involved, namely, two, but it sounded right. "The art police here are the best on the planet. Italy gets back more stolen art than any other country in the world."

"Val, I don't mean to be contentious, and I know you're just trying to put a good face on things, but couldn't that be because there's so much art to be stolen in the first place?"

"Well, that's a point, yes, but things really do work differently here. I'm not talking about the way the law works, which you probably know more about than I do, but about the way the cops work. They have a distinctive approach, and so do the art thieves, and they both make it more likely that paintings get returned. If we had time I could explain what I'm talking about, but trust me when I tell you—"

"Who says we don't have time? Uncle Sol won't be out for ten minutes yet, and from what you told me a minute ago, you're just sitting there in the dark waiting for them to come and check you out, so go ahead, explain. Please."

Fine. I was glad to keep talking to her, whatever the reason. In the U.S., I explained, the reasons a thief stole art were, most often, to sell it to a fence, or, secondarily, to demand ransom for it. Italian art thieves, more sophisticated and experienced, typically went about it differently. You stole the art (first making sure that it was insured), you waited an appropriate amount of time—a few months would be typical, although sometimes it was only a few weeks—and then you, or more likely, an intermediary, "found" it, dutifully reported it, as any good citizen would, and happily accepted the insurance company's reward. It was safer, less complicated, and more decorous than the nasty threats that went along with ransom, and far less dangerous than dealing with a fence. Over and above that, the money was better. A black market fence would pay out—at most—five percent; more likely three percent—of the estimated value, whereas the going rate for the major Italian insurance companies had risen over the years to ten percent.

No contest.

As for the art police, the *Comando Tutela Patrimonio Artistico*, they were different too: it was *art*, not art *crime* that was their highest concern. That meant that, for them, the apprehension of thieves was a distant second in importance to the recovery and return of the art. In fact, their critics suggested that they went out of their way to avoid pressuring or threatening the bad guys. And, from what I've seen, it was true.

A carabiniere I know in Milan once put it to me this way: "What does a narcotics dealer do with the bundles of heroin he's got stuffed in the hollowed-out printer on his desk when the police come pounding on the door? He flushes them down the toilet, he throws them out the window, into the stove, the fireplace—he does whatever is necessary to destroy the evidence against him. A thief with a small Rembrandt canvas under his bed will do the same. What are the consequences? When it comes to the heroin, the world is better off for its loss, isn't that so? But the Rembrandt, this irreplaceable masterpiece, what about that? Should we risk the destruction of a great work of art for the pleasure— the unlikely pleasure—of seeing a common thief go to prison for perhaps a year, if that?"

It made sense to me at the time, and still does, and I told Loren as much. She was not overly impressed. "Well, I hope the bastard doesn't wait too long to go to the police. Uncle Sol will be ninety in a couple of months."

"I know. I—"

"Val, the oven just beeped off." She was whispering now and speaking rapidly. "He'll be out in a minute. Look, I agree. I think you're right. What do you say we don't tell him at all right now? Give it a few days, a week, and then at least we'd be able to give him a progress report on how the police are doing, so at least he has a sense of progress being made, rather than just having the news—"

"Dumped on him," I said. "Yes, I like that, but you don't think he'll find out on his own?"

"Doubtful, I'd say. And I'll ask Esther not to tell him either. And, uh, there's one more thing I need to say." I expected a pause to allow me to ask what it was, but she barreled right on. "I only found out yesterday that you weren't being paid to do this. Uncle Sol was amazed that I didn't know that, but I didn't, I honestly didn't. I thought you were a . . . a . . ."

"I know what you thought I was. It's okay."

"No," Loren said, "I was terrible to you, and I want you to know I'm deeply, sincerely sorry. I'm ashamed. *Thank* you for what you're doing for us, and I'm so very sorry it's gotten you injured."

"No, I don't look at it that way, Loren—"

"Can we make it 'Lori,' please, Val?"

I was really floating by now, and I hadn't taken any recent meds I could blame it on. *Watch it, Val*, I heard myself warning myself, *don't forget, you're dealing with another lawyer here*. It had about as much effect as anything else you tell yourself. "I'd like that, Lori," I said eagerly. "I've always liked the name." A dumb remark, but, as it happens, true.

"Will you let me buy you dinner when you get back, to make it up to you?"

Will I . . . I gulped. "I'll have to consult my social calendar on that one, but I imagine that with a little juggling, I just might be able to squeeze you in. So, okay, it's a deal."

I heard Sol's voice in the background. "So who's that you're talking to so enthusiastically?"

"Just a friend of mine."

"A friend of yours called you on *my* telephone?"

I didn't get to hear how she got out of that. A quick "Bye" to me and she was gone.

I decided that a little more sleep might do me good, after all, so, rather than getting dressed, I climbed back into bed and quickly sank back into a more contented slumber than a newly concussed, contused, and lacerated hospital patient with a wobbly brain had any right to expect.

Chapter 15

At 7:00 a.m. I was still sound asleep when a couple of attendants came by to change the dressing on my stitches. Among the implements they brought was a mirror, which they offered to me when the old dressing came off. Did I want to see what my face looked like? Well, of course I did. I grabbed the mirror and took my first look. If my eyes were in any condition to bug, I'm sure they would have done it.

"Whoa! Yikes! *Buongiorno, signor Frankenstein!*"

The reaction made them both laugh. "Oh, it's not so bad," one of them said. "We see worse every week. Every *night*."

"Oh, far worse," the other concurred, preparing the fresh gauze. "*Far* worse. Do you remember the one last week where his whole—"

I raised a feeble hand. "Please. Don't. Have mercy."

"Oh, this doesn't look that bad, that's all I meant to say. And it's not even as bad as it looks, believe me."

I did believe him, but I sure hope I never see anything worse than that when I look in a mirror. Dr. Fannucci, despite all the talk about how beautiful they would be, had put in a string of black stitches running in a wavering, raw-looking row, from above and in front of my right ear almost to the middle of my forehead. Added to that, I had a truly ugly black eye on the right—for the first time I really understood why they're called shiners—and the eye had closed to the point of being not much more than an evil-looking, blood-red slit. The other eye was bloodshot as well, and the skin around both of them was not only tightly puffed up but bright pink. And then a separate swelling down my right cheek gave my head an asymmetrical appearance that made it seem as if one side of my face was farther away than the other.

I handed back the mirror. "Here, take it away. *Please.*"

Another laugh. "Seen enough, eh?"

"More than enough."

"Don't worry, my friend, once we get these stitches covered, people will barely notice."

⌘

COMANDO LEGIONE
CARABINIERI PROVINCIALE
STAZIONE CARABINIERI MOSCOVA

So read the marble plaque at which my sullen cabdriver was jerking his thumb to indicate that we had reached our destination, and that explained his mood. Somehow I'd gotten the idea that it was at least a two- or three-mile ride from the hotel, and although I felt pretty good, considering, I didn't think I was ready to try walking that far, not yet, not today. But instead of two or three miles, it had been two or three *minutes*; not even a mile. Even with the initial start-up charge (€3.20), the charge per kilometer (€1.06), and the per-minute cost (€0.46), the poor guy hadn't cleared €5, and here he'd been lined up in front of the hotel for who knew how long, hoping for a €25 fare to the airport.

I felt bad about it and gave him €15 as I climbed out, which earned me his first smile and a long-suffering *"Grazie."*

The plaque was bolted to the wall beside the entrance to a four-story, stuccoed palazzo of the grander sort, proportioned and decorated in the manner of a Florentine or Roman palace of the sixteenth century, but there were enough modern design and engineering touches to tell me that it was in essence an imitation, built in the middle or late 1800s, when the architects of Italy had turned for their inspiration—wisely, in my opinion—to those very buildings, particularly the great Farnese and Medici palaces of the High Renaissance. Imitation or not, it was an impressive pile of gray stone, what with its long rows of classically pedimented windows and a monumental arched entrance a good twenty-five feet high and fifteen wide.

It was all the more imposing because it stood alone among the non-descript 1950s–1960s apartment buildings that otherwise populated the via della Moscova. My guess was that the whole street had been leveled in the massive Allied bombings of 1943, and this had been the one structure thought to be worth restoring.

I was here because when I'd checked out of the hospital that morning I'd been told by the clerk that a message had been left for me the previous day by a *tenente*—that would be lieutenant—Fontanella of the carabinieri, requesting my presence at carabinieri headquarters at 9:30 a.m. A certain Dr. Bakshi had strictly forbidden its delivery until now, so as not to disturb my rest.

My eyebrows lifted. "That wouldn't be Luca Fontanella, by any chance, would it?"

"I believe so, yes."

Well, well. Luca was an old acquaintance. I'd met him on that earlier trip to Milan four years ago, to work on something or other with a couple of Brera curators. The museum had suggested that I come at that particular time because they were putting on a three-day seminar for the carabinieri, and an introduction to Impressionism was blocked out as a part of it. Not having much in the way of an Impressionist collection to curate, however, they didn't have any curators with much of a background in it, and they wondered, if, perhaps, by chance, it might be possible that the distinguished Impressionist scholar from the Metropolitan Museum of Art might be willing to honor them by . . .

And so I did. Luca Fontanella was in the three-hour session and he stayed afterward (the only one) to ask some perceptive questions, interesting enough to both of us so that we continued our conversation over a two-hour lunch the next day. And when he'd shown up for it, he'd come fully prepped, obviously having devoted the evening to researching the subject he was interested in. I was impressed. After that we'd met for a second lunch, and then done aperitivo together with a few other people one evening. Do you remember my mentioning the carabiniere who'd helped me to understand the art squad's seeming lack of interest in putting the bad guys away, with his heroin-Rembrandt comparison? Well, that was Fontanella; not a member of the art squad himself, but I'd be surprised if he didn't wind up there someday.

My mistake about the distance of headquarters from the Hotel Milano Scala had gotten me here with twenty minutes to wait. There was a little café a few doors down, the two boxed shrubs on either sides of its entrance providing a welcome touch of color and life to the drab gray façades around it. Standing at the counter I gulped down an espresso. Somewhat revived, but hardly feeling a hundred percent yet, I really could have used a second one, but thought I'd better get back to the carabinieri palazzo.

As it is with other grand structures of its era, walking through the broad entrance did not put you inside the building, but rather into a covered passageway that opened onto a gated, pillared courtyard, once used to leave coaches and their horsemen (which was, of course, why the entrances were built as big as they were). Today, as might be expected, the parked coaches, and there were a lot of them, all had four rubber tires and internal combustion engines. Before I got that far, however, there was a built-into-the-wall gatehouse on the right, manned by a smartly turned-out young carabiniere at a desk with four computer monitors and a small switchboard. As I approached the window, he slipped on his cap for formality's sake and turned with a ready smile.

"Come posso aiutarla, signore?"

When I explained that I had a nine-thirty appointment with Lieutenant Fontanella, he immediately got on the phone, and in a few minutes a middle-aged *maresciallo*, a marshal—a high-ranking noncommissioned officer somewhere between a sergeant and a lieutenant—showed up to open the iron grillwork gate and let me through. Girdling the courtyard were two large wings of the palazzo, invisible from the street. I was taken to the one on the right, in which we took an elevator up two floors, where it opened onto a corridor with cramped office cubicles on either side, six in all, with uniformed carabinieri, including one woman, in most of them. In the others were people in ordinary business attire, but with the unmistakable look of the bred-in-the-bone cop. (How do I know so much about the "unmistakable look of the bred-in-the-bone cop"? Same way you do; I've seen the movies too.)

At the end of the corridor there was a single office with real, ceiling-high walls and an actual working door, closed at the moment, on which the carabiniere rapped. A voice called out something indistinct from within, and the carabiniere shouted back that he had brought signor Caruso. He was answered by a few more muffled syllables (among which I thought I heard the word "caffè," which greatly brightened my outlook). The door was opened, and I was bowed into the room, after which the *maresciallo* left, softly closing the door behind him.

The office was nothing special one way or the other, just your basic bureaucratic midlevel manager's office, not much bigger than the cubicles; sufficient for work with a modest, metal desk at the window and a corner grouping of a few chairs around a coffee table, but with no attempt made at personalizing things beyond a hammered-copper pot of geraniums, obviously well-tended, on one corner of the desk. Behind it sat Fontanella, unchanged in three years. He was in uniform today, something not required of lieutenants, but then I'd never seen him otherwise. Carabinieri have famously handsome uniforms, and Luca obviously loved wearing his, with its brown leather Sam Browne belt polished to a satiny gleam and his medals and ribbons (they all seem to have medals and ribbons) aligned in precise rows on his chest. His blue tie was flawlessly knotted, and the trim, tailored, blue-gray jacket was buttoned up so tightly—even with him sitting down—that it was a wonder he could still breathe.

He stood up with a smile when I came in, tugged down his jacket, and reached a hand across his desk to greet me. "Ah, Tino, it's good to see you. Sorry about what brings you here, though." This was delivered in Italian. Luca spoke almost no English. With a gesture he invited me to sit.

I slipped into the visitor's chair, glad for the chance to get off my feet. "It's good to see you too, Luca."

It was, too. Seeing him now made me recall how pleasant he was to be around. A trim, affable man, a little older than I was, with a warm tenor voice, he gave you the feeling that, despite tons of evidence to the contrary, everything was under control, all would be well. And then he had a diastema, a space between his upper front teeth, that rounded out his persona by contributing a likable touch of goofiness.

His expression had gotten more serious as he took in my appearance. "Are you sure you're up for this? If I'd realized what a beating you took . . ."

I waved off the rest of it and gestured vaguely at my face. "It looks worse than it is, believe me. I have that on good authority."

The carabiniere was back with two steaming cups of espresso and a plate holding two brioches. Luca gestured his invitation. "I've gotten you up early. I thought you might like a little something."

"*Do* I," I said, gratefully reaching for a cup. The brioches looked great too. They were near enough to the back of my hand that I could feel their warmth, and the chocolaty aroma suggested they were filled with Nutella, that super-sweet kiddie spread that has so caught the fancy of our supposedly sophisticated European cousins. There are pizzerias, even in Milan, where you can order a Nutella pizza with no fear of derision. But then I love the stuff too (but not on pizzas), so I'm in no position to sneer. I hadn't had anything solid since that hurried panino at the Varenna train station the day before. My appetite had suddenly stormed back, and with a vengeance. I eyed those beautiful pastries, but I wasn't about to take the chance of getting into a police interview, even with Luca conducting it, with chocolate sauce drizzling down my chin.

While the sauce cooled and congealed and the brioches hardened (*damn!*) we chatted about what was going on in our lives over the coffee. It didn't take long. Despite the easy manner, Luca didn't have much in the way of small talk, and I sure had no knack for it myself.

"I guess we'd better get down to yesterday," he said as we wound down, and at my appreciative nod: "Let's start by going over exactly what happened. Your own words. Just talk. I've already spoken to signor Zampa, so I have a general idea of what occurred."

"Will do," I said with a laugh, "but I don't expect it's going to add anything to what Dante told you. I wasn't conscious at the time, you know."

"Let's just see, shall we?" He held up a small digital recorder for me to see. "I'll be recording this, all right?"

"Sure, fine." Naturally, it took me only a few minutes to go over what I knew, during which he did no more than nod from time to time or ask me for a couple of details, neither of which I could supply.

"The studio is protected by two automatic digital locks, as you know," he said as I finished up, "which means that whoever it was had to have access to the code. Which means he got it from Dante. Which narrows down—No?" he asked, seeing that I was shaking my head.

"No, I'm afraid it doesn't do very much narrowing down. Anybody who'd ever stood next to Dante when he opened those doors could know the code."

"Oh?"

I told him how easy it was to look over Dante's shoulder.

"So you know the code yourself?"

I thought for a second. "Yes."

"All right, let's hear it."

"Two-oh-one-four-something . . . eight, I think it was. The same one on both doors."

He flipped the wooden pencil he'd been toying with onto the desk and heaved a sigh. "Great," he said disgustedly. "I should have known this was too easy."

And seemingly out of nowhere a forgotten thought popped into my head: *Ulisse!* I'd planned to try his number again this morning, and if I got no answer, to check with Giulietta. And I'd clean forgotten, just hadn't given him a thought since—

"What's the matter?" Luca asked.

"It's a friend of mine. I just remembered. He didn't turn up for a meeting yesterday, and I've been worried—"

"This would be signor Ulisse Agnello and the meeting yesterday morning at the Serbelloni?"

"That's right. He's actually the owner of those paintings, and he was supposed—"

"Oh, I know who he is." It seemed to me that there was something suggestive in the way the words came out, an unstated "all right" at the end of the sentence. *Oh, I know who he is, all right.*

Before I could respond to it, he continued: "You don't have any idea where he might be, Tino? I'd like to know myself."

"Oh, Lord, you mean he still hasn't shown up? You might try a woman named Giulietta Barone. She runs an auction house here in Milan. They have a relationship, or at least I think they do."

He was nodding. "Yes, *she* called *us*. She's heard nothing from him either."

I shook my head. "That's worrisome."

"Oh, indeed." But it was a funny kind of "indeed," a tongue-in-cheek "indeed," as if to say there was more here than met the eye. What was he getting at?

"Uh, Luca—" I began.

He ignored it. "When did you talk to him last?"

"The day before yesterday. He told me he was going to Lugano that night, to some kind of arts council thing. He was planning to stay over and be back the next morning—yesterday—for the meeting."

"Stay over? Did he say where?"

"Yes . . ." I closed my eyes and concentrated, trying to pull the name from a memory that wasn't yet functioning in high gear. "No, I'm afraid I . . . the Splendide, that was it."

Having retrieved his pencil, he wrote it down. "Good." Then he made a show of arranging the papers on his desk, sliding them into two perfectly aligned little stacks. "Tino, you say he's your friend—"

"He *is* my friend," I said crossly. "What the hell's going on, Luca? You're making me nervous."

"I'm wondering exactly how much you know about him, Tino."

"I don't understand what you mean by 'exactly.' Look, I realize we're having a police interview here so you're the one who gets to ask the questions, but how about telling me what you're driving at? I'd really appreciate it."

Luca chuckled. "Let me answer that with another question. Do you find anything at all strange about signor Agnello and the two paintings all disappearing on the same day?"

I stared at him. "Whoa, let me get this straight. Are you suggesting he's the one who stole them?"

"Suggesting, no. Considering as one possibility, yes. There are others. You have to admit, it was a remarkable coincidence, a highly unlikely coincidence, wouldn't you agree? The very same day? Two very extraordinary events?"

"No, I would *not* agree," I said. "All coincidences are unlikely; that's their nature. Otherwise, they wouldn't be coincidences. An unlikely concurrence of events with no causal connection between them. And they most certainly do happen. That's why there's a word for them."

I was getting a little ticked off, but he remained his calm, amiable, slightly detached self. He sat now with his hands folded comfortably over his midsection and regarding me with a perfectly friendly expression . . . well, maybe just a little skeptical.

"Luca, think about what you're saying, will you?" I said. "Why would he steal his own paintings?"

"I don't think he did, Tino, but there is *something* there. This is an instance, not only of an unlikely concurrence of events, but of an unlikely concurrence of *two* unlikely events—and events with connections between them, at that. The Renoirs disappear; their owner disappears at the same time. A mere coincidence? Do you really believe that?"

He was beginning to get through to me. I remembered reading a novel by some hack mystery writer on a flight a few years ago. The book, otherwise forgettable, included one concept that has stuck with me ever since: "Goldstein's Law of Interconnected Monkey Business," I think he called it: the idea that when a lot of suspicious, or questionable, or "coincidental" things start happening in the same context to the same set of people, you better believe there's a connection to be found.

I thought about that and slowly nodded. "You're right, Luca. Sorry I flared up like that."

"You were standing up for your friend."

"Yes. I thought you were accusing him—"

He shook his head. "No. Just searching for possibilities."

"I understand. And another possibility is that he was . . . that he's been abducted over them, isn't that so . . . or . . . or killed?"

Something constricted inside my chest as I asked the questions. I realized that they had been on the fringes of my mind since yesterday, but saying them out loud brought them front and center, made the possibilities real. *Please,* I thought—prayed, I guess—*don't let it be so. Not Ulisse.*

A telephone in his desk drawer beeped, and Luca pulled it out and looked at the screen.

"Sorry, Tino, give me a minute. I think I should take this."

He swung his chair halfway around to keep his conversation private, so all I could hear was an occasional "yes," or "I see," and once a considerably more animated reaction: "He *what*?" followed by a burst of delighted, incredulous laughter. After about a minute he hung up and swung back around. "I have to check something out. I should only be a few minutes. Wait here for me, will you? I think this is something that's going to interest you."

"Of course."

"Have a brioche," he called to me from the doorway. "Have *both* brioches. I'll ask *maresciallo* Giordano to bring you another coffee." Whatever that call was about, it had certainly lit him up.

"No, thanks, I don't really need—"

But he was moving too fast for me, and two minutes after he left another coffee was brought in, a caffè latte this time, in one of those big, wonderful, white cups—more like a soup bowl with a handle than a coffee cup. It was getting a little late in the morning for Italians to be drinking caffè latte, so I realized this was a special treat for me as an American. I appreciated that, and the caffeine did me good. I glugged down nearly half of it, then turned my attention to the brioches, which were looking better every minute. The first bite slid down almost without any help from me—Nutella-flavored ambrosia—and I wondered for a moment whether, despite Fontanella's telling me to help myself to both, it was a little gauche, a little greedy, to gobble them both up. The moment quickly passed and two minutes later number two was gone as well. Ten minutes after that, so was the latte. While I drank it, I thought some more about Ulisse. It was easy to imagine still other possibilities, but the central fact was, there'd been no word from him in almost two days now; I wasn't imagining that, and it was worrisome.

When twenty minutes had passed since the lieutenant had left, I headed out into the hallway to find *maresciallo* Giordano and ask if there had been any word from Luca, when Giordano himself came striding down the hall toward me.

"Come with me, please," he said, turning on his heel. "There's something the *tenente* would like you to see."

We took the stairs down one flight to the public reception area, then proceeded through a waist-high gate beside the counter and into an open work space with eight or ten desks, all occupied by clerical employees clacking steadily away at their keyboards. Along the left-hand wall was a string of five small, windowed offices with open doors. From the farthest of them, the last in the row, streamed a sputtering torrent of invective.

"I hope that's not where you're taking me," I said to *maresciallo* Giordano.

"I'm afraid that it is. It would appear that a citizen is making his displeasure known."

"I'll say."

By now we were near enough to hear what was being said. There were two voices, one of which belonged to Luca, who was calmly, but not too successfully, trying to hold the fort against the onslaught.

"Signor Esposito, I'm merely trying to explain—"

"If there was no reward," interrupted the outraged voice of his adversary, "then why did your *sergente* Lombardo tell me there would be one if I brought them to you, can you answer me that?" From the exasperated, dogged tone I could tell that it wasn't the first time he'd asked the question. "Five hundred euros," he said.

"Signor Esposito, I assure you—yet again—that whoever called you was not 'my' *sergente* Lombardo. We do not *have* a *sergente* Lombardo in our—"

"Then why did he say he was? Answer me *that*." Immediately following which an implied but unuttered *Ha!* hung in the air.

Even from twenty feet away, Luca's long sigh could be heard. "Signore . . ."

"And even if the reward is no longer in effect, as you *now* claim, surely I am at the least entitled to some reimbursement for the time and cost of doing the carabinieri's work for it."

"But signore, surely it's the responsibility of every citizen to assist the police in their duty whenever possible?"

"Not if it means giving up three hours of work with no—"

At this point, Giordano bowed me into the room. On hearing us, Luca looked hopefully up, as if rescue might be at hand, at which Giordano made for the door before this affair, whatever it was, could be dumped in his lap. But Luca, despite that easygoing, relaxed manner of his, was too fast for him.

"Oh, *maresciallo*," he sang sweetly.

Giordano's shoulders drooped. His hand fell away from the door handle. "Yes, *tenente*?"

"I think you're the very man who can help signor Esposito. Signor Esposito, this is my trusted aide, *maresciallo* Giordano, who is our specialist in matters such as this . . ."

This produced a poisonous (but respectful) glare from Giordano.

". . . will be very happy to assist you. Take my chair, *maresciallo*, won't you?"

If Esposito even registered the change in his audience, you'd never know it, and by the time Giordano had gotten himself seated, he had picked up his rant, right from the point where he'd left it.

". . . with no recompense, no recognition, no *appreciation*, even . . ."

Luca grabbed me by the elbow, hustled me to a door at the back of the room, flung it open, and hurriedly closed it behind us. We were in a claustrophobic, windowless little room that held a minimal amount of furniture, all of which had seen some hard use: a wooden chair, a scarred interrogation table, and a landline telephone that appeared to be from the seventies. Nothing else, not even a second chair.

"Luca, what—"

"Look," he said and gestured at the table with his chin.

On it, I now saw, lay a couple of flat, rectangular objects. I walked up for a closer look.

And then, unless I'm misremembering it, my jaw dropped. I don't mean my mouth opened; I mean my lower jaw actually dropped, fell . . . *plummeted*, if you like. All my life I'd assumed the term was an allusion and not meant to be taken literally. But take it from me, there's a difference.

"Luca! . . . I . . . What . . ."

Luca laughed. "I gather those are what I think they are?"

It took me another moment to get my mouth back in working order, and then I said, "I can't believe it, but . . . *yes*."

Yes. The Renoirs were back.

Chapter 16

I drank them hungrily in, throwing questions at Luca all the time. Were these what signor Esposito was demanding a reward for? Why did he think there was a reward? Where had he gotten them? *How* had he gotten them? Did the carabinieri know who had stolen them? And why steal them at all if—

Luca shushed me with a wave of his hand so that he could answer some of the questions. The pictures had apparently spent at least some of the night outdoors, he told me. ("No rain, *grazie a Dio!*") There was a factory across the street from Dante's studio, with a high concrete wall in front of it; perhaps I remembered it. (I did; hard to forget a six-foot-high, two-hundred-foot-long, rainbow-colored celebration of the invention of aerosol paint.)

"Well, that's where they turned up this morning, right behind that wall, only ten meters or so down the street from the studio."

"Wait a minute. Are you saying whoever took them—and shot Dante, and put me in the hospital—just tossed them over the wall . . . threw them *away*—almost the minute he got down the stairs with them? That's what you're telling me?"

Luca was smiling at me. "Tino, yelling at me is not going produce the answers any more quickly."

That stopped me. "I was yelling?"

Now the smile turned into a laugh. "I'm beginning to think I'd be better off going back to signor Esposito and turning you over to Giordano." The closed door had done a good job of muffling the sounds from the room, but Esposito's noisy wheedling, if not its exact words, was still going full blast.

"The gentleman is a manager at the factory," Luca said. "He claims he got a call first thing this morning from a carabinieri *sergente* named . . . something—"

"Lombardo," I said.

"Thank you. And despite the considerable disadvantage of not existing, *sergente* Lombardo managed to tell him that someone had informed *him* that two extremely valuable stolen paintings the carabinieri were looking for had been hidden behind the wall of his factory the day before, and if they were really there, and if Esposito brought them to a *tenente* Fontanella at headquarters on via della Moscova, a substantial reward would await him."

I'd been focused hard on the pictures during most of the time that we'd been talking, and now I rubbed my eyes (my one good one, rather) and sat back in the chair, thinking. "So what's going on? Does this make any sense at all to you?"

"Not much, not yet. Do you have a theory to offer?"

"Well, it was the middle of the afternoon, there's that café right next to the studio, so maybe someone saw him run out with them—maybe even heard the shot just before—and that panicked him and he just wanted to dump them and get the hell out of there. Maybe the idea was to come back and get them later, in the middle of the night."

"So why didn't he? There's no security system that would have prevented his getting over the wall to collect them; we checked."

"Mm."

"Also, there were four people in the café, with each of whom we spoke, as well as the two waiters and the counterman. Nobody remembers seeing any such thing. It being Sunday, the cosmetics factory itself was closed and the shops were shuttered. So unless someone was sitting at an apartment window, looking out at nothing but an empty street, there was nobody *to* see anything. So . . ."

"Okay, scratch that theory. In fact, now that I think about it, what would he have been doing, anyway, running down the street with them? How could he not have had a car ready, right outside the door?"

"And that is precisely what I think he had," said Luca. "If he came out the door, got quietly into the car, and drove away—or an accomplice drove him away—who would have noticed? And if anyone did notice, would they have made a mental note of it? I doubt it."

"But then how did the paintings wind up behind the wall?"

"I think he did in fact return later—in the dark of night—but it was to *leave* the paintings there, not to get them back. A few hours later the call to Esposito would have been made, and—" He gestured at the Renoirs. *"Voilà."*

"Well, okay, I suppose that's *possible*, sure, but what kind of motive could there be for it? And how could he . . ." A filament of memory, tenuous and elusive, had interrupted my train of thought. It was from the time just before I got clobbered, when I'd sat down to look at the paintings. *Something important,* I thought. I stopped talking, trying to flesh it out, to get hold of it.

"How could he what?" asked Luca.

"I don't know. But something just came back to me—the very last thing I remember before I got whacked on the head. I was looking at the paintings, and I asked for a magnifying glass . . ."

"Is that unusual?"

"No, but I've got this feeling it's something significant, something to do with the robbery."

"Are you sure?"

"No, not at all." The filament was dying away, fading to nothing. "Just a feeling, very vague."

"But you don't remember what it was you saw, what exactly you wanted the magnifying glass for?"

"No . . ." I shook my head, staring at the paintings.

"Just a minute," Luca said. He went out into the clerical area, and came back with a rectangular magnifier, the kind used to read entire lines of type. He handed it to me.

"It was the sketch, the café sketch," I declared abruptly. "I just this second remembered."

"But you still don't remember what it was?"

"No."

"Well, you've got the sketch, you've got a magnifying glass. Have a go at it. In the meantime I'll go and deliver poor Giordano from his misery. I feel awfully guilty about that."

"Yes, I can tell from your grin," I said, propping the sketch against the telephone to make it easier to examine, and leaning forward with the glass.

I found nothing. Nothing odd, nothing suspicious, nothing even particularly interesting beyond the fact of its being a newly discovered Renoir. In case I'd been mistaken about which painting it was, I went over the self-portrait too. I was still examining it when Luca returned.

"Anything?" he asked.

"Not about the paintings *per se*, no, nothing at all. Maybe I didn't ask for a magnifying glass. Maybe I'm just . . . I don't know. Oh, one thing I can tell you: these were definitely *not* tossed over that wall."

He scowled. "Are you suggesting—"

"I'm suggesting that no oil painting tossed over a six-foot wall is going to survive without some damage to the frame or the stretcher bars, or the canvas itself, and these two show no damage at all. My guess would be that he didn't toss them over the top of the wall, he slipped them through one of those narrow breaks in it."

"Ah. And why do you consider this to be important?"

"I don't know if it is important, Luca. I just thought I should mention it. For one thing, though, it would seem to show he does have some concern about their condition."

"Yes, thank you," Luca said, unimpressed. Then he smiled. "Zampa will be happy too. I imagine it will save him a good deal of reconstructive work."

"I would sure think so. Have you called him about this yet?"

"Not yet. I wanted you to confirm what they were before I did that. But I'll want him in to make the formal identification, since they were in his possession at the time."

"Are you going to be able to release them to him? He's got to have them ready for the auction in a few days."

"Yes, that shouldn't be a problem."

I stood up and stretched. "Okay if I go now? I could stand to put my feet up for a while. Not quite myself yet."

"Of course you're not. I'll have a car take you back to the hotel."

"No, actually, I'd rather walk. I'll just take it slowly."

We shook hands and I said: "So, *tenente*, did the gentleman ever get his reward?"

Luca laughed. "It awaits him in heaven."

Across via della Moscova from carabinieri headquarters was a stark little plaza, a twelve-by-twelve grid made of six-foot-square quadrangles of featureless concrete paving blocks alternating with equal-sized patches of lawn, each with a slender young tree at its center. It was as if the municipal authorities couldn't decide on whether they wanted a park or a piazza and had settled on a little of each. The park contingent had the edge, because there was a grouping of concrete benches in the center, on one of which I sat to call Dante. I wanted to ask him if he remembered what had made me ask him for a magnifying glass (if indeed I really had; I was starting to wonder if it had actually happened or was merely some nonsensical output from my concussed and wobbly brain). I wanted to see how he was doing too, of course; I knew he'd appreciate that. And if I reached him before Luca did, so much the better; it'd be fun to be the one to give him the good news about the paintings.

I had only one number for him, the one that was on his card, and my call was answered by a woman who took my name and number, and told me that signor Zampa wasn't available; he had gone off to Rome on business and wouldn't be back until the weekend, five days from now. I told her that I had important information for him that I knew he would be very glad to hear, and couldn't she just put me in touch with him before then, or at least give him a message?

No, she couldn't, she said, getting defensive about it. She was an employee of Centro Fiera, a telephone answering service, she told me. She didn't know signor Zampa personally, had never spoken to him, and was only following his standing, very explicit written instructions: When he was away from Milan, telephone messages were to be held for him until his return, when he would be given the list of callers and their business with him. Those he approved, and only those, would then be forwarded to him. And no promises were to be made to callers to the effect that they might expect a return phone call from him.

It was only at that point I remembered that Dante was reputed to be a world-class telephonophobe. He never answered his own phone, even back when he was in New York. A friend of mine had asked why not, and Dante's answer wound up, in several variations, on the "Dante Zampa Outrageous Quotations" list. The version quoted to me by my friend was: "Answer the telephone? Are you serious? Me? And speak to any moron with ten eurocents in his pocket who happens to feel like talking to me? Don't be ridiculous."

I thanked the woman and let it go. If he was well enough to travel to Rome, I didn't need to worry about his condition, and as for the paintings, I was sure that Luca would have an easier time reaching him than I would. The thing about the magnifying glass was getting less important by the second. I'd now given those pictures, especially the café sketch, a long, hard look . . . and there just wasn't anything there.

I headed slowly back to the Milano Scala.

Chapter 17

I have to confess something here. You know the way I reacted—not very politely, I'm afraid—to Luca's implying that there was something shady about Ulisse? Well, the umbrage was real enough—Ulisse and I go back a long way and I do love the little guy, but it was a little on the disingenuous side too. The fact is, as much as I liked Ulisse, I was aware that there was something of the sharpster about him. I'd sat in on some of his meetings with collectors who were considering putting their things up for auction with Dell'Acqua, and it sure seemed to me that the negotiations on some of the issues involved could get a little dodgy, a little, say, more flexible than I would have thought proper.

It's tricky: very few of those issues are cut and dried. Take the number-one thing, the estimated price for the object to be auctioned. The catalog will generally publish an estimate of what the house expects it to go for in the form of a range. On a painting by Marc Chagall, for example, you'd probably see something like "Low Estimate: $500,000, High Estimate: $600,000." A giant, shiny, purple, puppy-dog balloon figure by Jeff Koons, on the other hand, would more likely show as $50,000,000 to $60,000,000. (Don't look at me. I'm not the one who comes up with these numbers.) These estimates supposedly provide a guide to would-be buyers as to what they need to be prepared to spend.

Fair enough. But don't they also give buyers an impression of the inherent *worth* of the painting (as opposed to its expected price), and thus, whether or not it might be a good idea to bid on it themselves, and if so, how high to go? And aren't those three very different things that can have very different effects on how the sale goes? The answers are yes, yes, and yes. They can and do affect the level of excitement the auction generates, the interest in the specific items, the level of the bidding, and the perseverance of the bidders. And, of course, the profit to the house.

Well, how do the houses arrive at those high and low estimates? They all do it their own way, naturally, but I can tell you this much: none of them relies on any supposed robotic algorithm that puts previous artist sale prices, market trends, economic indices, and whatnot into a digital blender that grinds them up and spits out the answer. Sure, those are all taken into consideration, but in the end it's human beings who make the decision. In a major art sale by a big house, that generally means the chief appraiser—at Dell'Acqua in the old days, that would have been signor Ulisse Agnello.

And once you get human beings involved, there's always going to be wiggle room, something that Ulisse wasn't averse to making use of when it was there for the taking. What he did was to maneuver and engineer things so that Dell'Acqua made a good profit, and, where favored clients were involved, so that they came out of the experience better than they might have without his machinations. The estimates weren't the only things that were involved, either. There was the reserve price too—the minimum bid that had to be reached before the object would be sold. If it wasn't reached, the object would be withdrawn. This was always a secret between the seller and the auction house. There's also the question of whether a guarantee of sale would be provided to the seller by the house, and what it would cost the seller to get it, and a dozen other things peculiar to the trade.

The first time I saw him playing fast and loose like this, I was stunned; new to the business, I had assumed that, at a well-known house like Dell'Acqua, any prospective buyer or seller would be treated the same as everyone else. To see that it wasn't so, that different standards were in place for different players, simply didn't seem to me like fair play.

Of course, now I know that it's standard practice in the auction world, and legal too, as long as you don't cross over any fairly well-defined red lines. Me, I still don't like it. I still think it's both unfair and unethical. But then, as Ulisse would (and did) say, and Esther too for that matter, I've always been a little naïve about these things.

As far as I know, there was never any personal profit in the way Ulisse handled these matters—no kickback from the house, no cut of the selling price from the sellers, and I would have been shocked to learn otherwise. But that initial surprise—make that disappointment—that I felt when I first saw him merrily bending and stretching the house's rules and guidelines had never gone away; it was a part of him that I never could get to mesh with the annoyingly, amusingly punctilious man I knew.

And so, when I first read about this amazing find of his, there was a part of me that couldn't help wondering if maybe he'd played a bit fast and loose with the two paintings as well. I mean, really, think about it—a man happens to be at a flea market, at which he picks up two old, discolored, presumably worthless paintings ("for their frames"). A little later he "accidentally" discovers that *both* of them are unknown Rembrandts, or Titians, or Renoirs that are worth a hundred thousand times what he paid for them. And it's all just honest luck? Are you kidding me? Didn't I see that movie? Pierce Brosnan, wasn't it? Michael Caine, maybe?

It was just too damn improbable, and so, almost against my will, there was no way I could help speculating as to whether there wasn't something, well, fishy about the way Ulisse had come by the paintings. Had he somehow known that the Renoirs were there, under those seascapes? Even perhaps been the one who'd painted them over? The idea really troubled me. I felt guilty for even thinking it about him, and so it was with great relief that I read an article on the Louvre's forensic findings that showed me I was wrong.

These particular findings pertained to the age of the paint, the pigment. Because different paint molecules decompose at different rates, analyzing a few small paint samples from a painting for radioactive decay can give you an approximation of how long ago they were applied. It's the same principle that, on a much grander scale, allows the carbon-dating of 60,000-year-old fossils.

Well, the age of the underlying paintings, the two presumed Renoirs, had been determined early on: 1855 to 1880, which very nicely encompassed the 1864 day on which Maurizio said he received the sketch from twenty-three-year-old Auguste's own hand.

That was good news for art historians, me included. But for me and me alone, the more recent findings on the age of the overpainted seascapes were even better: the range that the scientists came up with, with a very high level of reliability, was 1990 to 2005, which meant that Ulisse couldn't have had anything at all to do with the overpaintings, since he hadn't bought them until 2013.

Whew. Ulisse was off the hook. Case closed. Hallelujah.

Only to be reopened a couple of hours ago when Luca's thinly—diaphanously—veiled allusions connecting Ulisse's disappearance to the theft had hit their mark and left me wondering once more about his involvement in the entire affair, from the purchase of the pictures at the flea market four years ago, to the dramatic revelation of the underpaintings, to the theft. I'm not including what happened after that—the stashing of them behind the wall. That part was just too weird for me to process.

Anyway, the more I thought about it, the more I thought Luca might be onto something, even if neither of us knew what it was.

As the mysterious Professor Goldstein had decreed, there was a connection to be found. What it was, I couldn't come up with, but I

couldn't get around the notion, try though I did, that whatever nefari-
ous doings were involved, Ulisse had something to do with them,
something that put him at the center of them. Something he'd done,
or something that had been done *to* him? I couldn't decide . . . Hell, I
didn't want it to be either one of them.

All this heavy thinking had been done while lying comfortably
on my back, eyes closed, hands clasped behind my neck, a couple of
pillows propped up behind my head, on the very comfortable double
bed in my room. Inevitably, nature took its course; the next time I
opened an eye to look at the bedside clock it was 1:15 p.m.; I'd been
asleep for almost an hour. My mind must have stayed on the case,
though, because I woke up brimming with pertinent what-if questions
that I hadn't thought of before. What if I'd been reading things wrong,
drawing the wrong conclusions? What if my affection for Ulisse made
me immediately reject one unwelcome possibility that had jumped to
my mind when I first heard about his finding of the paintings? I had
guiltily dismissed the very thought as disloyal and duplicitous, but
now that I was in the thick of things myself, I saw it as something
that I couldn't refuse to look into, however traitorous it was going to
make me feel.

And I even knew how to do it. With a crisp nod of reassurance
to myself—yes, Val, chin up, you're doing the right thing, nothing to
feel guilty about—I sat up on the side of the bed and used the room
telephone to call Montefiore Arte, the house that would be auctioning
a single Renoir portrait if I had my way, or a portrait plus a café sketch
if I didn't. Getting to Giulietta Barone, the CEO, took a bit of doing
but my Met accreditation did the trick.

"Giulietta, it's Valentino—"

"Have you heard something from Ulisse?" she asked after a tiny
catch in her throat.

"No, nothing. I gather you haven't either?"

"Oh, my God, Valentino, I'm so worried. *Something's* happened to him, I know it. Oh, this is all so terrible. And now with the paintings gone—oh, and you were hurt, weren't you, and they *shot* poor Dante. My God, I can't, I can hardly—"

"No, wait. Dante and I, we're both okay. And the paintings, they're back. And they're fine too."

One beat, two beats, and then a hushed, "What did you say?"

"I said Dante and I—"

"No, the other part, the paintings." Not too hard to tell where her primary concern lay. But it was easy enough to understand. She had a very big, very profitable auction on the line . . . but not without the Renoirs, or at least the self-portrait.

"They found them this morning, just a few hours ago. They're perfectly fine," I said again.

She fired a dozen questions at me, barely waiting for my replies, not that I had anything to tell her beyond the basic facts.

"I don't understand," she said when she'd heard everything I had to say, and I could tell she was shaking her head as she said it.

"You, and me, and Dante. And the police. Nobody can figure out what's going on. Look, I'm sorry I didn't tell you about it sooner. I have to take off now. Could you let Benvenuto know, please?"

"Yes, certainly. Valentino, this is so very strange. I . . ." She hesitated, then blurted out her suspicion, apparently as unwelcome to her as it had been to me. "Val, did Ulisse have anything to do with this? What do you think? You know him better than any of us."

"I don't know," I said curtly. I didn't want to admit I was chewing the same thing over myself.

"I'm asking you what you *think*."

"Giulietta, I don't know what I think. I'm as befuddled as you are."

I heard her sigh, and took it as the chance to change the subject. "Look, I'd really appreciate a favor. I haven't seen the auction catalog. Could you send me a copy? Here to the Milano Scala?"

"Certainly. I can have a courier drop it off for you this afternoon."

"That would be great. The earlier the better."

"I'll see to it right now. Listen, Valentino, if you do hear . . ."

"If I hear from him," I finished for her, "I'll let you know right away, I promise."

Twenty minutes later, having made a second phone call, I splashed water on my face, combed my hair, and applied a fresh, supersized adhesive pad to cover my stitches. And five minutes after that, I was climbing into a taxi in front of the hotel and giving instructions to the driver.

"A Porta Nuova, per favore; via Joe Colombo 14."

The current address of the Dell'Acqua Casa d'Arte.

Chapter 18

I'd known, of course, that Dell'Acqua had left its romantic past behind when it had vacated its lodgings in the Galleria, so redolent of its turn-of-the-(twentieth)-century beginnings. I'd known too that its new quarters were on via Joe Colombo in the gleaming, sterile concentration of modern high-rises in Porta Nuova, the city's twenty-first-century business center, so redolent of its ten-year-old building boom. But knowing it and seeing it were two different things, and I was sorry to find its leased offices only dimly visible behind one street-level row of the thousands of smoked glass panels that made up the façade of its thirty-story building, and of many of the tall, sleek buildings around it. If it was *trying* to look anonymous it couldn't have done much better.

(Oh, in case you're wondering: no, the street is not named for the infamous Mafia boss, but for the industrial designer Cesare "Joe" Colombo, a favorite son of the city.)

Once inside the building, Dell'Acqua's lobby was more of the same: clean, spacious, uncluttered, and unexceptional, with three curvy, lemonwood-and-steel Danish Modern chairs for visitors and a kidney-shaped lemonwood desk with a pretty receptionist behind it. A wheat-colored Berber carpet, a few small abstract sculptures on low tables, and three nice Italian Post-Impressionist paintings well-sited on the walls. Certainly, there was nothing especially objectionable about the place, but all in all, a pretty minimalist production. Had Edward

Hopper painted an office scene, which I don't believe he ever did, it would have looked like this. If you'd told me that it was an upscale ad agency that I'd wandered into by mistake, I'd have had no trouble believing it.

When I told the receptionist that the CEO, Cipriano Cosetti, was expecting me, she picked up the telephone, said a couple of words, and a few minutes later, out he shuffled. Cipriano and I had been interns together at Dell'Acqua during my second summer there and had become friendly, often having our brown-bag lunches together, or even going out for a meal once in a while (usually right after payday). Cipriano had stayed with the company, had survived the purge that had come later, and had gradually risen in the organization, finally arriving at the top-of-the-heap position two or three years ago.

We'd spoken on the phone several times since our internships, but it had been ten years since we'd seen one another, so a vigorous, pro forma handshaking and back-thumping was in order. Once that was done we stepped back to take each other in. On the phone when I'd called earlier, I'd headed off any shock on his part by very briefly explaining how I'd gotten injured and subjecting him to the now familiar "it's not as bad as it looks" spiel.

But I was the one who could have used a warning. Cipriano was five years younger than I was, and as a twenty-four-year-old he had been a bright, funny, gawky kid with a love of practical jokes, which was mitigated by his being just as ready to laugh when the joke was on him. But today . . . today he looked in no mood for practical jokes, or any jokes at all.

The years had not treated him kindly, probably in particular the wear and tear of shepherding an art auction house through its crazy rags-to-riches-to-rags-and-back-again (you hoped) existence. Once fizzing with life, he was now sunken-chested and stoop-shouldered. When I said he'd shuffled out, I meant it literally. I'd heard the soles of his designer shoes scuffing over the carpet as he came down the corridor. For me it was a sad reunion, and I hurried us through the *so-how-are-you-doing* phase. He didn't seem to mind either. In fact, I got us down to business without our ever having sat down or left the reception area.

What I wanted, I told him, was to look at the catalogs for their fine-art auctions (in other words, just art; no furniture, dead-celebrity sell-offs, and such) from 1999 to 2005. I didn't tell him why and he didn't ask, so I didn't have to invent anything.

He frowned. "I'm afraid that won't be possible, Tino. Our catalogs only go back ten years. After that, they are, ah, disposed of."

"Not even digital copies?"

"Nothing earlier than 2007."

Well, that sure put a crimp in my plans. "Damn," I mumbled, with a drawn-out sigh.

"Would sales invoices be of help?"

I brightened. "You bet!"

"Good. Those we keep forever. Sometimes, ah, issues arise years later, even decades later, you know."

Did I ever. "And can I see those?"

"Of course you can. You'll have to thumb through the original paper copies, however. I'm sure you remember how hidebound the firm has always been; it didn't start converting from paper until three years ago, after I took over, can you imagine?" He smiled. "One of my little innovations to try and get us into the *twentieth* century. And I'm still trying."

"Good luck with it," I said, although I was only being polite. What he called hidebound I thought of as traditional. It went along with the dark mahogany and the smells of old books and furniture polish that I'd loved about Dell'Acqua. Here in their current offices, the wood was blond, and I couldn't detect any smells at all.

"Very well. Rachele will show you where they are kept," he said, indicating the young woman behind the desk. A curt set of instructions to her, and then a pretend-glance at his watch, a supposedly frustrated shake of his head, and a series of subdued mutterings. ". . . Very busy. Very. Too bad. If only you'd called earlier . . ."

We shook hands again, told each other how great it was to see one another and how we needed to do it again soon, and back down the corridor he shuffled, and that was the end of our reunion.

Rachele took me down one level to a concrete-block-walled room in the basement, filled with rows of metal bookcases holding thousands of red rope folders, the old-fashioned kind with a flap that you tied down with a little red string that wound around a couple of flat cardboard rings. At the front of the room was a steel desk, behind which sat an erect, portly woman in her sixties, every bit as formidable-looking as I remembered her having been back when I was a summer intern.

"Signora Lombardo, this is *dottor* Caruso," Rachele said. "He wants to see the art sale invoices from 1999 to 2005. Signor Cosetti said it's all right to let him have whatever he wants."

The older woman looked up from the catalog cards she was writing on. "Very well, you may go," she said dismissively. "I'll take care of him."

Hearing her voice brought back a flood of memories. *Dismissive* was the word for Madolina Lombardo, all right. *Intimidating* would be a pretty good one too.

"It's nice to see you again, signora Lombardo," I said. "I used to work here—well, when it was in the Galleria—some years back. I was a summer intern . . ."

"I remember you," she said, getting out of her chair, as expressive as a doorknob. "You may take a seat at the table there." I was surprised she remembered me at all.

I was smiling as I went to the library table at the side of the room. *Same old signora Lombardo,* I thought. Forbidding old bird. Daunting.

When I was in my late twenties, she'd had the knack of making me feel like a twelve-year-old trying to hide some guilty secret. She still had it.

She was also still as efficient as they came. In a minute she was back from the shelves with the requested folders, three for each year, on a cart.

"Thank you, signora Lombardo."

"Hm. Yes," she said with her chin in the air, and went back to her desk, leaving me to get down to it. I opened the first folder, from 1999. I'd chosen that year as the starting point because it was the year Ulisse had joined Dell'Acqua.

In those days (not anymore) Dell'Acqua had held about a hundred auctions a year, and each auction had twenty or so lots, each with its own invoice, so we're talking about two thousand paper slips a year to be thumbed through. Slow going, in other words, and it took forty minutes to get through 1999, with no results. Ditto 2000 and 2001. By that time I was tired of sitting, and hungry as well. I'd skipped lunch, trusting in those two brioches at Luca's office to carry me through to dinner. I was wrong.

I took a break then, leaving the building and going to a café a few doors down, where I stood at the counter and ate a ham and artichoke panino. (How do they keep the rolls so fresh and crusty all day in those unrefrigerated, glassed-in counters, and why haven't *we* figured out how to do it? It's a mystery.)

Afterward, an espresso to finish off, and then, on impulse, I bought a double espresso to take back to the signora, thinking she might appreciate a bit of a break herself. And darned if she wasn't touched. She'd been writing longhand in an account book for a while, her half-moon reading glasses sitting low on her nose. When I put the coffee on her desk, she looked utterly amazed, as if no one had ever done this for her before. (*Could be,* I thought.) Then she let the glasses, attached to a

chain around her neck, fall to the ready shelf of her bosom, and gracefully reached for the cup.

"Why, *thank* you, Valentino. I can certainly use that."

Pleased, I went back to the library table, feeling her eyes following
me all the way there. "You know, Valentino," she said as I pulled out my
chair, "I've watched your career with interest. I'm very proud of you. I
always thought you were a good boy."

I was twelve years old all over again, although this time I didn't
mind. "Thank you, signora Lombardo."

I had flipped through the first couple of dozen invoices from 2002
before she spoke again. "Valentino?" she said offhandedly. "You may
call me Madolina, if you like."

"Thank you, signora, I'll try, but it won't be easy." I got back to
work with a smile on my face.

I'd developed a system to move things along, holding a bundle of
thirty or so invoices in my left hand and using the thumb of my right
hand to riffle through them, front to back, as if they were a deck of
cards. I was nearing the end of 2002, my attention starting to wander
again, my focus slipping, beginning to think about one more coffee
break, when one invoice stopped me cold, snapping me to attention.

Pay dirt.

I'd found what I was looking for. And my God, it made me feel
like hell.

Date: 28 November 2002
Lot: 43
Bidder: 144. Identity:——
Total Hammer: €2,200
Buyer's Premium: 330
Sales Tax: 440
Invoice Total: €2,970
Amount Paid: €2,970

Lot description:

Two late XIX–early XX century French oil paintings, unsigned. Probably by the same artist, a follower of Georges d'Espagnat.

1. Portrait (head and shoulders) of a young man, 40.64 x 30.48 cm.

2. Café scene with man drinking coffee, 38.11 x 29.21. (Oil sketch)

So what did that tell me that was so important? Well, I now knew that on November 28, 2002, two paintings were sold to Bidder 144, identity unrecorded, for €2,200 plus premium and tax. The descriptions of the paintings were suspiciously—remarkably—like the two Renoirs. And the dimensions seemed right too; they would translate to about fifteen by twelve inches for the self-portrait and twelve or thirteen by eleven or so for the café sketch, which fitted the way I remembered them. But I would be checking that out later for myself.

For now, I had enough to know that what I'd been fearing to learn was almost certainly true: my good-hearted old friend, my proper, judicious mentor, had been a façade. Behind it all along had been a corrupt, immensely greedy thief and a cunning swindler. It's hard to put into words what I was feeling—a profound mixture of grief, anger, letdown, and stupidity (my own, for being so purposefully blind to what I should have at the very least surmised, a long time ago).

Ulisse, however, had been anything but stupid; I had to give him that much. He'd been as smart as Pierce Brosnan or Michael Caine any day, and probably more patient too. He'd pulled off what had to be the art scam of the century, so far, anyway. As to how he did it, there are a lot of details we'll probably never know (*definitely* never know, if Ulisse didn't turn up alive), so I've gone ahead and put together what I think is a plausible scenario—it squares with the facts, at any rate—for the way he handled it.

It probably would have had its beginning in late October or early November 2002. As chief appraiser of paintings, Ulisse would have been the person to whom a walk-in visitor, a potential seller with a promising-looking painting or two under his arm, would be directed for an evaluation, and it was probably in that way that the Renoirs (not yet painted over) came to him. Ulisse would have thought from the first that they were early Renoirs, but not ones that he recognized. This he would have kept to himself. I imagine he would have told his visitor that they appeared to be minor Impressionist paintings that he would be happy to add to the upcoming Impressionist auction at the end of the month . . . but not to expect too much for them.

Then he would have gone to the Bernheim-Jeune *catalogue raisonné* of Renoir's works and pored over every page of the five volumes—all 4,019 of the paintings known to have come from Renoir's brush. Neither picture would have been among them. Of two things he is now convinced: First, that these two pictures are the genuine work of Pierre-Auguste Renoir, of his formative years. Second, and still more exciting, they are *not* in the *catalogue raisonné*, which is another way of saying that they were unknown to the art world. No history, no sales record, no provenance, nothing. He had come into possession of that most coveted of art finds: previously undiscovered works by one of the great masters.

He then added the two paintings to what was already Dell'Acqua's biggest Impressionist auction of the year, and scheduled them late in the day, by which time most of the important buyers, the knowledge-able collectors, gallery owners, and museum representatives who came to put in bids on the big-ticket Manets, Monets, Sisleys, and Renoirs of the earlier lots would have left.

To make sure that none of the serious, deep-pocket buyers had any interest at all in sticking around for Lot 43, likely some four hours into the auction, Ulisse cleverly described the paintings as "probably attributable" to "a follower of Georges d'Espagnat," which

I think he must have regarded as a clever little inside joke to himself. Which it was.

"Attributable to" is just about the lowest, vaguest, least concrete descriptor an auction house can put on a work of art, a big notch lower even than "attributed to." And to make it even more spineless, it's preceded here by "probably," a combination of fudge-words I'd never seen before. "Probably attributable to a follower of Georges d'Espagnat," it says. And who is Georges d'Espagnat? Georges d'Espagnat was a minor Impressionist and Post-Impressionist painter who, when he's referred to at all, is usually identified as a follower of Renoir. Thus, the Renoirish look of the paintings is explained, but their maker is described as a follower of a follower, two levels of abstraction, so to speak, removed from the sainted Pierre-Auguste, and thus not worthy of serious consideration.

D'Espagnat's paintings, with very few exceptions, generally sell for less than $10,000, usually far less, sometimes only in the high three figures. His *followers'* paintings, when they sell at all, are unlikely to make it up that high. His *probable* followers, especially unnamed ones . . . well, how would we even know?

Another important point about this last-lot-of-the-day, fuzzy-attribution business is that it would be hardly any time at all before it was forgotten, even by the few people who'd stuck it out until the end. Give it ten or twelve years—which was Ulisse's plan, if for once in his life he could hold out that long—and *no* one would remember it.

The mysterious Bidder 144 who came away with Lot 43 at the auction would have been a paid proxy of Ulisse's. It's perfectly acceptable to have a proxy bidding for you and to keep your own identity secret, but *not* when you happen to be the chief appraiser for the auction house putting on the sale. When you then throw in the fact of the buyer-*cum*-appraiser's having knowingly undervalued the objects by ten or twelve million euros or so, what it adds up to is big-time fraud, and that leads to disgrace, financial ruin, and more than likely, a prison sentence.

But for that to happen, the malefactors have to be found out, and it looked as if Ulisse and his pal got away with it. From what I could tell, nobody ever knew that there was anything to get away with.

Then would have had to come the hiding away of the paintings for more than a decade while he bided his time. A flat, medium-sized safe deposit box at his local bank for €100 a year would have done the job, but my gosh, for a fretful, congenital worrywart like Ulisse, a wait like that must have had him climbing the walls.

Before they went into the vault, though, to ensure against any conceivable possibility of discovery, Ulisse, who was a fair-to-middling amateur painter himself, would have painted them over with the seascapes. (That probably would have been in December of 2002 or January of 2003, which fitted in just fine with the scientists' date range of 1990–2005.)

And there they lay, these multimillion-dollar little trifles, until 2013, when he put into effect the ultimate stage of the plan he'd been formulating, and refining, and re-refining for a decade. His annual buying tour to Eastern Europe provided the cover he needed. Another proxy (or the same one, for all I know) was recruited to consign the two small "seascapes" to a seller at the Budapest art fair. Ulisse would then have bought them, probably within minutes of their being put up for sale, to make sure that nobody beat him to it.

And that was it. The rest of the story, everybody knows: the "discovery" of the underpaintings, the forensic analysis by the *Laboratorio di Tecniche* in Florence, the art-historical evaluation by the Musée d'Orsay, the story in the *New York Times* . . . and finally, me, here in Milan, in it up to my eyeballs and, really, with only a hypothetical scenario to show for it. But I knew, or thought I knew, the questions I needed to ask in order to confirm it positively, and there were only two of them.

One of them I could ask right then, simply by turning my head.

"Signora, excuse me for interrupting. Does a record still exist of the names of the buyers in these old auctions? The ones who are identified only by number?"

"No. There are only the invoices, nothing more."

What I expected, but too bad. I would have loved the chance to talk to Bidder 144. However, a cipher he would remain.

The answer to the other question, and it was the crucial one, would be waiting for me at the hotel . . . if Giulietta had lived up to her promise.

Chapter 19

She had. When I got to the Milano Scala, I was told that a courier-delivered envelope had indeed arrived for me and had been sent up to my room. There I found it, slipped under the door. The second I got in, I bent down and snatched it off the floor, resulting in a blinding, star-producing stab of pain across the back of my eyes, a salutary reminder that I'd had my head split open just yesterday. I still had some healing to do.

In the envelope was the Montefiore auction catalog I'd requested from Giulietta. The two Renoirs were not only Lot 1; they graced the cover too. They'd come quite a way from their modest, retiring Dell'Acqua days as Lot 43. I took a couple of ibuprofen to deal with the steady ache that the one stab of pain had settled into, and sat down at the desk to read the entry.

> **Lot 1: Estimated sales price €10,000,000–€15,000,000.**
> Two newly discovered masterpieces (authentication papers from the *Laboratorio di Tecniche Nucleari per l'Ambiente e i Beni Culturali* and the Musée d'Orsay are provided) by Pierre-Auguste Renoir (1841–1919). These are historically and aesthetically significant paintings from Renoir's formative years, 1864–1867.
>
> The café sketch is probably a study, or perhaps several combined studies, for the more polished café

scenes of his future, but already one can see the developing use of loose, broken brush strokes to capture movement and light in everyday scenes that were to become a hallmark of his mature Impressionist years.

The self-portrait, probably done a few years later, is altogether a more finished work. His earliest known self-portrait, its vivid, brash palette highlights the vibrancy, not to speak of the . . .

Blah blah blah. Interesting if you like that kind of thing, but not the reason I'd asked for the catalog. It was the details I wanted, and they were at the bottom of the page. Before checking them, I placed my never-leave-home-without-one vest-pocket notepad next to it, and opened it to a page of notes I'd made at Dell'Acqua.

Okay, Moment of Truth. The Montefiore catalog first.

-Self-portrait, 40.62 x 30.47
-Café scene, 38.11 x 29.20

And my notes from Dell'Acqua:

-Self-port. 40.64/30.48
-Grandpa 38.11/29.21

That settled it. A total of four millimeters' difference in the listings; not even a rounding error. There could be no question about their being the same paintings Ulisse had first gotten—had embezzled—for €2,200 in 2002, re-gotten for €90 in 2013, and was hoping to sell for €10,000,000 to €15,000,000 in 2017.

Or rather, *had* been hoping.

Chapter 20

So where did I go from here? Obviously, back to Luca with what I'd learned. I called his number but was told that he was gone for the day. Could they give me another number at which I could reach him? No, they could not, but they would be happy to take a message. I declined; I'd get hold of him in the morning.

It was probably best anyway. I was really too tired to face Luca or anyone else, or even to have any dinner. I'd gotten out of the hospital only that morning, amazing as it seemed, and it had been a long, draining day. I felt like one of Dante's old bunged-up, squeezed-out paint tubes. All I was fit for was bed.

I couldn't even face undressing or brushing my teeth. I did manage to take off my shoes, though, before flopping flat on my face onto the bed. Which is exactly the way I woke up, stiff and groggy, thirteen hours later, at seven o'clock in the morning. It took me a while to get myself together enough to try seeing if my limbs still worked. But once I'd dragged myself out of bed, showered and shaved, and gone downstairs to the breakfast room for an embarrassingly colossal breakfast (three trips to the buffet table) I was raring to go, practically my old self.

I carried my fourth cup of coffee out to the pleasant sitting area, sat digesting for a few more minutes, then called Luca to tell him I needed to talk to him about Ulisse.

"And I need to talk with you," was his response. "Also about signor Agnello. Are you free right now?"

"Yes, but give me twenty minutes to get there; I can really use a walk."

"So could I, Valentino. I've been here in the office for a while. I'd love to get out for some fresh air. It's a beautiful morning, and there's a quiet, pretty little park I walk to sometimes when I want to think. It's one of my favorite places in the city, practically in the shadow of the Pinacoteca di Brera, but not easy to find. It's not far from you either. All you need to do—"

"Ah, but I do know it, and it's one of my favorite places too. See you in ten minutes?"

"I'm on my way."

The *Orto Botanico di Brera* is a lovely spot of quiet greenery shielded on all sides by trees and buildings, in which it's easy to forget for a while that you're in the middle of one of the world's busiest and most industrious cities. I like it too because it's old, and although it's changed hands many times since it was laid out in the seventeenth century—going from the Jesuits, to the Austrians, to the French, back to the Austrians, and finally to the Republic of Italy—even with all that, it still retains its original simple, unfussy design and its purpose: the display of plants. In the 1600s, they were medicinal; now they're mostly ornamental.

I got there before Luca did and wandered around just taking things in. The grounds had been freshly mulched and I was standing in front of a cluster of flowering *Hepatica transsilvanica* (the groupings are labeled; otherwise, I wouldn't recognize a *Hepatica transsilvanica* if it bit me), lightly stirring the odd-looking pale mulch with my toe, wondering what it was . . . not bark, not composted soil . . . hay . . . ?

"Rice husks," said Luca, coming up behind me. "We have to find *something* to do with them."

"I bet you do," I said with a laugh. What spaghetti is to Naples, rice—that is, risotto—is to Milan, and only a half-hour's drive south of the city lie the largest and richest rice fields of the Western world. No problem getting rice husks around here.

We began walking slowly down one of the lanes together. "Listen, Luca, you were . . . you were right about Ulisse." The words stuck in my throat; I was still having a hard time making myself believe them. "I've come up with some awfully damning—"

"Let's sit down," he said. "I walked a little faster than I'm used to." He pointed to a pair of white wrought-iron garden chairs in front of a trellised wall and once we'd sat, I briefed him on what I'd learned yesterday, and what I thought it meant.

He agreed with me. "The sizes of the paintings—that's what cinches it. No question—they're the same ones he auctioned—to himself—at Dell'Acqua all those years ago. Hunh. A patient man."

"Now that's something I never thought I'd hear anybody say about Ulisse Agnello," I said with a thin smile. I'd been saying a few things I'd never expected to say about him.

Luca sat for a while, leaning over, elbows on his knees, head bowed, musing and, I thought, enjoying the sun on the back of his neck. When he straightened up he looked directly into my eyes. "It's Ulisse I wanted to talk to you about, as well."

His tone, his posture, were impossible to misread. "He's dead," I said. By now, this was the way I knew it would turn out anyway.

"That's right. We found his body. I'm sorry."

I hunched my shoulders. So that was that. Ulisse and I, we'd come full circle. That's all she wrote, folks. How did I feel? Dull, numbed, I guess; nothing more, really. I'd already said goodbye to the man I'd known. "How? What happened?"

"Apparently, an accident, an automobile accident."

It had occurred very early Sunday morning, Luca told me. Ulisse's car had veered off the road on his way back from Lugano, at around 2:00 a.m., give or take a couple of hours either way. It had happened on the Swiss side of the border, on a winding, uneven section of the road between the villages of Bissone and Maroggia. The car had plunged over the edge of a ten-meter rise, rolled over several times, and had landed right side up in a thicket alongside the lake, where it had lain undiscovered until about eight thirty in the morning, when a passing motorist spotted it. Unfortunately for him, he hadn't been wearing a seat belt—

I broke in. "Wait, eight thirty *Sunday* morning? If you already knew about it then, why didn't you say anything about it when—"

"No, I didn't yet know about it when I saw you at headquarters after the robbery. The Swiss had no reason to contact the carabinieri on it. They simply went through the usual channels for automobile accidents, which means they informed our *Polizia di Stato*; they're the ones that handle expressway accidents. I didn't learn about it until very late yesterday, and then only because I'd put Agnello's name into an interagency search. The body got back to Milan early this morning and our *medico legale* should be doing his autopsy right now. You're frowning."

"I'm wondering. Our meeting at the Bellagio wasn't until ten. Why would he have been heading back at two o'clock in the morning?"

"Ah," said Luca with a forlorn smile, "I was hoping you'd be able to tell me."

"No, I'm sorry." I chewed the corner of my lip, thinking. "Luca, if the car didn't get found until eight thirty, how do they know *when* it happened?"

"The Swiss police doctor. That was her time-of-death estimate when she came out to the scene: somewhere between midnight and four . . . Excuse me."

His cell phone had signaled, and he flipped it open. "Yes, *dottore*," he said into it. "Have you found something?" After a minute he followed that with an "Is that so?" accompanying it with a look on his face that was as good as words: *Well, now, that's interesting.*

Naturally, my own interest perked up and I leaned toward him to hear better, but all I got for my trouble was a string of "I see's" and a final "Yes, definitely, send them along, please. Right now, if you can. But better neaten them up a little first, all right? Many thanks, Giorgio."

He put the phone away and looked quizzically at me. I got the feeling I was being assessed. "Something important?" I ventured.

He hesitated, then appeared to come to a decision. "That was our *medico legale*. He's completed the autopsy. He's concluded it was *not* an accident. Your friend Ulisse died as a result of severe injuries to his head." With his eyebrows raised and his lips pursed, he waited for my reaction.

"Are you saying he was murdered?"

"That's right. You're frowning again. Something puzzles you?"

"Yes, why is he so sure it was murder? The car drove off a cliff and rolled over several times, he didn't have his seat belt on, and he died of head injuries. I would have thought—"

"No," said Luca. "He was bludgeoned. Do you know what a depressed skull fracture is, Valentino?"

"I know what a skull fracture is."

"Of course. And when you think of a skull fracture, a fractured skull, what comes to mind is a skull that may be anywhere from simply cracked to one that is actually broken into pieces, would I be correct?"

I nodded. "Correct."

"A depressed fracture, on the other hand, is one in which the segment of bone that has been struck is not cracked but is pushed inward by the force of the blow. You follow?"

I followed.

"And the interesting thing about such fractures, from a forensic point of view, is that the nature of the object that created the injury can sometimes be identified from the shape of the depression. An ordinary hammer, for example, would be likely to produce a round depression that matched a hammer's head. A square-headed mallet, however, would more likely create a square depression. You understand?"

"Luca, for God's sake—"

"All right, all right, you understand."

"Yes, I understand. And what you're obviously coming around to telling me—eventually—is that a depression in Ulisse's skull *is* the kind you get when you're hit with a mallet, or a hammer, or a poker, or some other murder weapon that's now been identified."

"No," he said with a superior smile, "what I'm telling you is that it isn't."

"Isn't what?"

"Isn't the kind of wound that would normally be associated with a murder weapon at all. In fact, it's quite distinctive. Our *medico legale* himself has never seen such a wound before."

I sat back with a sigh. "Okay, you win. Now *I* don't understand. How do you come up with murder from that?"

He held up a finger. "Give me a second." He got out his phone again and hit a few buttons. "Ah," he said, looking at the screen with satisfaction, "even sharper than I'd hoped. This will explain things better than I can, Valentino. Here." He handed me his phone. "Giorgio's cleaned things up for you so it's not too grisly."

That told me it was a photo from the autopsy, but it still took me a few seconds to understand what I was looking at: a close-up showing a part of Ulisse's skull—somewhere near the top, it looked like. The scalp had been peeled back beyond the borders of the photo, and although the skull itself was coated with pink, glistening skin rather than being the clean, pure ivory that I would have expected, it wasn't too bad. Still, I couldn't keep down the turbid roiling in my stomach when I realized, truly realized, that this was Ulisse Agnello's dissected head I was looking at. I guess I wasn't quite as numb as I'd thought. But my full attention was soon caught by the injury itself, the depressed fracture. And it looked nothing like what I imagined.

Despite my irascible protestations to the contrary, I *hadn't* understood what Luca had been talking about. When he'd said "depressed" and "depression" I'd pictured a sort of dent in the skull, a dip, a concavity, but this was nothing like that. A depressed fracture, it turns out, is a chunk of bone, discrete and separate, that has not been *pushed* down, but *punched out* of the surrounding bone and thrust down below the rest of the surface. If it had been made by that hammer that Luca had been talking about, it would have looked like a disk, a coin made of bone, that had created its own hole in the skull and been driven down into it.

The depressed piece of bone in Ulisse's skull, however, looked nothing like a coin. I could see why neither Luca nor the pathologist had any idea what might have made it. I sure didn't. It was tiny, smaller than the head of any hammer I ever saw, a rectangular chunk fifteen millimeters long—a little more than half an inch—and about half as wide. (A ruler had been propped alongside it for scale.)

But what especially caught my eye was . . . what *was* that? . . . I looked up at Luca. "Is that an opening in the middle of it? Like a . . . a slit? A slot?"

"Yes, like a slot." He reached over and tapped the screen. "Here's another photo, this one taken with a low-magnification microscopic lens."

Now the depressed chunk took up the entire screen, and it was clear that the hole in it was, like the chunk itself, rectangular. An open slot in what looked like the exact center of the chunk, with its four borders perfectly parallel to the edges.

"And it punches all the way through the bone," Luca said.

I gave the phone back to him. "And you have no idea what would make a slot like that?"

"The slot itself? No, no, there are plenty of things that could do that. The point of a knife would be the most obvious example. Not that I think it did in this case."

I frowned. "I would have thought the point of a—"

"A knife in cross section is rectangular, is it not? So while the extreme tip of a ferociously sharpened point might leave a round, pinpoint opening, once it penetrates beyond the very tip, the opening it leaves must be rectangular, you see?"

"I see, yes. All right, maybe a knife could have made the hole *in* the chunk, but how do you explain the chunk as a whole?" (In Italian, there wasn't the semantic confusion this would create in English.)

"Now you see our problem, Tino," said Luca.

I sat back and crossed my arms. "I sure do. But look, I still don't understand why you've settled on murder. Just because the wound was made by something you can't identify, that hardly means—"

"Valentino, there's a second fracture a few inches away, not as well-defined as this one, but very obviously from the same object. In other words he was struck twice."

"Even so, why couldn't he have hit his head more than once on the same thing? The car was bouncing around and rolling over, he had no seat belt—"

"Let me finish. Giorgio put our crime scene people to work on Agnello's car, exploring every square millimeter of it in search of any object—knob, projection, anything—that might, however implausibly, have inflicted such an injury during the accident—and not once, but twice. And there was nothing. Nothing." He sat back and waited for me to figure this part out for myself.

Easy enough, now. "*Ergo*," I said, "it wasn't the accident that killed him. Something hit him in the head *before* then. Twice. When the car went over the edge he was already dead."

"Exactly, and that some*thing* was surely wielded by some*one*."

I nodded. "Murder."

"Murder." He put his hands on the arms of his chair, getting ready to push himself up. "I think I'd better get going. I appreciate the information on Agnello's scheme. I have no doubt it will prove useful."

I rose with him and we shook hands. "Luca, about his death: Is that confidential or can I talk about it? There's somebody I think should know."

"The girlfriend, Giulietta."

"Yes."

"You can tell her, or anybody, for that matter, that he was killed in an automobile accident on his way back from Lugano. That's as much as the press will hear, for a few days, anyway. But as to the indications of homicide, I'm going to try to hold that back from the media for the time being, so please—you'll keep that part to yourself, all right?"

"Will do, Luca."

He handed me a business card. "My personal cell phone number," he said. "If you need to talk to me." An eyebrow lift, a crisp nod, and he was gone.

I sat back down and called Montefiore Arte to set up an appointment with Giulietta. I wasn't looking forward to it, but I certainly wasn't going to give her news like this over the phone.

Chapter 21

The Montefiore auction house was in the Brera district, on via Senato, one of the handsomely rebuilt eighteenth-century streets that had been pulverized in the last months of the Second World War and now housed a cluster of upscale art galleries. When I'd called ahead I'd been told that she would be available to see me, but when I arrived a receptionist informed me that an unexpected meeting had been called and Giulietta would be unavailable for another hour at the least. I said that I thought it best to see her right away, and although there was some reluctance on the receptionist's part, my Met ID did the trick, as usual, and I was directed to a door adjacent to the smaller of two auction chambers.

When I opened it I found myself at the rear of a small private viewing room, that is, a room that had been set up both for auction rehearsals and for private screenings of upcoming items for favored clients. There were two rows of folding chairs, four to a row, eight seats in all, and at the front a lectern with a floor easel on either side of it, each one holding a painting. Giulietta was sitting in the first row, with Benvenuto next to her. The other seats were occupied by people I didn't know, probably Montefiore staff. And an earnest young woman in a pantsuit was at the lectern with a felt-tipped classroom pointer, holding forth on the superlative qualities of the two paintings being displayed—which, as it happened, were the two Renoirs.

I stood at the back for a while, hesitant to interrupt, just looking at the paintings and waiting to be noticed, but the woman at the lectern refused steadfastly to give me any attention, and the others were all facing forward, away from me. I was about to announce my presence when my eye, instinctively following the sweep of the pointer over the café sketch, was caught by something in the painting that stopped me just as I started, so that only a little bark escaped before it lodged in my throat.

I couldn't believe what I'd seen. It was totally unexpected, and yet it gave me the answers to all my key questions. I goggled at it, leaning forward over the back row to make sure that I was really seeing what I thought I was seeing, and that movement, along with that little bark, was finally too much for the presenter up front.

"Signore?" she said frigidly. "May I help you?"

"Yes, I'm sorry to interrupt, but—"

Giulietta turned. "Oh, hello, Valentino," she said with a smile. "Come in and sit down. Dante *finally* finished with the pictures yesterday, if you can believe it, and our transport service just brought them in. Aren't they wonderful? I'm so excited. I can hardly bear to think about parting with them."

"Giulietta, I need to talk to you." My mind buzzed with what I'd just seen, but I did the best I could to put it aside.

"Can it wait just a little while? We shouldn't be more than another twenty minutes."

"It's about Ulisse."

She paled, and I mean literally. Her voice came down half an octave. "We'll pick this up later," she said to the assembled group, and they got right up and docilely filed out, even the presenter—all except Benvenuto, who remained seated next to her.

I pulled around the chair on the other side of him and sat down. "It's not good news," I said.

"Go ahead," she said tonelessly.

"I'm afraid he's dead. I'm sorry."

Giulietta closed her eyes and said nothing. Benvenuto said, "Oh, my God, what happened?"

I told them as much as Luca said was okay: that his car had gone off the road on his way back from Lugano.

"How did you find this out?" Giulietta asked.

"Lieutenant Fontanella told me."

"Told *you*? Why would he tell *you*?"

"I went to see him about something else, and he heard about it while I was with him."

Benvenuto's head came up. "Something else—about the paintings?"

"No, something different altogether."

A flat-out lie, but I didn't want to get into Ulisse's razzle-dazzle maneuverings with the Renoirs and with the questions they raised. If Ulisse's criminal acquisition of the paintings meant, as I assumed it did, that he didn't meet the definition of a good-faith purchaser, did that mean that he hadn't been the bona fide owner and therefore had no right to sell them? Where did that leave Giulietta and the auction house, even with their "ironclad" contract? And what about Benvenuto, where did he stand? Was his twenty percent share valid, given that Ulisse, as a bad-faith purchaser, would have had no more right to give away shares than he did to sell the paintings outright? I imagined that the lawyers would be wrangling about all this for years to come.

As for Sol, at his age, ever getting that picture of his grandfather, well, I didn't even want to think about that.

"This is extremely disturbing," Benvenuto said accusingly, directing it at me. His speech had an edge that was new: still prissy and high-pitched, but tight in a way I hadn't heard before. I wondered if he was thinking about exactly those questions I hadn't wanted to raise.

I still didn't. And I had other things I needed to do. "Well," I said, stirring, "I don't want to take up any more of your time. I just wanted to let you know. I'm so sorry—"

"Don't turn around." The voice was male, no doubt about that, and he had squinched it down into a snarling growl.

We froze, the three of us, not moving a muscle, just staring into each other's faces.

Again? I thought. *Seriously?* But since I was conscious this time around, I felt that some show of resistance was called for. "What's this all about?" I demanded.

Pretty limp, I admit, despite my own try at a snarl, and stupid besides, inasmuch as (a) a civil reply was not in the offing, (b) the answer was obvious, what with two highly portable objects worth eleven or twelve million dollars, both of which could be tucked under an arm, just sitting there for the taking, and (c) irritating the guy was probably not the wisest course of action.

"Shut up," was the reply, not unexpected. "Get down on the floor, on your faces—*now!*" This was accompanied by a compelling *snick-snock* of the slide on an automatic pistol, indicating that a cartridge had been inserted into the chamber and was sitting there just waiting for the trigger to be pulled.

"Don't shoot, there's no reason to shoot," Benvenuto said from high in his throat. "We're getting down, we're getting down, you see?"

He got jerkily to his hands and knees—a button popped from his trimly fitting suit jacket—and then he stretched out flat, his arms extended beyond his head.

Giulietta did the same.

And so did I, but I had more to say. "Look," I said, talking into the carpet, "at least leave the little one. It's just a sketch, it's hardly worth—"

"I said shut *up*! I'm not going to tell you again. I *mean* it!" There was a quaver in his voice; he was getting more tense. I took him at his word and shut up.

His voice was continuing to come from the back of the room, but there were rustling sounds from the front as well. There were at least two of them, then, and the second one was helping himself to the Renoirs.

I heard him quickly walk back around the side of the room to rejoin his partner at the rear.

"We'll be watching this door," said the growler, who seemed to be the spokesman. "Anyone who sticks his head out in the next two minutes is going to get it blown off. Nobody's gotten hurt so far. Don't spoil it."

And the door was pulled closed.

We raised our heads and looked at each other. I can't tell you what thoughts were running through their minds, but I know what I was thinking:

Two major art thefts in three days, and I was present, front and center, for both of them—probably the two most sensational events of my life—and I never got to see a damn thing.

Unbelievable.

The carabinieri who responded, a *sergente* and a *maresciallo,* were already familiar with the paintings and knew about the bizarre theft-and-return a couple of days earlier. And Giulietta, Benvenuto, and I, having had our faces stuck in the carpet throughout, couldn't tell them much about today's theft, so our interviews were quickly done.

Same with the staff in the outer area, ten of them, who, like us, had been forced onto their faces by another member of the gang for the five minutes it took to pull the whole thing off. He'd worn a mask, they'd said. Giulietta, Benvenuto, and I couldn't even tell the police that much.

But unlike the staff, unlike Giulietta and Benvenuto and the two carabinieri, unlike even Luca, I now thought I had a handle on what was going on: what this robbery was about, what the earlier robbery had been about—even why the paintings had been left behind the wall; what the overall plan was that had set everything going . . . and who was behind it. I still had no notion of who had killed Ulisse or why, but for the rest, *push* was definitely coming to *shove*.

And I knew a way to put at least some of it to the test. And where to do it.

Getting out of the building was a hassle. Not on account of the carabinieri, but because the media had shown up en masse, buttonholing anyone who would stand still for them. Out on the street, blocking the doors, were two reporters with microphones, backed up by their photographers, and by two double-parked TV trucks, one black and one white, both of them sprouting electronic gadgetry from their roofs.

To squeeze through, I had to slide sideways between the reporters with apologetic shrugs and *no-spikka-de-italiano* gestures. Then, a dash across the street, between the trucks, and I was free.

The media had gotten there in surprising numbers and with astonishing speed, arriving perhaps five minutes after the carabinieri; and new cars and trucks were continuing to pull up. Even that was starting to add up to me.

I'd noticed a taxi rank a short way up the street when I'd gotten here (in Italy, you don't flag them down; you go where they are), and I headed quickly for it.

Push had arrived at *shove*.

Chapter 22

2 . . . 0 . . . 1 . . . Holding my breath, I punched in the final two numbers: *. . . 4 . . . 8.* And on the eight, with an unobtrusive click, the latch guarding the street entrance to the studio of *D. Zampa, Restauratore della pittura,* popped open. I'd been counting on Dante's celebrated inattention to "trivial" matters to mean that he hadn't gotten around yet to changing the combinations on his locks, even after the robbery of two days ago, and I was right.

Two seconds later I was inside, with my back against the door, trembling just a little and breathing through my mouth as quietly as I could. This kind of escapade was new to me and I was more nervous than I'd anticipated. Dante would be in Rome for another few days—I knew that from his answering service, but I couldn't be one hundred percent sure; people's plans changed. And so I continued to stand there, as still and silent as the flowers on the wallpaper behind me, listening intently for any rustle, any creak, or thump, or crunch, or quiet cough—anything that might indicate the presence of another human being upstairs.

I waited five full minutes. It seemed like twenty, but I was timing it on my watch. I could hear sounds from the café next door, and from the street, but the silence inside was total. The place was empty.

I went quickly up the steps, confident that I had the place to myself. Confident too that the combination for the door to the studio itself hadn't been changed either.

And again, I was right. In two seconds I was in. The place was much as it had been before. I'd hoped to quickly find what I was looking for and get the hell out of there, but no, there was nothing at all in the workshop area that interested me. I even looked under the rumpled coverlet on the bed in the corner. Nothing.

This all took longer than you might think, because it seemed as if every few seconds I'd imagine I heard something from below: a voice humming, or the click of a lock, or a footstep on the stairs. Or, most unnerving, from just outside, the slam of a car door. I would stand stock-still, barely breathing, but each time it would pass without there being any follow-up, and I'd go edgily back to work, trying to leave everything exactly as I'd found it.

I prowled through the tiny kitchen too, pulling open cabinets and drawers. At the back of one of the drawers was a matte-black handgun; a semiautomatic Glock 17. (My friend Sal's detective-father had the same model and had let us look at it once. If I remember correctly, good old Sal didn't even charge us that time.) Finding it set me back a little, made me more uneasy than I already was. I was sure by now that the man was a crook and a scam artist, no less than Ulisse had been, but I just hadn't thought of him as the kind of person who'd have a gun, a serious one like this, in his kitchen drawer. Still, it wasn't what I was interested in. I put it out of my mind.

There was another place to look: Dante had mentioned a storage room on the ground floor. I hadn't seen it, but when I went down to the ground floor and around the side of the stairway, I found a locked door at the rear of the building, right next to the back exit. Beside it was a keypad. *Gee,* I thought, *I wonder what the combination could possibly be . . .*

Yup, right again. The room that the door opened into had no windows, but there was a light switch in the usual place beside the doorframe, and when I flipped it a bank of fluorescent tubes on the ceiling hissed to life. The room was closet-sized, maybe eight feet by six. Along the long wall on the left was an ancient worktable, scratched, and stained, and gouged, with shelving above it holding tools and sundries—sandpaper, clamps, etc. In front of it was a metal stool, and on the opposite wall a jumble of floor easels partially blocking the door, and then, at the rear, a rack for the vertical storage of paintings.

It was the rack to which I headed. There were about two dozen paintings lined up in it, each in its own padded slot, with their edges facing out so that their surfaces weren't visible. I noticed that they were in two groups, a larger one with beat-up old wooden frames, and a smaller one, eight paintings in all, the frames of which, judging from the edges that were visible, were gilded.

A hollow, fluttery feeling in my chest suddenly blossomed; my heart rate had speeded up the moment I saw those gleaming edges. If I was going to find what I'd been hunting for, it would be here: the mother lode, proof that Dante Zampa was putting together what I suspected him of, a confidence game that goes back more than a hundred years and returns us, full circle, to the story we started with. Remember? Vincenzo Peruggia's audacious theft from the Louvre of Leonardo da Vinci's *Mona Lisa*.

Let me pick it up from where we left it: the theory that the theft itself, sensational as it was, wasn't the point at all, but rather the lead-up—the preface, so to speak—to an elaborate scam perpetrated by an elusive figure who advertised himself as the *Marqués* de Valfierno. Made up as it surely was, the title has stuck to him and to his elegant scam as well.

One of Valfierno's longtime accomplices was a brilliant forger whose name we do know: Yves Chaudron. The plan he helped Valfierno cook up was arduous but magnificently simple and began long before the theft was to take place. Chaudron would spend several months at the Louvre, sitting among the reverential art students who were always to be found with their paints and easels, copying the famous painting as part of their training. But Chaudron outdid them all, making not one but six meticulous copies. More than that, the oils that he used he'd made himself, strictly following French formulas from the sixteenth century. And the pictures themselves were painted on panels made of centuries-old poplar wood. (The *Mona Lisa*, like most of da Vinci's pictures, was done on wood, not canvas.)

Once they were finished, so the story goes, Valfierno paid Peruggia to steal the painting, take it home, and hide it. He also gave him a camera and had him photograph the back and send the photo to him, so that Chaudron could reproduce the original's back as well, something that had never been seen by the public, as an added touch of authenticity. He then told the hapless Peruggia that he'd be in touch a little later with additional money for him. When two years had gone by and it hadn't yet happened, according to the theory, Peruggia got tired of waiting and decided to sell the painting on his own.

In the meantime, after the theft and the expected storm of world-wide publicity, Valfierno had gotten hold of half a dozen wealthy, not overly ethical art collectors and offered *each* of them the "original" *Mona Lisa* for his very own private, clandestine collection. It's believed that he sold them all, at $300,000 each. Once it was accomplished and the money had changed hands, the scam was foolproof. If any of them got suspicious that maybe they'd been cheated and they *didn't* really have the genuine article, what could they do, go to the police?

There's some evidence, not altogether convincing, that Valfierno soon retired to a palatial spread in North Africa for the rest of his life.

Frankly, none of this is altogether convincing. The *Mona Lisa* was stolen, and Vincenzo Peruggia stole it and hung on to it for two years: that much you can take to the bank. The rest is, um, speculative, and the details vary in different versions, but Valfierno and Chaudron are always at the heart of them. If you google "Valfierno" and "Mona Lisa" you'll see that its veracity is still being debated.

But whether or not the master forger and the flamboyant "*marqués*" really did pull this off, other con men certainly have, but always (as far as we know) as small-time rip-offs, never with anywhere near the breathtaking impact of the theft of the *Mona Lisa*.

Until now. If I was right about this, Dante was currently in the process of putting one together. I stood for another few seconds with my hand on the gilded corner of one of the frames. Then I blew out a long, shallow breath and slid it out of its slot.

It was the Renoir self-portrait. Well, okay, fine, nothing wrong with that. Except that the second one was *another* Renoir self-portrait. The next four were café sketches, and the final two were self-portraits. Four of each, eight paintings in all. It was the mother lode, all right. And there were probably two more out there, since I doubted that the ones taken at Montefiore could have gotten here so soon, or were necessarily headed here at all. Ten altogether, if you included the originals—where once there had been but two.

So Dante had been busy secretly making copies of the paintings, and it didn't take much of a leap to get from there to what the point of it was: the *Marqués* de Valfierno lived again—in the person of D. Zampa, *Restauratore della pittura*.

The copies would be sold as the real thing to shady collectors who were wealthy, gullible, greedy, and obtuse. This is a combination of traits not so rare as you might think; indeed, you could make a good case that it's what keeps the market for contemporary art humming along.

Practically puffing up like a blowfish with satisfaction (I mean, how smart was I to figure all this out on my own?), I laid them slowly out side by side on the worktable. I did have to shake my head at Dante's skill. The self-portraits couldn't have been more alike if they'd come out of a printer; he had done an incredible job there. Was one of them the original and the other three copies, or were all of them copies? I thought I could tell, but I couldn't be sure; not without magnification and some serious scrutiny.

And the sketches? Ah, well, there I knew, because one of them was subtly different from the others, and that one was the original. Dante had taken some liberties when he made his copies, probably thinking: Well, with Renoir's earliest known self-portrait as the big attraction, who was going to be looking very hard at some casually tossed-off, not terribly successful preliminary study that young Pierre-Auguste probably simply never got around to throwing away?

Me, that's who, and those self-indulgent liberties of Dante's were instrumental in helping me to get a handle on his scam, and also in getting my head busted open the day I first looked at the café sketch in his studio. Not in that order, of course. What he had done that had alerted me that fateful day was to use techniques from two different stages of Renoir's career in his copies of the sketch, and one of them hadn't even begun to emerge until the mid-1880s, twenty years after the young Renoir had painted it. In the 1860s, Renoir had still been using the soft, feathery strokes that were to become hallmarks of early Impressionist painting. But by the 1880s, he'd concluded that Impressionism, with its fuzzy details and ambiguous representations, had made its point and was losing its energy. As a result, Renoir's own figures then became cleaner, more linear, and more three-dimensional. In artspeak, less painterly, more representational.

Well, on what I now recognized as the original café sketch, sitting right here in front of me on the worktable, the woman sitting vacantly over her absinthe had been painted even less fastidiously than Grandfather Maurizio or the two men playing cards in the background. She was like an out-of-range figure in a photograph, her face blurred, her hat so indistinct it was impossible to say much more about it other than that it was a hat. This was what I'd expected to find—*should* have found—when I looked at it in Dante's studio.

But when it came to making his fakes, Dante had taken it upon himself to "improve" her. Her face on the copies was admirably rendered, heavy-lidded and apathetic, but still somehow showing that not so long ago she'd been a beauty. And the hat—it had morphed from a formless what-is-that-thing to what was known as a lady's sailor hat, a flat-crowned, wide-brimmed straw hat like those worn in the nineteenth century by male boaters, but with the addition of some fabric flowers on top and a pair of dainty ribbon streamers coming down the sides. All quite admirably accomplished—but nothing at all like the way Renoir would have rendered her in 1864.

Doing all this had taken a lot of painstaking work, so why, exactly, had Dante done it? My guess is simply that his justly celebrated hubris had gotten the better of him. A perfectionist himself, he had been offended by Renoir's sloppiness as Dante saw it. If Renoir wasn't going to paint up to his abilities, then Dante Zampa would do it for him. He would out-Renoir Renoir. It was an example of the esteem in which Dante held himself, and it was going to be his undoing.

But it was only in the last hour that all of this had become clear to me, falling into place piece by piece. Remember when I'd been looking at the sketch in Dante's studio just before that first robbery, and I'd seen something that made me ask him for a magnifying glass? Only I couldn't remember what that something was? At the time, I couldn't even remember asking for the magnifying glass. (Thank you, retrograde amnesia.) What I understood now, of course, was that it was Dante's modifications that had set off my alarm bells, shortly to be extinguished by a couple of knocks on the head.

Then, the next morning at carabinieri headquarters, when I had the chance to view the pictures again after they had been returned by the unhappy signor Esposito, the memory of having asked for the glass did pop to the surface again, and along with it was that vaguer memory of having spotted something in the scene that was "off." And so, with the aid of another magnifying glass, I checked it out again; I mean I really looked at the thing *scrupulously*, and it was just fine, nothing funny about it at all. I wound up doubting that I'd really seen anything before. Who knew, if concussions could give you retrograde amnesia, maybe they could give you retrograde delusions too.

But then today, just a few hours ago, when I showed up at the back of the room at Montefiore and saw the sketch on the easel up front, I knew exactly what was "off" about it; namely, Dante's "improvements" to the original, and I did it from twelve feet away without the aid of a magnifying glass.

And that was the clincher, the linchpin that brought it all together. My original confusion—Had I seen something? Had I *not* seen something?—came from having had different café sketches in front of me at different times, when I naturally assumed that I'd been looking at the same one each time. But in Dante's studio it was one of his copies that I'd been looking at, and what had caught my eye just before that knock on the head were his anachronistic touches to the woman's face and hat. At carabinieri head-quarters the next morning, the sketch in front of me, the one that had been retrieved from behind the wall, wasn't the one I'd been looking at the day before; Dante had put the original there, so that even careful scrutiny—by the carabinieri, perhaps by me—would pick up nothing unusual. Which is exactly what I picked up: nothing.

But the one that had been on the easel at Montefiore earlier today . . . ah, that had been one of the fake ones again, with Dante's alterations. As soon as I looked at it I saw what had bothered me about it, and that was when everything had come together.

It occurred to me only now to wonder if he was in this on his own. What about Ulisse? Had he been aware of it? Had he been *part* of it? Was it what had gotten him killed? Could it have been Dante who killed him? No, I just couldn't see it. Dante as a forger? Sure, if for no other reason than the satisfaction of proving to himself how brilliant he was. But as a man who would smash a friend's head in? Nope, couldn't see it. Then again, I hadn't been able to see him as a man who would have a slick, black semiautomatic in his kitchen drawer either, so maybe it wasn't as improbable as all that.

I shook myself. Without realizing it, I'd been standing there musing; dreaming, practically, and the sooner I got out of there, the happier I'd be. I started slipping the paintings back into their slots in the same order and in the same way I'd slipped them out, which meant turning them around so that their backs were toward me as I slipped them in. As I'd guessed, Ulisse had put new, blank backs on the originals years before, and Dante had been happy to follow through with similar backs on the copies, making things a lot easier for him than they'd been for Yves Chaudron. I hadn't paid much attention to the backs before, but now I noticed that he had used glazier's points, a twentieth-century invention, to keep them in place, instead of the simple nails that had been used in Renoir's day. My first thought was that it was a surprisingly careless error on the part of a perfectionist like Dante, but no, I realized that in this kind of enterprise, a recent repair like that, with no attempt made to make it look old and authentic, would be seen as evidence of honesty: no wool was being pulled over the prospective buyer's eyes. Right.

I gave my head another shake; daydreaming again. Into their slots the rest of the paintings went. Then I took a quick look around the cramped space to make sure everything was the way it had been when I came in. With a final—

Wait a minute. I hauled the last painting back out, one of the self-portraits, gently laid it on its face on the worktable, and took another look at the back, especially those glazier's points.

A glazier's point, so named because it's most commonly used to temporarily hold a new pane of window glass in its frame until the putty hardens, is a small fastener that's next to impossible to describe (I tried, believe me), so here's a picture of the thing:

It's really tiny, not quite a quarter-inch wide—about the width of the fingernail on your pinky. With the painting lying on its face, the back side of a glazier's point is placed flat against the painting's backing and driven into the inside margins of the frame. That flat upper part is what holds the backing in place, and those little ledges stop the point from going too far into the frame. You put one in every two or three inches. A nice, handy device, but the problem is getting it in without marring the painting's backing, which is hard to do with an ordinary hammer, because of course you have to do it sideways. So a lot of interesting tools have been devised to make it easier, including one particular kind that . . . that . . .

It took me only a minute to find it on one of the shelves above the workbench—a small hammer looking superficially pretty much like one you'd find at Home Depot, but with a few differences. First, the handle was slightly offset from the head, so that the side of the head, which was flat and smooth, could be laid flat against the back of the picture without scraping your knuckles against the surface. Second, and infinitely more significant, the hammer's "face"—the business end of the head—wasn't what you'd ordinarily see on a hammer—that is, a smooth plane great for banging in nails. You couldn't use this one to drive in a nail, because the face had a slot in it, and I knew what it was for. I could feel my pulse rate jump as what had been a possible but not too likely supposition suddenly reshaped itself into a firm conclusion.

There were a few glazier's points lying scattered on the shelves. When I placed one in the slot, backward, as intended, so that the point jutted out, it fit tightly, held in place by an interior spring. Rap it deftly against the inside rim of a frame, use your thumb to press a little button that released the spring, remove the hammer, and the point would be left behind, neatly in place in the wood. Whack it not so gently against a human skull, *don't* press the spring release, and what would be left behind would be a rectangular depressed fracture, half an inch wide, with a rectangular slit in the middle of it—the result of being punctured by the glazier's point. (The surrounding rim of the hammer-tool that holds the point in place would account for the additional width.)

I stood staring off into space, the hammer in my hand. My God, it was Dante who killed Ulisse, after all. But why? How utterly weird. How did this all come together? Wheels within wheels. Goldstein's Law of Interconnected Monkey Business strikes again. I hefted it in my hand, wondering whether—

"*God damn you, Caruso!*"

Chapter 23

I spun around at the words, coughing, almost tripping over my own feet. "Startled" doesn't even come close.

Dante's body filled the narrow doorway. At the sides of his throat, muscles strained and bulging arteries pumped. His breath came forcefully, through quivering nostrils; his lips were laid back over bared teeth.

I mean, the man was *mad*.

"God damn you to *hell*," he ground out, in case his first try at it had been insufficiently emphatic.

Clamped in his right hand was the matte-black Glock 17 that I'd seen in the drawer upstairs. He had it trained more or less in my general direction, but waggling from side to side, considering his options, none of which appeared to please him, and none of which, I expected, was going to make me happy either.

"Look—" I began, but where was there to go from there? *Look, I know this looks bad, me standing uninvited in your workroom, but you weren't supposed to be in town? Look, pay no attention to this forged multimillion-dollar painting I just found hidden away in the corner, or this unusual object right here in my hand, that I turned up on that shelf right there and that proves you're a murderer and will probably wind up sending you away for a lot of years? Look, I haven't figured out a thing, honestly, not a thing, so what do you say I just go my way and maybe we can get together for lunch one of these days?*

We stared at each other across the five feet that separated us. I was . . . well, I don't know what I was. Scared, yes, but not as much as I'd have thought. *Stunned* would be more like it; stunned and incredulous. I was having a hard time believing this was happening for real, and the gun just added to the absurdity of it. This was the second time *today* I'd had one pointed at me. It was so theatrical, so clichéd. So *silly*. Regular people didn't get themselves into situations like this in real life, did they? I felt as if I were in the middle of an old Laurel and Hardy two-reeler: *Well, Stanley, this is a fine mess you've gotten us into.*

But then he did that *snick-snock* thing with the Glock, and shook his head, sighing disgustedly, as if to show how terribly annoyed he was that it had come to this, but after all, I had nobody to blame but myself, now did I? And when he shifted the gun to level it at the center of my upper lip, boy, did that snap me out of it. I could feel the instantaneous rush of adrenaline as the fight-or-flight response took hold. It would have to be *fight*, I understood somewhere in the primitive part of my brain. Standing, as I was, in a six-by-eight room with him blocking the only exit, flight was not in the cards.

"You've really made a problem for me," he said, marginally calmer. "I'm sorry to say it, but I don't see any other choice than—"

I flung the hammer at his head and myself after it, my own head down, aiming to butt him in the belly. The hammer got there first, *thunking* off his forehead with a noise like a wrench bouncing off an Abrams tank.

My body launch was not as successful, partly because Dante was twisting away, partly because my eyes were squeezed shut and every muscle in my body was clenched against the shot that would surely come—but didn't—and partly because my left shoulder got caught in the tangle of easels beside the doorway. It knocked me off balance and off course, sending me scrambling sideways over the floor like a crab, and barreling into his right hip. We both went sprawling, but I was in better shape (not having been bonged in the head with a hammer a half-second or so ago), so that while I wound up on my hands and knees, Dante was half sitting, half lying on the floor, shoulders propped against one of the stanchions that supported the stairway. Judging from the swaying of his neck and the dopey look in his eyes, he was still seeing stars.

He hadn't dropped the gun, although I could see that his fingers had loosened around it. Did he know he still had it in his hand? I wasn't going to wait to find out, so I made a two-handed dive for it. His fingers closed around it, probably instinctively, but in another moment his body jerked and he was wide-awake again.

We struggled for the gun. I was on my knees beside him with one hand on the gun barrel and the other on his wrist, trying to wrest the gun from him while doing my best to keep it pointed anywhere but at me. Dante, red-faced, was hanging onto it hard while pounding on me with his other fist, swatting me in the chest, the shoulder, the forehead, the upper lip (now, *that* hurt!), and anywhere he could reach, while I was ducking and jerking my head around, trying to get it out of the line of fire.

He was stronger than I was, no surprise there, but not *that* much stronger. My two hands clawing at the gun outdid his one-handed grip, and I managed to get my fingers under his and scrape the thing out of his hand. He grabbed after me, but I rolled quickly away and jumped to my feet.

"Don't!" I shouted, waving the gun at him when he too tried to get up. "Stay there, Dante; I'll shoot you if you move, I mean it!" I was so short of breath that I barely managed to choke all that out, but it seemed to impress him, either because I sounded so intense that I might actually follow through and plug him, or so nervous that I might jerk the trigger by accident. Even now, I can't honestly say which was closer to the truth.

In any case, he stayed where he was and made soothing motions with his hands. "Come on, pal, don't act like that." You'd think he hadn't been a trigger-pull away from shooting me five seconds ago. He crinkled up his eyes to go with a strained smile and tried for an easy tone. "So where do we go from here?"

"You, you're going to jail," I said, pulling my phone out of its belt holster.

"Oh, now wait a minute, there's no need for that." He still had that false but self-assured smile on his face. No doubt about it: he was better at this than I was. "Let's give it some thought," he said. "Has it occurred to you how much money there's going to be to go around once—"

His foot suddenly lashed out at my ankles and caught me by surprise; I was barely able to leap out of his way. As I staggered backward, my finger must have jerked the trigger, because the gun went off. Loudly.

I don't know which of us jumped higher.

"Are you crazy?" Dante yelled, frantically patting at his lower body, searching for holes. "What's *wrong* with you?" Pretty disingenuous, I thought, from a guy who had committed murder a couple of days ago.

Having seen the puff of plaster pop from the wall well off to one side of him, I knew he wasn't going to find any holes. "Try something like that again and the next one goes into your thigh," I said coldly, "and the one after that into your other thigh, and the one—"

Dante's expression had quickly gone from shock to grumpy trepidation. "All right, all right, I get the point," he muttered. "Jesus Christ, you don't have to . . ." He let the sentence die away. "Christ."

I had scared him; that was clear, and my own self-assurance took a leap. On my phone, I scrolled down the list for Luca's number, the personal one he'd given me. When you're doing that using just one hand, one thumb, and one eye, while you're trying to keep your other eye on the dangerous character on the floor, you realize how long "instant" dialing can take. I wasn't yet halfway there before Dante started in again, speaking quietly so as not to upset me.

"Tino, give yourself a minute to think. Ten million euros! You and I, we could—"

I jabbed the muzzle of the gun in his direction, pointing it just above belt level. "Dante, if you don't shut up, I swear to God . . ."

"Okay, okay, but—okay, all right." Head bowed, he sank despondently back against the stanchion and seemed to shrink into himself. "I just don't know," he said meaninglessly.

I finally reached Lucas's name, tapped it, and waited, the phone to my ear, sending thought waves across the city to his office. *Pick up, dammit!* I didn't know how much longer I could handle this. What if Dante decided his best bet was to fight, to rush me? Would I really shoot him? *Yes, I would,* I thought, and felt my jaw muscles set in resolve. But what if he simply jumped up and ran? Could I, could I really shoot him in the—

Much to my relief, my thought waves worked. Luca answered on the second ring.

"It's Tino," I said. "I'm at Dante Zampa's studio. Can you get over here, like right this minute? And bring along some help. You've got an arrest to make."

"What? Who? Why?"

"Just get here, please. The guy is making me jumpy and I don't want to have to shoot him."

"*Shoot* him? Shoot who? What's going on? Who am I arresting?"

"Dante himself. He killed Ulisse. He's behind everything."

"Dante *Zampa?*"

"No, Dante Alighieri. Luca, for Christ's sake—"

"All right, I'll have a couple of carabinieri there in two minutes, and I'll be there myself in ten, at the most. Don't shoot him! Don't shoot anybody! *Maresciallio!*" I heard him shout as he hung up.

By the time I put the phone away, Dante had revived a little and was showing signs of desperation, enough so that I was starting to worry that he might somehow try to catch me unawares in the few minutes that were left to him. I made him turn over on his stomach with his head away from me, which required more shooting threats from me. I could sense that they were losing their motivational oomph by virtue of repetition, and although I meant them (I think), I really didn't want to have to follow through.

With him now lying facedown and unable to see me, I backed quickly into the storeroom and snatched a roll of duct tape from a shelf. Then I pulled his ankles together around the stanchion, and with the aid of my teeth tore the tape and wrapped about a thousand layers of it around ankles and stanchion together. That didn't stop him from jabbering, mostly in the form of telling me how much money was in it for me if I would only etc., etc. But by now I'd relaxed, so I just let it flow over my head. By the time the two cara-binieri, whom I didn't know, got there, I was sitting on the stool from the storeroom, calmly watching him from ten feet away, the gun in my lap.

Needless to say, confusion and tumult ensued, with Dante loudly claiming from the floor that this was his studio and home, I had broken into it, had assaulted him, had forcibly restrained him with tape, as they could plainly see, and had been continuously threatening him with the gun.

All perfectly true, of course, if somewhat slanted. I was still trying to make my case, not altogether successfully (it was *complicated*), when to my relief Luca and *maresciallo* Giordano arrived. Luca spoke calmly and succinctly. Reason prevailed. Dante left, handcuffed, with the two carabinieri, and Luca turned to me with a half-scowl.

"You want to tell me what just happened? This had better be good, Tino."

Chapter 24

Before we left the storeroom I told them I had one more thing I wanted to show them. I picked up the glazier's point hammer, inserted a point, and whacked a soft piece of scrap wood with it, holding the result up for them to see.

I waited for their reaction. They studied it. They fingered it. They looked at one another. "I think we're supposed to ask him why he's showing us this," Luca said to Giordano.

"*Dottor* Caruso," said the ever-compliant Giordano, "why do you show us this?"

I was surprised; I'd thought it was obvious, but now I realized that the impression made in wood was different from the one made in bone; softer, less clean-cut. Still, the size was right, the shape was right, and, above all, that deeper, rectangular slit in the middle was right.

"Imagine that this isn't wood," I said. "Imagine that it's bone—a skull. Now look at that impression and tell me it's not—"

"Of course!" Luca exclaimed. He took the hammer from me. "This is what killed Ulisse Agnello. This, or something exactly like it. Where did it come from? Did you find it here?"

"Right on that shelf," I said. I turned over one of the paintings. "He must have been using it to drive in those points."

"How about that?" he murmured, running his fingers over it again. "Unfortunately, this won't be of much use as evidentiary proof in a courtroom now that we've gotten our fingerprints all over it, but I suspect it will help convince Dante that he might as well be cooperative."

"I would think so," I said, "but may I suggest you take the point out before you hit him with it?"

Luca's eyes flicked upward. "Very funny."

There was a lot more to tell him, mostly things that had come together for me only this afternoon, and I didn't have them quite straight in my own mind yet. Also, that adrenaline rush hadn't gone into full reverse yet, so my nervous system was still in overdrive, and I was kind of, well, squirrely. When I tried to explain things, I wound up telling them in the wrong order, interrupting myself, reversing course, and in general bouncing all over the place.

Luca took pity on me. "Why don't we go over to headquarters? My office will be more comfortable."

"Fine. And maybe *maresciallo* Giordano here would be good enough to find me an espresso when we get there. A double, if that's doable." I knew perfectly well that a caffeine hit is not what's called for when your nerves are as tight as piano wire that's been tuned up three steps too high, but I also knew what I wanted: coffee.

"It would be my pleasure," the *maresciallo* said.

I saw Luca's eyebrows go up and down, and from the side of his mouth that was away from me, he whispered a single word to Giordano: *"Decaffeinato."*

With Giordano at the wheel of the unmarked black sedan and Luca in the back seat with me, the first few minutes of the drive to via della Moscova were silent. I could see that Luca was turning things over. I could also see that he was suffering some confusion, which he soon confirmed.

"Valentino, you've really done some amazing work here, but there are a few things that I'm a little, ah . . ."

"Confused about? Right, that makes two of us."

"Let me ask you one thing. You said that when you went to Zampa's studio this afternoon, you knew that the entrance codes hadn't been changed, despite the earlier robbery. How did you know that?"

"At the time, I didn't *know* it; I suspected it because of Dante's reputation as a procrastinator. Now, of course, it's clear that there was another reason: he just wasn't worried about a second attempt to steal the paintings."

"Clear to you, maybe. Why would he not have been worried about a second attempt?"

"Because there never was a first attempt."

Luca had been looking out his window while we spoke. Now he swung around to peer hard at me. "There never was a—?"

"No, there wasn't. I told you, that wasn't a real . . . I didn't already tell you about this back at the studio?"

"No, you did not tell me about this back at the studio."

"Oh, I must have—"

"Ferruccio, did he tell me about this back at the studio?"

"I don't recall the *dottore's* doing so," was Giordano's tactful reply.

I shrugged. "Well, maybe I didn't. I was a little . . . overwrought at the time, I guess."

"Perhaps a little, yes," said Luca. "So: Why do you say it was not a real robbery? And what would have been the point?"

"And who was behind it?" Giordano chipped in.

"Dante was behind it," I said.

"But Dante was right there in the room with you when it happened," Giordano said. "How could—"

"Ferruccio," said Luca a bit snappishly, "I believe I can handle this."

Giordano bowed his head. *"Tenente."*

"Thank you. Now let us all be clear about it. What *dottor* Caruso said was that Dante was *behind* it, not that he *executed* it."

"Yes, but I meant that he was behind it *and* that he executed it."

With Luca taking a moment to puzzle that out, Giordano couldn't restrain himself. "But then who shot *him*? And struck you? And made off with the paintings?"

"Dante. And Dante. And Dante," I said. This was fun. This was why Poirot and Holmes always seemed to be having such a high old time when they wrapped things up for their astounded audiences. Still, I felt I owed it to these two to explain my deductions—and deductions they were—without making them tease them out of me.

Now that my nervous system had had a chance to come down, I was able to do it. First off, I pointed out that while, yes, Dante was there in the room at the time, I myself didn't happen to be conscious, so I never saw what happened. And what happened, I assumed with growing confidence, was that while I was waiting for him to bring a magnifying glass, he came up behind me, not with a magnifying glass but with something heavy enough to lay me out cold. Apparently it took two tries, because there were two contusions in my scalp. He grabbed the paintings, quickly hid them somewhere—right under the bed in the corner, maybe; there wouldn't be any reason for the police to search the place afterward—then knelt down beside me, all excited, pretending there'd been a robbery. Oh, and somewhere in there he would have shot himself to make it look good. He'd had that gun right there in his kitchen drawer. All of it could have been done in ten or fifteen seconds.

"And the object of all this?" Luca asked.

"To keep me from looking any more carefully at the sketch and picking up the discrepancy in brushwork that had caught my eye. Then later, probably when it was dark and no one was around, he slipped out and left the two paintings behind the wall—only this time the café sketch was the real one."

"Knowing, as he did," Luca said thoughtfully, "that you'd be at our headquarters the next morning, and assuming, correctly, that when Esposito brought them in, I'd have you take a look at them. And when you found no such discrepancy, you'd have to doubt your earlier impression, probably attribute it to your head injury."

"And I did. Damn good thinking on his part," I said with a nod.

Giordano was shaking his head. "Shot himself," he said doubtfully. "That's easy enough to say, but not many people—"

"No, he may well be right," Luca said. "Zampa didn't *shoot* himself; he *grazed* himself. You know, I wondered about that when it happened. The wound was as superficial as a bullet wound can be. And if you think about the placement, on his hip, angling down and back, isn't it precisely what you'd get if you laid a handgun alongside your hip and fired downward as shallowly as possible, without missing your leg altogether? I suspect they would have spotted powder burns at the hospital if there'd been any reason to look for them."

"My thoughts exactly," I said. "And I wouldn't be surprised if there's still a slug in the floor."

Luca gave me a long, appraising look. "You're smart, Valentino. I admire your ability to put things together and produce a conclusion, and what you say makes sense. But other theories may also make sense. Is there any evidence for what you're saying, or are these . . . conjectures?"

"They are conjectures, Luca, but they're not made out of thin air. You're right, I *have* put a lot of things together, mostly just today, so maybe they're not too coherent yet. But they do account for everything that's happened, and if there's another theory out there that can do that, I'd love to hear it."

"Still—"

"Look, how about listening to the rest of my 'conjectures,' and then you can draw your own conclusions."

He nodded. *Proceed.*

"Give me just a minute, though." I wanted to be able to put my thoughts in a more cogent order, but by the time I was ready to give it a try, Giordano was pulling the car into Luca's slot in the carabinieri parking area.

"Hold off a little," Luca said to me. "Let's continue upstairs. And Ferruccio, you can get us both those coffees. Bring one for yourself too."

"*Caffeinato* for me," I said firmly. "*Super-caffeinato*, if you can manage it."

Luca shrugged. "Give the man what he wants."

In the office, we sat around the corner coffee table in surprisingly comfortable armchairs. I refused to continue until I got my coffee. While we waited, Luca called downstairs to check on how Dante's initial interview was coming along. "Nothing," he said when he hung up. "They're still waiting for his lawyer to get there."

"So he's asked for a lawyer," I said. "That must mean—"

"It doesn't mean anything, Tino. In Italian law, if you're a suspect being interviewed, you can't waive your right to an attorney. You get one whether you like it or not."

When Giordano arrived with the coffees, I reached for mine before he could set it down on the table, and practically inhaled it in two bracing, head-clearing gulps.

"Wow," I said, and I was actually licking my lips, "that is really—"

"It's *caffè corretto*," Giordano said. "I thought you could use it."

"And you were right." *Caffè corretto* is espresso with a shot of grappa, usually just a spoonful, but happily Giordano was a heavy-handed pourer.

"And it didn't occur to you that *I* could use it?" Luca said grumpily.

"You haven't tasted yours yet, *tenente*."

Luca smiled. "Good man, Ferruccio."

When he began to lift it to his lips his phone emitted a soft *cheep*. He grabbed a quick sip of the drink and pulled the phone from his pocket. Then he listened silently for a while, making inscrutable faces as he did. Disbelief? Amazement? *Are you kidding me? All of the above,* I thought.

The phone went back into his pocket. "I have to go. You two stay; this concerns you. I shouldn't be more than a few minutes." He gulped down the rest of his *caffè corretto*, jumped up, straightened his jacket, and hurried to the door.

"What's it all about, *tenente*?" Giordano called after him.

The answer came floating back over Luca's shoulder. "You won't believe it."

Giordano and I sat looking at each other. Time passed. "Ah, would you care for another coffee, signore?"

"I don't think I'd better, thanks."

He hesitated. "A bit more *grappa*, perhaps?"

I could feel my eyes light up. "Now that sounds good, *maresciallo*. A little energy is exactly what I need. Just a small shot, please."

"Of course."

It's not that I'm a coffee addict or a drunk, honest, but the day—the last few days—had drained me dry. I was flush out of physical resources; now I required chemical ones. The caffeine had done its job. Now a bit more alcohol was just what I needed to get my equilibrium back where it belonged.

He came back in a few minutes with two new white porcelain espresso cups. Mine held grappa—a nice, clear amber. His looked like straight black espresso, but I suspected he might have touched it up a bit.

He lifted his cup in a semi-toast. I matched the gesture.

"*Cin-cin.*"

"*Cin-cin.*"

We had just tossed our drinks back and put down our cups when I heard Luca coming down the corridor. He seemed to be laughing.

He was. He was still doing it when he came into the office. "I know I shouldn't be laughing," he said, "but I can't help myself. It's all too ridiculous."

He dropped into his seat, still smiling to himself, although the smile was a bit equivocal now. Giordano and I waited for him to speak. It was obvious he wasn't going to need any prompting. He cleared the smile from his face and leaned forward, hands clasped, elbows on the arms of the chair. "You both know Montefiore Arte, yes?"

We nodded, and Giordano said: "The auction house; the one that was supposed to sell the Renoirs."

"Exactly. The two Renoirs." His eyes had begun to dance. He was having a hard time keeping from laughing again. "Well, a few hours ago the damn things were stolen *again* . . . and this time for *real*."

"*No!*" Giordano whispered.

"Yes, I know," I said quietly.

So quietly that Luca, eager to spill his story, didn't register it right away. "There were three men this time. They . . ." His eyes swung around so hard that his stare went past me, but it came quickly back and bored straight into me. "You what?" he said, even more softly than I'd spoken.

"I know about the robbery."

"How can you know about it? It just happened three hours ago. You've been with us for the last three hours."

"No, I've been with you for the last two hours. Three hours ago I was at Montefiore. I was there when it happened. There just hasn't been time to tell you yet. I was coming to it."

"You were *there* when it happened? Two robberies of the same paintings, from two different places, in the last three days, and you were at both—"

I raised my hand. "I know; this has just been one of those lucky days for me. But Luca, this one wasn't real either. At least I don't think it was."

Not surprisingly, that brought an eruption of skeptical questions and objections from the two of them.

I folded my arms, lowered my head, and waited them out before responding. "Look, I know it sounds a little improbable—"

"A *little*?" Luca said.

"—but it was a perfect way for Dante to—"

"Dante again," Luca muttered with a shake of his head.

I laughed. "All right, maybe I have a one-track mind, but give me a chance, will you? I'll keep it short."

"Go ahead," said Luca. "I look forward to further astonishments."

⁂

"Okay, here's what I think," I said slowly. "I think that what happened at Montefiore this afternoon was the capstone, the final piece, of the plan. Unless the pictures were stolen . . . *ostensibly* stolen . . . there was no scam. The robbery today—"

Luca waved a finger at me.

I nodded in response. "Luca?"

"He had already fabricated the first robbery at his studio. Why would he not have simply used that, rather than go to the trouble and risk of organizing an additional, far more hazardous and complex enterprise at a major auction house?"

"A major auction house, a well-known one—that was the point," I said. "The thing at his studio was strictly impromptu. He came up with that to get him out of a difficult situation with me."

"And it worked," said Giordano appreciatively.

"Sure did. But what kind of press coverage did it get?"

"None, as far as I know," said Luca, "but that was because there wasn't time. The paintings were returned early the very next morning. As far as I know, the press never even learned of it."

"Right, but you can bet this afternoon's robbery, just a few hours ago, is already all over TV and the internet, and it'll be in the evening papers. By tomorrow morning it'll be news all over the world. Why the difference? Because this time the press *was* alerted. Luca, they were crawling all over the place five minutes after the carabinieri arrived. How did that happen? Well, I'll give you ten to one that if you check with them, you'll find that more than one of them got an anonymous call telling them about it."

"Like the anonymous call to signor Esposito about the paintings in his backyard," Giordano observed.

"Exactly. And while Montefiore Arte isn't quite the Louvre, it is a well-known house, and it makes for a lot more sensational story than if they'd been taken from the workshop of an obscure restorer totally unknown outside of the art world, and a very small segment of the art world at that. Three armed, masked, efficient robbers, more than a dozen people forced at gunpoint to lie on the floor . . . pretty good news material. I'm surprised they didn't video-record it." I sat back and stretched to work the kinks out of my shoulders, which had started to stiffen up from the beating they'd taken from Dante's flailing fists. "And that's about it, Luca."

"What? Do you mean to say you aren't going to tell us where the Montefiore paintings have been stashed?"

"Hey, that's your job. I mean, what are they paying you for, anyway?"

A telephone cheeped again, but this time it was Giordano's. He listened for a few seconds and then said: "*Capitano* Molinari's office, *tenente*. Signor Zampa's attorney has arrived. They would like you down in Interrogation Room B."

Luca nodded and stood up. "Your conclusions have been truly help-ful, Tino. They make sense, and they give us a great deal about which to chat with Zampa. I'm sorry to keep you here any later than it already is, but I would like to have you deposed before you leave. So if you don't mind—"

"I'll stay. Of course. But what are my chances of getting a panino or two to keep me going? I barely remember the last time I ate."

"I'll take care of it, *tenente*," said Giordano.

Two prosciutto and cheese panini did keep me going, but making the deposition and waiting around to sign it still took almost three hours, so it was after eight by the time I finished up. I took advantage of Giordano's offer to have a carabiniere drive me back to the hotel, where I practically collapsed onto my bed again. I slipped in and out of sleep for almost two hours, and when I forced myself awake at ten thirty, I was more beat than when I lay down. I was bruised all over, and the shoulder that had encountered those easels seemed to have something not quite right with the works inside. As with last night, all I wanted was to sleep. Instead, I picked up the phone. With the publicity that the Montefiore "robbery" was going to get, I needed to let the folks back in New York know that it was a put-up job, and there wasn't much doubt that the pictures would soon be recovered.

But after all the explicating I'd already done that day, I couldn't see my way to any more long explanations, so I took the coward's way and called the switchboard at IRSA, leaving a message for Esther with just the essential details, and saying I was going to bed. But I got what I deserved; five minutes later she called back demanding answers to a zillion questions.

Half an hour later, when I finally did slip into bed and turn off the lights, I saw that the red message button on the room telephone was blinking. Hard to resist, even when you're dead tired. When I pressed it, the call-in time was shown to be ten o'clock this morning, and this was what I heard:

"Signor Caruso? This is Signora Nucci at Centro Fiero, the answering service. I'm afraid I gave you some misinformation when you called signor Zampa's number the other day. He has returned from Rome early. Would you still like me to convey your message to him?"

"Thanks a million, signora Nucci," I said to the recording, "but I don't think that will be necessary. I've conveyed the message on my own."

I was still laughing when I drifted off to sleep a few minutes later.

Chapter 25

Possibly you remember the Pinacoteca di Brera's touring exhibition that was the reason for my being in Milan in the first place? The assignment that had paid my way here and was supporting my extravagant Milanese lifestyle? Well, despite my varied misadventures, I hadn't been totally ignoring it. The meetings had been called off for a few days out of consideration for my jarred and shaken brain, but over that time I'd managed to snatch a few minutes whenever I could to exchange what added up to several dozen emails, texts, and phone calls, not only with the Met, but with the other four U.S. museums for which I was the liaison.

I haven't told you any of this because it's pretty tedious stuff, and while I was obligated to suffer through it, you certainly aren't, so why do it to you?

You're welcome.

After four days off, however, I was judged fit to participate and another meeting was held, mostly to deal with the outcomes and issues my exchanges had produced. All told, what with the many new adjustments that had to be made, coordinated, and readjusted, three essentially all-day meetings were needed. This is pretty much the way this sort of thing usually goes, and for those who thrive on it, it's stimulating, satisfying work. For those who don't (such as Guess Who) . . . not so much.

Each afternoon at four, practically the minute the meeting let out, I was on the phone to Luca for an update on how things were progressing at his end. The investigation was now under the direction of the public prosecutor, but Luca remained closely involved. Here is what I learned, day by day:

Day 1:
Dante had sworn on his mother's grave that he had not killed Ulisse. He had, however, admitted to painting the forgeries for possible use in a version of the Valfierno scam. Since the scam itself had not yet been perpetrated, however, Luca doubted that he could be successfully prosecuted. In Italy, as in the United States, making a copy of a painting, say a Renoir, and signing Renoir's name to it, and even claiming to others that it's an original Renoir . . . none of that is a crime. It becomes a crime only when it is offered for sale as a Renoir. And that, as far as anyone could prove, Dante had not yet done. He'd freely admitted that he'd intended to do it, but an intention wasn't likely to count for much in a courtroom either.

The good news was that the paintings taken from Montefiore Arte had been recovered unharmed (they'd been in the trunk of one of the robbers' cars). Although the robbery had been carried out at Dante's instruction, it was unlikely that he'd pay much of a penalty for that either. In Italy's version of plea bargaining, he had informed on his three colleagues, and—more important—told the police where to find the paintings. In return, he had been promised a much-reduced sentence, and perhaps no prison time at all.

If I were willing to come back to testify as the injured party, Luca told me, they would charge him for assault in the "robbery" at his studio. I was willing, and was also willing to come to carabinieri headquarters to separate the wheat from the chaff, i.e., to identify which of the ten paintings they now had in an evidence room were the two originals and which were the eight forgeries. I was able to do it that very evening, after which I treated a worn and frazzled Luca to a dim sum dinner at a Chinese restaurant.

Day 2:

First, there were some relevant legal developments regarding Ulisse's devious acquisition of the paintings back in 2002. A preliminary hearing had ruled that, having failed the good-faith purchaser test, he did not have—never did have—legal possession of them. Which meant that he didn't have the right to "pass on title" to them, which meant that he couldn't legally sell them, in whole or in part. Thus, Benvenuto's newly put-in claim to twenty-percent ownership because of his loan to Dante would likely be disallowed. And Giulietta would have to call off the auction, and who knew what else the repercussions might be. Dismay, confusion, and tons of paperwork all around.

As to Dante, no change; he had stuck to his story. He had sworn to it on the grave of his grandmother.

"What did he have to say about the hammer?" I asked.

Luca smiled. "Ah, that's a surprise we've been saving for him. Oh, and what do you think of this? Our laboratory has matched it—matched that particular hammer to those particular wounds. There is an irregularity in the hammer's head, you see, a nick that produced a spur of metal that projects from the rim. It matches exactly the depressions in Ulisse's skull. They made a cast of the more well-defined wound and placed the hammer's head against it. A perfect fit, inarguably unique; I saw it for myself."

Ain't science wonderful, I thought. "When do you plan to tell him about it?"

"Tomorrow. I expect he'll come up with a new story."

"Think you'll believe it?"

He laughed. "Not even if he swears it on his great-grandmother's grave."

Day 3

On being presented with the hammer, Dante did indeed change his story. After an hour-long consultation with his lawyer, he confessed to killing Ulisse, but insisted it was in self-defense. Ulisse had been in on the scam from the beginning, he said; it had been his idea. Late in the evening of the day he'd gone to Lugano, he made an agitated call to Dante from his Swiss hotel to say that he'd been scouting for potential buyers at the meetings and it had come forcefully home to him what a hazardous job that was, how open it made him to informants, or blackmailers, or undercover police. Dante's part, on the other hand—painting the fakes—was virtually danger-free. It was over and done, it had been accomplished behind the scenes, and nobody would even know who had painted them.

Ulisse now believed it was only fair to set new terms for their split, which had originally been set at 60-40 in Ulisse's favor. But if he were going to continue to line up buyers—and he was the one with the contacts to do it—he now felt that the risks he would be taking, risks that Dante didn't face, entitled him to eighty percent. Dante would still come away with two million euros or more for two months' work, so what was his problem?

Upset—"betrayed" had been Dante's word—he had immediately driven to Lugano and cornered Ulisse in his hotel room. They had argued over it, the argument had gotten rough, and Ulisse, quite beside himself, had grabbed a fireplace poker, swung it wildly at him, missed, and come at him again. Shocked, Dante had desperately searched for something with which to defend himself and had found the glazier's point hammer in his pocket. He had tried to warn Ulisse off with it, but Ulisse had kept coming. Dante had had no choice. He had struck Ulisse with the hammer. Twice. The first elicited little reaction, but unfortunately, the second blow had killed him instantly. Ulisse had collapsed in a heap onto the carpet.

Dante had panicked. He had waited in the room until midnight and then, using a service elevator at the back of the hotel, had hauled Ulisse down to Ulisse's own car, driven partway back to Milan, put Ulisse in the driver's seat, and sent the car over the closest thing to a cliff he could find. He had then walked along the road to the nearby Swiss village of Maroggia, gotten a taxi back to Lugano, and driven back to Milan in his own car.

And that was truly the way it had happened, he declared with his hand on his heart, but for this telling he was so subdued, so dejected, that he finished without swearing on anybody's grave at all.

"What do you think?" I asked. "Do you believe it?"

"Some of it. I think we're getting closer to the truth."

"What about the self-defense claim? Believe that?"

"No."

"Because," I said, "if he drove to Lugano just to talk things over, why did he have that hammer with him? Why did he bring it up to Ulisse's room? It's not the kind of thing you'd ordinarily carry around in your pocket."

"Yes. Exactly."

"So then, how does it stand? What's your next move?"

"The next move is up to the prosecutor, Tino. As it happens, at this point his inclination is to charge him with unpremeditated murder."

"So he's going to trial?" Funny. Despite how much I've been mouthing off about my disappointment in Ulisse, I needed to *know* that the man who killed him was going to have to face the law over it.

"Oh, I believe so, but it's not so simple here. First there is a preliminary hearing at which a judge must be convinced there is sufficient reason to pursue the charge. Then, after that there are a number of—" With a smile, he stopped himself. "Let me simply say that the Italian government is unceasing in its efforts to maintain its hard-won reputation for *lungaggini burocratiche*."

Red tape. I smiled too, which I might not have done if I'd known how much of it I'd be wrapped in over the next few days.

In the meantime, the Brera meetings proceeded at their own frustrating pace as, one by one, the many and varied glitches were resolved. On the second day, I invited Adriano Riccardi, the judge who'd presided over Sol's appeal, to join me for lunch.

"I'll buy, but there's a catch," I told him. "I have some questions I'm going to spring on you."

He frowned. "The subject being?"

"Good-faith purchasers, bad-faith purchasers, and subjects appertaining."

The frown vanished. "Ah, Ulisse Agnello. Yes, I've been mulling over a few thoughts about him myself," he said brightly, "and I have an idea, a proposal, actually, that I believe will be of interest to you."

Was it ever.

Chapter 26

Funny how your perspectives can change on you. It was barely two weeks ago that I was doing all that whining about how crummy my life was. Well, I still haven't been promoted, and I'm as divorced as ever, and now I'm forty years old plus thirteen days.

And yet today was the best day of my life.

I left Milan at nine this morning, arriving at JFK at a little before two in the afternoon, giving me time to have the limo stop at my borrowed condo to drop off my luggage, take a fast shower, change clothes, and hop back into the waiting car to get to my five o'clock meeting with Sol, Lori, and Esther. Originally, it had been set for Esther's office, but a fall drizzle had built into a gloomy, steady rain and Sol was sensing the onset of a cold, so it had been changed to his Lower East Side apartment.

He'd lived since the 1970s in a prewar building on Ludlow Street, the kind with a brown-brick façade and fire escapes out front. Once upon a time it would have been called a tenement, but the Lower East Side had seen considerable gentrification, and Sol's building, like the adjacent ones, while they looked the same on the outside as they had in 1930, were dumps no longer.

Still no elevators, though, which must have been tough on him. Fortunately, he lived only one flight up, above a taqueria, but in the rear of the building, looking down on a quiet, green pocket garden. I knocked on the door, bringing a shouted response from Esther. "Just a minute."

But I was too excited and eager to wait and jiggled the knob, trying to get the door open myself, which was silly. Who leaves a door unlocked in New York?

"Well, you're in a hurry, aren't you?" Esther said, pulling it open. "Does that mean good news? I hope?"

"Not bad," I said.

Sol's one-bedroom apartment, which looked as if it had been through a modernizing not long ago, was modest all the same. He had furnished it tastefully but sparely, and there were plenty of windows, so the place had an airy, spacious feel to it. *Eminently livable,* I thought, and tucked away a mental note: *Pleasant, lively neighborhood, why not see what an apartment costs around here? Couldn't go on living in Gerry's borrowed condo much longer.*

Esther led me to a sofa and armchair grouping in the living room, where Lori and Sol waited, both standing. There were the expected murmurs of concern about my face, which actually looked worse than it had a few days ago. The hotel doctor in Milan had removed my stitches, so that now instead of a bandage I sported an angry-looking red furrow across my forehead. My two black eyes had gotten less puffy but a lot more colorful: a rainbow medley of purple, brown, yellow, and green.

The commiseration phase didn't last all that long, because they couldn't keep their eyes from wandering to the package I had under my arm, a flat, two-by-two-foot fiberboard carton. Their expressions, all three of them, were giveaways to the questions they were afraid to ask. *Surely that isn't . . . ? Could it be . . . ? Was it possible that you actually managed to . . . ?*

Well, yes, it was possible, and it was so. Thanks to the prodigious assistance and heavyweight influence of *il giudice,* Adriano Riccardi,

I had sliced through knots and tangles of *lungaggini burocratiche* in record time: two and a half days for something that would normally take six months. He'd even arranged to ease my way through American customs at this end. The poignant and unusual history of this particular case had been a big help. Bureaucrats have hearts too, especially Italian bureaucrats.

Esther was eyeing the carton with particular intensity. "Something tells me that's not a pizza."

"Let's all sit down," I said, laying it on the low table at the center of the grouping of chairs. "Sol, why don't you open it for us?"

He looked down at it and then at me, and started to tremble. *Dear God,* I thought, *is this too much for him to handle? Have I made a mistake? Should I have broken it to him in stages?*

"Sol," I began, but he had already lifted the carton's lid. (When I'd stopped off at the condo, I'd removed the tape that had sealed it for the journey from Milan.) The lid was laid very gently to one side, as if even it was something special. But of course, the something special was in the lower half of the carton and still hidden from view by the sheets of glassine paper in which it was wrapped, the wrapping held in place by masking tape.

From the size and shape, there couldn't be much doubt about what was inside, but no one wanted to say anything for fear of being wrong—*or more likely,* I thought, *for fear of making it not happen.* Yes, I know, these were all intelligent, educated people who very properly scoff at magical beliefs, but that's what was on their minds, all right. I knew because if I'd been in their place, that's what I would have been thinking too.

"Do I cut the tape?" Sol asked. "Do I need scissors?" I could barely hear his whisper.

"No," I told him, "you just tear the tape where it holds the flaps down." Rule One of handling artistic masterworks: nothing with points comes within striking distance of it.

Sol nodded and leaned forward to do it, but his hands were really shaking now, and he sat back with a little laugh. "Lori, dolly, you know, I'm a little nervous. Maybe you could . . . ?"

Lori quickly moved around the corner of the table, knelt next to Sol, and pulled apart the four pieces of tape that held the glassine sheets down, so that they could be lifted with ease to see what lay underneath. But she left that part to him, giving his knee a squeeze and going back to her seat. "It's all yours, Unc."

"So it's all mine, is it? Well, then." But he sat there for another few moments, looking at each of us with that innocent, angelic expression of his and a sort-of smile, an equivocal, ineffable Mona Lisa smile. Then, with hands that he seemed to be controlling with sheer willpower, he peeled back each of the four glassine flaps while the rest of us held our breath.

And there it was. A single sob burst out of him. With a visible effort, he managed to keep it to just that one. "Excuse me," he whispered, buying time by taking off his glasses and wiping the lenses with a tissue. "I'm a little . . . Val . . . Dr. Caruso . . . there's no way I can thank you for . . . for . . ."

"You've already thanked me," I said, and my voice wasn't all that steady either. "You're thanking me right now." I reached across the table and gently grasped the back of his hand for a second. If this kept up I was going to turn into a toucher.

"Congratulations, Sol," Esther said. "Congratulations to you, Val. Didn't I tell you you'd pull it off?"

"You may have said something along those lines," I said, smiling. When was the last time I had felt this warm, this good?

Lori said nothing; she just dabbed at her eyes and sat there beaming at her uncle. Then she turned toward me and mimed a kiss. Not a sexy kiss, not even a flirty one, but it went through me like a lightning shaft. Why, her eyes were *green*. And blue—a luminous, bewitching turquoise.

How could I not have noticed, if not at Eileen's Cheesecake, then here, the minute I walked in?

Well, I guess I knew why. From the second I boarded Alitalia 7602 this morning, with the picture seat-belted into the paid-for first-class seat next to me—it's the usual way big-time pictures like Renoirs travel with big-time curators (like me)—my mind, my heart had been filled to capacity with anticipation and imaginings of Sol's reaction when I presented him with the picture; of this very moment, in fact. There just hadn't been room for anything else, even Lori.

But now . . . my God, she was smashing. No more sweatshirt and baggy flannel sweatpants. Today it was a nicely tailored skirt-suit and a silky, collared shirt, and . . . I think . . . high heels. No rubber-banded ponytail either; her sandy brown hair was untied, curving gracefully down to just above her shoulders. Other than looking maybe a little too much like a smart-aleck lady lawyer, which raised a few jitters that I quickly put down, the woman was a knockout. Did she usually dress this way when she wasn't taking classes? Was it, could it possibly, hopefully, wishfully, implausibly be that she'd done herself up for me? Was—

"I'm sorry, what?" I asked. I'd realized that Sol had said something and it had been directed at me.

"How long can I keep it?" he said.

"As long as you want. It's yours, Sol, you own it. I have that for you in writing."

He looked shell-shocked. "Own it?"

"Yes, Agnello is dead, Sol—"

"I know that."

"And it was never legally his, anyway. The last known legal owner was your great-grandfather, and so . . . it's yours."

"Yes, yes, all that I understand, but I never thought it would be so soon that . . . I don't know what I never thought." A manic little laugh escaped him. "This is unbelievable, Val. Wonderful. Thank you from the bottom of my heart for what you've done."

"You couldn't possibly be more welcome, Sol. It's been a tremendous pleasure to be able to help."

"Yeah," Esther said. "All you have to do is look at that beat-up mug of yours to see how tremendous it was."

"No, even so. I stand by what I said. It's been a tremendous pleasure, a privilege, and, Esther, I thank you for talking me into it."

"How did you do it so fast, though?" Lori asked. "I know something about Italian export regulations, and you don't get something like this done in a week." Her eyes, fixed on mine, twinkled. "Uh, look, if it turns out to cause you any, um, trouble with the law, I promise to do what I can to get you out of jail."

I twinkled back at her. "I'm relieved to hear that, but it's completely legal. I got a great deal of help from an influential judge, Adriano Riccardi."

"Riccardi?" Lori exclaimed. "But he was the judge who, who—"

"*Giudice* Riccardi," Sol said, nodding. "You know, in spite of everything, I always thought that underneath that black robe and that funny napkin thing around his neck, he was a nice guy, a man who was honestly trying to do the right thing."

"Exactly what I thought," asserted Esther. "A nice guy. You can tell about people."

I stifled a laugh. A mealy-mouthed, nitpicking hypocrite he might be—but a nice one.

"By the way," Lori said, "what about the other picture, the self-portrait? Will that go to Uncle Sol too?"

"I don't want it!" Sol said instantly and excitedly. "No, no, I can't be responsible for that. I have what I want."

"You could always sell it," Esther said. "Ten million dollars? That'd buy a lot of cheesecake."

"No," Sol said, getting more upset. "No, I don't want it. What would I do with it? Can I give it to the Metropolitan Museum?" he asked me. "Would they take it?"

"I don't think we'd turn it down," I said with a laugh, "but it'll be going around in bureaucratic circles in Italy for a while, so why worry about it now?"

"Right," said Lori. "Sorry I brought it up. We'll work all that out later."

Esther clapped her hands. "I'd say this calls for one hell of a celebration. Let's start. Where's that bag I brought, Sol? In the kitchen?"

"Bedroom. On the bed." He was more in control of himself than he'd been a few minutes ago, but he'd never altogether stopped trembling, and the tears still glimmered on his eyelids.

Esther started to get up but Lori beat her to it, going into the adjoining room and coming back with a cooler tote bag. "This it?" (She *was* wearing heels. Not that I was particularly watching.)

"That's it, give it here," Esther said.

From it she pulled four stemmed glasses and set them on the table, and then a bottle.

"Champagne!" Lori said. "Perfect!"

"Whoa," I said, "not only champagne, but Veuve Clicquot! You went all out, didn't you?"

"It's no more than what the occasion deserves." She handed me the ice-cold bottle. "Val, will you do the honors?"

I'd torn off the foil, twisted off the wire basket, and begun to work the cork before a question occurred to me. I put the bottle down. "Hey," I said.

"Are you addressing me?" Esther inquired magisterially.

"Yeah, you. This is pretty fancy champagne. How did you know there'd be anything to celebrate that rated a Veuve Clicquot Vintage Brut?"

She looked down her nose at me, as if peering at me through a monocle. "I knew because I had utter confidence that you would bring it off. As I did from the start, may I remind you."

"Right, so *utter* that you hid it in another room where no one could see it, until you were sure there'd be a reason to bring it out."

"*Ree*-dickaluss. I just didn't want to spoil your surprise, that's all."

We laughed, all of us except Sol, who had barely taken his eyes off the painting and probably hadn't heard any of this. He'd looked up and smiled at us a few times, but without really seeing us. His thoughts were far away, in time and place, that much was easy to see; beyond that they were unreadable.

"It shouldn't have this gold frame on it," he said. "It should just have a wood frame, plain, like it used to in the kitchen."

"You're right," I said. "The fancy frame is all wrong for it. I'll get one of the conservators at the Met to reframe it for you."

"And you'll want some insurance for it, and a good security system," Esther said. "IRSA will take care of that for you. All part of the service." She was very happy too.

"Thank you both," Sol said, "for so much, for everything." He smiled at Lori. "Thank you too, darling. What wonderful people I have around me."

I had poured the champagne for everyone, and we'd all clinked glasses and taken a token sip, but apparently none of us was in the mood for drinking. I guess there was no way alcohol could improve on the high that we were already feeling.

"It's six o'clock," Esther said. "I think a commemorative dinner is in order. How does Amelie sound? What say I give them a call and see if they can take us at six thirty or seven?"

There was no objection and Esther placed the call. "Six thirty," she said, hanging up. "We should probably get started."

Lori, Esther, and I began to get to our feet, but Sol stayed put, hunched over the picture. "Everybody?" he said. "I don't know how to put this, but . . . would you mind very much if I didn't go?"

"Of course we wouldn't mind," Lori said. "We can order some takeout for here. That'd be fun. Everybody can choose what kind of food they want."

"No, it's not that. I'm not hungry at all. I guess I'm too excited. What I would really like . . . well, this sounds so ungrateful, after all you've done for me . . . is just to stay here, by myself. I don't know how to explain it; I just want to . . . to . . ."

"Be alone with your memories," I finished for him. "Memories that none of us can share."

"That's it exactly," he said. "You know, this picture . . ." He ran his fingers over the surface, a crime for which I would have murdered anybody I'd caught doing it to a Renoir at the museum, but which didn't bother me at all here. ". . . this picture—it's not only what it's a picture *of* . . . it's the picture itself, the physical picture. That this very thing, this very object I'm touching now, was actually hanging in our kitchen all those years ago . . ." He smiled. "It's not easy to explain."

"I don't think you need to explain, Uncle Sol," Lori said, and Esther and I nodded along with her.

Everybody got up then. Lori and Esther warmly kissed Sol, and when it was my turn, I damn near did too, but instead we gently embraced. Eyes glowing, he shook his head at me as if to say, "What can I say?" and I clasped his thin shoulders just a little more firmly.

Downstairs in the street, Esther said, "I don't know about you two kids, but I don't really want to go out to dinner either. I'm exhausted. I just want to go home, take off my shoes, and *plotz*. Maybe some takeout Chinese."

We stayed with her until she got a taxi, and then Lori and I were left alone. I was as nervous as a gawky fifteen-year-old trying to get his courage up to propose a date to the prettiest girl in the entire high school.

"Uh, Lori . . ."

She saved me from blurting out whatever stupid thing I was going to say. "Val," she said, looking up at me and smiling, and turning my knees to milk with those fantastic turquoise eyes, "don't you think it would be a pity to let all four of those reservations at Amelie go to waste? I believe I owe you a dinner, and I would love it if you'd dine with me right now."

"I'd love it too," I said.

And then, with her eyes downcast she softly said, she actually said: "The first of many, I hope."

Definitely. The best day of my life.

AFTERWORD

As always, I needed plenty of help in trying to get things right, and as always it was freely given. I want to thank four people in particular:

Vincenzo Panza, Knight of the Order of Merit of the Italian Republic, former president of the National Carabinieri Association, and longtime international executive management consultant, for his great kindness in putting aside his busy schedule for an entire day to help me in my research, and doing it with great charm and pleasantness.

Colonello Biagio Storniolo, *comandante, Provinciale Carabinieri di Bergamo*, who not only patiently answered my questions and resolved my confusions about police matters in Italy, but hosted me to a splendid lunch in the city.

Cristina Perissinotto, PhD, president of the Canadian Association of Italian Studies, and associate professor of Italian studies and director of the Italian program at the University of Ottawa, for her affability and wit in once again helping me to find my way through the nuances and vagaries of Italian language and culture, and for the pleasures of our ongoing correspondence.

Jay Gates, who has served as director of three of America's most distinguished museums: the Phillips Collection in Washington, DC, the Seattle Art Museum, and the Dallas Museum of Art, for sharing his insights on museum exhibitions. Jay has been my fount of knowledge for art history and museum affairs for thirty years now.

ABOUT THE AUTHOR

Aaron Elkins's mysteries and thrillers have earned him an Edgar, an Agatha, a Nero Wolfe Award, and a Malice Domestic Lifetime Achievement Award. His nonfiction works have appeared in *Smithsonian* magazine, the *New York Times* magazine, and *Writer's Digest*.

A former anthropology professor, Elkins is known for starting the forensic-mystery genre with his 1982 novel, *Fellowship of Fear*. He currently serves as the anthropological consultant for the Olympic Peninsula Cold Case Task Force in Washington State.

Elkins lives in Washington with his wife, Charlotte, who is his occasional collaborator and shares in his Agatha award.